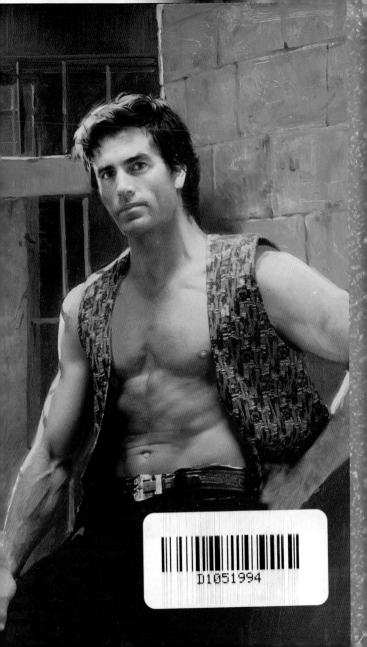

ROMANTIC TIMES PRAISES MADELINE BAKER'S PREVIOUS BESTSELLERS!

SPIRIT'S SONG

"Madeline Baker consistently delivers winning, heart-wrenching, passionate romances and *Spirit's Song* is no exception."

UNDER A PRAIRIE MOON

"Madeline Baker writes of a ghost, a curse and a second chance with such power and passion readers cannot help but be mesmerized."

CHASE THE WIND

"This sequel to *Apache Runaway* is pure magic and packed with action, adventure, and passion. Madeline Baker fans, get ready to laugh and cry from the beginning to the surprising ending."

THE ANGEL & THE OUTLAW

"Readers will rave about Madeline Baker's extraordinary storytelling talents."

LAKOTA RENEGADE

"*Lakota Renegade* is as rich, passionate, and delicious as all of Madeline Baker's award-winning romances!"

APACHE RUNAWAY

"Madeline Baker has done it again! This romance is poignant, adventurous, and action-packed."

CHEYENNE SURRENDER

"This is a funny, witty, poignant, and delightful love story! Ms. Baker's fans will be more than satisfied!"

UNFORGETTABLE

"Darlin', you feel so good."

"Hmm, so do you."

He had to leave her, he thought, and soon, or he'd go crazy. Even now, knowing there was no time to waste, certain the sheriff would come after him as soon as he was able, he was tempted to spread his saddle blanket on the ground and make love to her there and then. But she deserved better than a quick roll in the sagebrush. He wanted their first time together to be something she would never forget.

He rested his chin on the top of her head and grinned. On sagebrush or satin sheets, she was never going to forget it, he would see to that.

UNFORGETTABLE

MADELINE BAKER

LEISURE BOOKS NEW YORK CITY

A LEISURE BOOK®

September 2000

Published by

Dorchester Publishing Co., Inc.
276 Fifth Avenue
New York, NY 10001

ISBN 0-8439-4762-4

The name "Leisure Books" and the stylized "L" with design are trademarks of Dorchester Publishing Co., Inc.

Printed in the United States of America.

This book is dedicated to:

All the ghosts in Bodie, real or imagined, and

The Friends of Bodie
for their dedication in preserving the town
and to all the wonderful rangers
and park aides who so kindly and
patiently answered my numerous questions.

And to:

Carol Amato
who gave me the idea in the first place,

Flo Robinson
who helped me with the research
(even though the train didn't make it),

Mitch Dearmond
for his poem at the end of the book,

And to Mary
who has been my best friend
and fan for, lo, these many years.
It's a dirty job, but someone has to do it.

Time Passages

I saw him in the distance
His image blurred by time and space
I heard his voice
so soft and low
I yearned to see his face

A lonely walk down a deserted street
And I saw him just beyond
I felt his spirit call to me
I reached
But he was gone

I crossed time's dusty threshold
And walking toward me he came
And I knew
Deep within my heart
I would never be the same

A dream, a wish, or was it fate
That scattered
The mists of time
That sent me back in history
To reside within his clime

How or why, it matters not
Together forever we'll be
Our hearts and souls
Now bound by love
For all eternity

—M. Baker

UNFORGETTABLE

Prologue

She needed a vacation, and she meant to take one. Preferably, a long one. She was fed up with the rut she found herself in, with life, with deadlines, with men. Especially men! If she never saw another one until she was a hundred and three, it would still be too soon.

Leaning back in her desk chair, Shaye Montgomery closed her eyes and pictured the lake at Plumas Pines. The water in Lake Almanor was as deep and blue as a midsummer sky. Tall pine trees stretched upward, their emerald green branches ever reaching toward heaven. It had been years since she had been up there, but it was a place dear to her heart, and it was time to go back. Time to fish in Deer Creek, where the water was so clear you could stand on the bank and watch the trout take your bait. Power bait, she mused;

that was what they liked. Time to take long walks in the twilight, time to feed the deer and the squirrels. Time to go into Chester and wander through the shops, indulge in some of the rich chocolate fudge at The Grey Squirrel, browse the antique stores, bask in the pleasure of devouring one of the huge pancakes at The Kopper Kettle.

She could stop off at Bodie State Historic Park on her way. She had always wanted to go there. The last time she had been this fed up with the demands of her job, she had thought she might give up reporting and try her hand at writing a novel set in the historic ghost town. She had long ago given up on the idea of writing a book, but she loved ghost towns, and Bodie was one that had always intrigued her.

Yes, she thought, a vacation up in Northern California was exactly what she needed. She smiled as she thought how pleased and surprised her mom and dad would be to see her. Her parents had always loved it up north and they had moved there a few months after her father retired from the Los Angeles Police Department. Three months later, they bought a cute little combination antique shop and cafe in Chester. Just thinking about some of her mom's homemade apple pie made her mouth water.

Reaching for the phone, she dialed her editor's number before she could change her mind.

Chapter One

Shaye grimaced as her Range Rover bounced over the rough road that led to Bodie. She had negotiated thirteen miles of crooked road after turning off Highway 395. It had been fairly smooth going until the last three miles or so, and then the paved road had run out.

"I guess this is so tourists will get the full flavor of 'roughing it,'" she muttered as she swerved to the left to avoid the worst of the ruts. "But I think a mile would have been more than enough."

At the entrance, she paid the two-dollar admission fee, noted in passing that it would have cost her an additional dollar if she'd had a dog. She gave the attendant a dollar for a guidebook to the park, wrote the three dollars down in the little notebook she carried to log her expenses.

She parked her car in the lot, grabbed her backpack, which contained her wallet, camera, extra film, a couple bottles of Evian water, her cell phone, and some other odds and ends, and opened the door.

The weather was perfect, warm but not hot, with a mild breeze. She followed the other tourists toward the path that led to the town, glancing at the guidebook as she went. *Bodie State Historic Park*. There was a quote at the bottom of the booklet that read:

> *And now my comrades are all gone;*
> *Naught remains to toast.*
> *They have left me here in my misery,*
> *Like some poor wandering ghost.*

She stood at the top of the path for a moment, gazing down at what was left of the town. There were a number of buildings and houses still standing. According to the guidebook, only five percent of the buildings from the original town remained, "just as time, fire, and the elements have left it—a genuine California gold-mining ghost town."

Even though she didn't believe in ghosts, a shiver slid down her spine as she read the last two words.

Reading on, she learned that Bodie had been designated a state historic park in 1962.

She continued reading as she walked slowly down the hill. Bodie had been named after Waterman S. Body, also known as William S. Bodey, who had discovered gold there in 1859. Some thought the change in the spelling of the town's name was due to an illiterate sign painter, but the booklet said it had been a deliberate change on the part of the town to ensure proper pronunciation.

Shaye grinned, amused that people of that time and place would have worried about such a thing.

Reading on, she learned that Bodie had boasted a population of about ten thousand by 1879 and was "second to none for wickedness, badmen, and the worst climate out of doors." One little girl supposedly wrote, "Good-bye God. I'm going to Bodie" in her diary. The booklet noted that killings occurred with monotonous regularity, and that robberies, stage hold-ups, and street fights provided variety, while the town's sixty-five saloons offered many opportunities for relaxation. In 1881, the Reverend F. M. Warrington saw it as "a sea of sin, lashed by the tempests of lust and passion."

She felt a shiver as she read the last few sentences: "Bad men, like bad whiskey and bad climate, were endemic to the area. Whatever the case, the streets are quiet now. Bodie still has its wicked climate, but with the possible exception of an occasional ghostly visitor, its badmen are all in their graves."

The booklet made for fascinating reading. At one time, there had been thirty mines in operation, and enough saloons, pothouses, restaurants, gin mills, and ale stoops to cater to the miners. The names of the saloons conjured up images of long bars and spittoons, billiard tables and floors covered with sawdust—the Occidental, the Grand Central, the Parole Saloon, the Rifle Club, the Senate, the Champion, the

Sawdust Corner, the Bonanza. Three breweries had supplied the saloons.

Booklet in hand, she turned left at the end of the path and began the self-guided tour marked by numbered posts. She fell in love with the Old Methodist Church on the corner of Green and Fuller. Quaint was the word that came to mind. Several houses came next—the McDonald house, the Metzger house, the Miller house. She paused at Site Number Six—residence of James Stuart Cain. According to the guidebook, Mr. Cain and a Mr. Maguire had leased a block of ground from the Standard Mine and Mill and took out ninety thousand dollars in gold in ninety days. She was surprised by the large bay window that looked out on the street. Moving on, she passed a small sawmill used for cutting firewood. The Donnelly house was notable in that, in its prime, the garden in front of the house had been the only green spot in town.

Referring to the booklet yet again, she read that winters in Bodie were harsh, with snow often up to twenty feet deep, winds up to a hundred miles an hour, and temperatures plunging to thirty and forty below zero.

She took pictures of practically every structure, more fascinated than she would have thought possible by a bunch of old buildings pummeled by the passage of time. She was surprised at how large most of the houses were, many having rooms that looked to be about twelve by twelve. Wallpaper covered most of the walls. Of course, the paper was badly faded now, and most of it was peeling.

In one of the few dwellings open to the public, she ran her hand over the paper above the fireplace, which felt much thicker than the wallpaper she was used to, and seemed to be backed by cotton cloth. To the left of the fireplace was a bedroom with a double bed. To the right was a dining room with a rectangular table and four chairs. There was a hutch of sorts across from the table, and a stove for heating. Beyond the dining room was the kitchen, which contained a sink, a cupboard, and a small round table and three chairs. Another bedroom was located off the kitchen.

It was hard to believe that people had just packed up their clothing and personal belongings and left town, but it was obvious that was what had happened. Beds, tables and chairs, stoves, dressers, pictures, a wrought-iron crib, all had been left behind. There were pots and pans in the cupboards, dishes on the table in the kitchen.

She wiped off the window of the mercantile and peered inside. In the dusky light, she could see the items stacked on sagging shelves—canned goods, jars, bottles, boxes of baking soda, most with faded labels still intact. Another shelf held piles of clothes.

There were a number of caskets left in the morgue.· All empty, she hoped.

Pausing in the shade of the Moyle house, she read the paragraph about Chinatown, which had been located off King Street. Apparently, several hundred Chinese had lived in Bodie at one time. Theirs had been a town within a town, with its own stores, gambling halls, and saloons, as well as a Taoist temple. The main sources of income for the Chinese had been peddling vegetables, operating laundries, and cutting, hauling, and selling firewood.

Shaye grinned as she read two of the street signs—Virgin Alley and Maiden Lane. Even without being told, she would have known this had once been Bodie's red light district.

She paused at the jail. It was made of weathered wood with a peaked roof. The door to the sheriff's office was locked, of course. The window beside the door was boarded up. She moved to the second window and peered through the thick iron bars. Inside she could see another door, which had a window with iron bars, that she assumed led to another cell. She walked around the building and found another barred door. Looking inside, she saw another cell.

She checked the guidebook, which stated, "the Town Jail may not look like much now, but it had its day." It went on to say that only one prisoner was known to have escaped. Bail for "guests" was five dollars. A man named Joseph DeRoche had been taken from the jail by a vigilante group known as the Bodie "601" and hanged.

She walked back to the front of the building and looked inside again. There was no furniture of any kind. She tried to imagine how the cells must have looked. She supposed there would have been a cot in each cell, perhaps more than one. Possibly a chair or two. Maybe a small table. And a chamber pot.

She was about to turn away when she felt a breath of cold air and for a moment, just a moment, she thought she saw a man standing against the far wall ... a tall man dressed all in black, with long dark hair. His eyes were brown. Deep, dark brown beneath straight black brows.

I didn't do it. Maldición! *How many times do I have to say it?*

A chill ran down her spine as the words echoed and re-echoed in her mind.

She blinked, and the faint, wavery image was gone.

Telling herself it had been nothing but her own shadow and an all too active imagination, she turned away from the weather-beaten jail and forced herself to walk, not run, to the Stuart Kirkwood Livery Stable and Blacksmith Shop, which was just across the way. It had been nothing but an illusion, she assured herself, wrought by the light of the sun pouring in through the window. But try as she might, she couldn't shake the feeling that she had actually seen one of the ghosts she didn't believe in.

She felt better when several other tourists came into view, even managed a grin when she overheard one of them remark that having the stable right next door was really handy in case of a jail break.

The schoolhouse was a large two-story building that had originally been the Bon Ton Lodging House. Peeking in the window, she saw several rows of old-fashioned desks, the teacher's desk at the head, and beside that, an easel with the day's reading assignment. The first school, originally located two blocks away, had been burned down by an early-day juvenile delinquent.

She noticed there were signs on several of the houses that read "Employee Residence." In one such house, old and new lived side by side . . . the room on the right side of the front door depicted the scene as it had been a hundred years ago; the room on the left was furnished with a new cot and an exercise bike.

She gazed up at the old buildings scattered on the far hillside, at the remains of the Standard Mine and Mill on the west slope of Bodie Bluff, and tried to imagine what it would have been like to live in the town a hundred years ago. Hot summers with no trees to provide shade, no air-conditioning. Freezing winters, the snow whipped by fierce winds. No forced-air heat, only fireplaces or cast-iron stoves for warmth. No indoor plumbing, no hot running water. No radio or TV, no computers. No malls.

"I would have hated it," she muttered. "In spite of smog, global warming, road rage, and all the other ailments that plague modern civilization, I'll take today over yesterday."

There might be a lot to be said for a slower, more pastoral life but, given a choice, she'd take a microwave oven over a cast-iron stove, and flush toilets over an outhouse any day of the week.

Bodie. It was a nice place to visit, but she wouldn't want to live there.

Chapter Two

She drove into nearby Bridgeport for dinner, then found a quiet motel to spend the night. Tomorrow, she would continue up Highway 395, maybe stop in Reno and try her hand at one of the blackjack tables before going on to Plumas Pines.

Later, in her room, she pulled out the books she had bought in the Bodie museum: *Boomtowns of the Old West; The Cowboy, An American Legend; The Guide to Bodie and Other Eastern Sierra Historic Sites*; and three reproductions of Bodie newspapers.

She picked up the first paper, the *Bodie Morning News*, dated Tuesday, August 12, 1879, noticing that it contained mostly advertisements and only a few articles. She glanced at some of the ads, noting that The Bodie Bank boasted capital of $50,000, while the Mono County Bank had $100,000 in capital.

23

Koppel & Platt's was having a clearance sale. There was a note at the bottom of the ad, signed by Koppel & Platt, which read, "This is an opportunity seldom offered, as the stock now on hand is finely assorted and of the best quality. Gentlemen will please call and examine goods and prices to satisfy themselves that it is no humbug and we mean business."

The American Hotel was for sale.

Turning the page, she saw a lengthy article titled, "A Chinese War! War Breaks Out Among the Chinese Last Night—A small battle in Chinatown—Three Known to be Killed, and More to be Heard from."

She skipped the article itself and picked up the second paper, dated August 13, 1879. An ad at the bottom of the first page caught her eye. "$100 Reward . . . Taken from our barn in the lower end of Bodie, on the night of the 7th of August, one black horse, Mexican saddle, and blankets." The next few sentences were illegible, but it went on to say, "We will pay $100 for the return of the horse in Bodie, and will pay $50 for the arrest and conviction of the thieves. Moresi Brothers. Dairymen, Bodie, California."

She laughed out loud as she read an audacious ad by a Mr. Jonas Cohn, who claimed to be "The Pioneer Clothing Man of Nevada." Mr. Cohn went on to say he was there to let all his old friends know he was still around, and that he was going to "sink or swim with all the old timers." He also claimed to have an entirely new stock of clothing, gents' furnishings, boots and shoes, and claimed it was as good as anything to be found in San Francisco. He closed with an invitation to call at the Poor Man's Store and shake an honest man's hand.

She couldn't help thinking that Mr. Jonas Cohn must have been the Colonel Tom Parker of his day.

Yawning, she turned the page and read, "The Cheap Column. Under this head we will publish notices not exceeding FIVE lines."

The third paper was the *Daily Free Press* dated Thursday Morning, March 16, 1882, making her wonder if the *Bodie Morning News* had gone out of business. This paper, too, was mostly ads:

Philadelphia Beer Depot
Opposite Wells, Fargo & Co's.
This Celebrated Beer is not on tap, and for
purity and flavor
IT HAS NO EQUAL

Chas. H. Kelly
Leading
UNDERTAKER
Main Street, Bodie
Everything in the undertaker's line
fully attended to. Embalming and
the preparation of bodies for trans-
portation will receive special attendance.

Madeline Baker

WOOD! WOOD!
At
N. Ambler's
Nevada Wood Yard
Nut-pine, Cedar & Mahogany Wood
Cut to order and delivered at lowest rates.
Yard on Mill Street, South of Hospital

Mrs. Brophy
FASHIONABLE DRESSMAKER
LaGrange House

HOSTETTER'S STOMACH BITTERS
The name of Hostetter's Stomach Bitters
is heard in every dwelling. It finds a place
in every household, and its praises are
sounded throughout the whole Western
Hemisphere, as a general invigorant,
a cure for sick headache, a specific for flatulency
and sour stomach, an appetizing stomachic,
an excellent blood depurent and certain
remedy for intermittent fever and kindred
diseases.
For sale by all Druggists and Dealers
Generally

She thumbed through *The Guide to Bodie and Other Eastern Sierra Historic Sites*. She grinned when she saw that this book, too, mentioned the quote from the little girl's diary that was supposed to read, "Good-bye God! We are going to Bodie." According to this book, the editor of a Bodie newspaper rejoined that the little girl had been misquoted. What she had really said was, "Good, by God! We are going to Bodie."

Yawning, Shaye closed the book and put it on the table beside the bed, turned off the light, and snuggled under the covers. No sooner had she closed her eyes than the ghostly image she had seen at the jail appeared in her mind, as tall and dark and handsome as before, his eyes shadowed with despair.

"Go away," she murmured. "You don't exist."

She slept later than usual and woke feeling vaguely uneasy over a dream which had been set in Bodie. She supposed her dream wasn't all that surprising, since she had spent the day wandering through the ghost town, but, try as she might, she couldn't remember any details except that she had been desperately searching for someone . . . someone with long black hair and dark brown eyes.

She showered, brushed her teeth, and dried her hair. She pulled on a pair of black shorts and her favorite Beauty and the Beast tee shirt, laced up her Nikes, and went in search of breakfast, hoping to be on the road no later than eleven.

After a quick breakfast of French toast and orange juice, she made a stop at the nearest gas station. She smiled as she glanced at her watch. Ten forty-five.

She pulled out of the driveway and followed the signs to the highway. Switching on the radio, she found a country station.

"Next stop, Reno."

She was singing "Smoke Rings in the Dark" along with her favorite country singer, Gary Alan, when she realized she was on the road heading back to Bodie.

With a shake of her head, she pulled off the road, intending to turn around. Instead, she sat there for a moment, wondering how she could have made such a mistake in the first place, wondering if, subconsciously, she wanted to go back, wanted to see the jail one more time, if only to prove that what she had seen, or thought she had seen, had been nothing more than her imagination.

Frowning, she switched off the engine and gazed into the distance. Bodie was there, nestled in a shallow valley surrounded by a range of barren, windswept hills where nothing grew but sagebrush.

She leaned to the right and peered in the rearview mirror. "Have you lost your mind, Shaye Montgomery? You're supposed to be going to Reno. What the devil are you doing here?"

What, indeed? She closed her eyes, and the image of a man's face flashed through her mind. A face that looked familiar, yet one she knew she had never seen before.

Except in her imagination.

And last night.

In a dream.

The same attendant was on duty when she reached the entrance to the park. "Welcome back," she said.

Shaye grinned as she handed the woman two dollars. "Thanks. I didn't expect to be back so soon."

"Well, the place kind of grows on you," the woman replied. "Do you need a guidebook?"

Shaye held up the one she had bought yesterday. "No, thanks. Got one."

"Well, have a good day then."

"Thanks, you too." Shaye hesitated a moment. Then, feeling like a fool, she blurted, "Has anyone ever seen a ghost here?"

"Of course, honey," the attendant said with an indulgent grin. "It is a ghost town, you know."

"I'm serious."

"I've worked and lived here for the past five years," the attendant replied soberly. "And I've never seen one, but some of the year-round employees claim to have seen the Angel of Bodie."

"What's that?"

"Well, the way the story was told to me, one of the miners and a little girl became good friends. Seems she followed him wherever he went. One day she followed him just a little too close, and as he was swinging his axe, he accidentally hit her in the head and fractured her skull. She's buried in the Bodie cemetery."

"Have you seen her?"

"No, but a few years back, a couple of tourists claimed to. A man and his daughter were visiting the cemetery, and he said his little girl was laughing and seemed to be playing with an invisible playmate. He didn't think anything of it at the time. Later, his daughter supposedly asked who the little girl in the cemetery was."

"Do you believe it?"

"I don't know. But if there's such a thing as ghosts, this is the place for 'em."

With a nod, Shaye put the car in gear and drove up to the parking lot. As clearly as if she were seeing the words in print, she recalled the last few lines on the first page of the guide book: ". . . but with the possible exception of an occasional ghostly visitor, its badmen are all in their graves."

She parked the Rover, grabbed her keys and backpack, and locked the door. For a moment, she stood at the top of the hill, and then she hurried down the path and made her way to the museum housed in the Miners Union Hall on Main Street where she had bought books the day before.

"Can I help you?"

"Yes." She smiled at the man behind the counter. He was a nice-looking man, about her height, with wavy blond hair and hazel eyes. His badge identified him as Clark McDonald. "Do you have any books on . . ." She hesitated. "On ghosts?"

"You believe in ghosts, do you?"

"No, I don't, actually."

"Just curious?"

"It's research," she said, thinking quickly. "I'm a writer."

"Is that so? What do you write?"

"Actually, I'm an investigative reporter." She held out her hand. "Shaye Montgomery."

"Clark McDonald. What are you investigating here?"

"Nothing. I mean, it's like I said, I'm doing research. I've decided to try my hand at writing a novel set in Bodie."

"I see." Clark studied her a moment, his eyes narrowed, his expression thoughtful. Stepping our from behind the counter, he motioned for her to follow him.

Curious, she followed him outside and around to the back of the building. "You've seen something, haven't you?" he asked. "Felt something?"

"What do you mean?"

"Haven't you?"

She nodded, her mouth dry, her heart pounding.

"Where?"

"At the jail."

McDonald drew in a deep breath, let it out in a long sigh.

"Have you seen it?" she asked.

"I'm not sure. I thought I did once, maybe cause I was hoping to, but . . ." He shrugged. "It was probably just my imagination."

"When did it happen?"

"At the jail, just a year ago. On August twelfth."

"I saw him yesterday," she said. "Well, I don't know if it was him, but I saw something. At least I think I did."

He nodded. "Yesterday was August twelfth."

"Who is he? I mean, who was he?"

Clark glanced up and down the street. "His name

was Alejandro Valverde, but most people called him Rio. He came to Bodie in late eighteen seventy-nine, near as I can tell. He was a gambler, quick with a knife and a gun. He owned half-interest in a saloon for a while. His partner was a prostitute. He was accused of killing her. He swore he was innocent right up to the end, but no one believed him. He was hanged in eighteen eighty. On August twelfth, three days after they arrested him for her murder."

Shaye stared at him, her heart pounding wildly. "How do you know so much about him?"

"He was a distant relative. His mother was an Indian. I think her name was Lark or Dove or something like that. His old man was Irish and Spanish. Our lines cross somewhere on the Irish side. Alejandro was born in South Dakota, near the Black Hills."

"Do you know what Valverde looked like?"

"Just that he was tall, with long black hair."

"And brown eyes?"

Clark shrugged. "Might have been. I have an old photo, but it's black and white, you know, so it's hard to tell."

She felt a thrill of excitement. "I'd like to see it."

Clark glanced at his watch. "I've got to get back to work. Are you planning to spend the day here?"

"I don't know. Why?"

"The picture's up at my place. I've got an old diary you might be interested in, too. I could show them to you after work."

"All right."

"Why don't you meet me here at, say, seven? We can have dinner and talk."

Shaye nodded. "Sounds great. Thanks so much."

With a nod, he walked toward the street.

Shaye stood there a moment. It was only a little after noon, which meant she had seven hours to kill. She tapped her foot impatiently, then took a deep breath.

"Relax, Shaye," she muttered. "You're on vacation."

There was nothing to do but take the self-guided tour again. Pulling the guidebook out of her backpack, she walked back to Green Street and the post marked One. The Dolan house. The guidebook had little to say about this family other than that it produced two Mono County sheriffs around the turn of the century.

The Methodist Church was next. It was the only church still standing in the town, and the only Protestant church ever built. The last service had been held in 1932. In the ensuing years, the interior of the building had been badly vandalized. According to the booklet, the Ten Commandants, painted on oilcloth, had once hung behind the pulpit. Apparently, whoever had stolen it did not hold with the Eighth Commandment—Thou shalt not steal.

The next stop was the McDonald house. The guidebook said that McDonald had been injured when two tons of dynamite, still a recent invention in 1879, blew up the old Standard works. The house was later owned by the Burkham family. S. B. Burkham had operated a store on Main Street in the 1880's and

1890's. His son, Cecil, ran the first automobile stage out of Bodie in 1912.

She really should write a book, Shaye thought. The town and its former inhabitants were fascinating.

Shaye continued on down Green Street. She paused in front of each building, waiting to see if she would feel anything, sense anything out of the ordinary. Maybe what had happened at the jail yesterday had just been her imagination, after all. And maybe Clark McDonald was just some guy who was a little wacko from spending so much time in a ghost town.

She stopped in front of the Cain house, located on the corner of Green and Park Streets. It was her favorite, with its large square glass window. There was a photograph of James Cain and his wife, Martha, on page five of the guidebook. It was a wedding picture. The caption stated they had been married in Carson City on September 17, 1879. The groom was sitting down, looking stern. Martha stood beside him, her forearm resting on his shoulder, her long white veil trailing down her back. They made a handsome couple. She wondered if they had been happy in Bodie. According to the guidebook, Cain became the town's principal property owner.

She passed the sawmill, the Seiler house, the Cameron house, the Lester Bell house, the Mendocini house, the house of Pat Reddy, a one-armed attorney who had been well known through the West for his ability to defend criminals, union members, and the underdog in general.

It was with a sense of trepidation that she approached the jail. Today, there was no one else nearby, no other tourists in sight.

She approached the barred window slowly, took a deep breath, and looked inside.

Nothing met her gaze but an empty room. She felt a deep sense of relief, and a vague sense of disappointment. "You really do need a vacation," she muttered.

And then she felt it again, a sudden whisper of cold air that raised goose bumps along her arms and sent a chill down her spine. She grasped the iron bars in her hands. They were firm. Cold. Tangible.

She clung to them as the air inside the cell began to shimmer, and then she saw him, standing against the far wall, his hands shoved in the pockets of his trousers. He looked solid and real, not ghostlike at all. As if sensing her there, he looked up, his gaze catching hers. Something intangible flowed between them. She felt his anger at being imprisoned, his bitterness. His despair.

This can't be happening. Yet even as the thought crossed her mind, she knew it was real . . . maybe the most real, or unreal, moment of her whole life.

And then, as quickly as the image had appeared, it was gone. She stood there for several minutes, trying to convince herself she hadn't seen what she had seen. Her hands were trembling when she let go of the bars. Her legs were too weak to support her and she sat down, her back against the jail's rough-hewn wooden exterior. Closing her eyes, she took several deep breaths. She couldn't deny what she had seen this time. It hadn't been her imagination. She had seen him. Alejandro Valverde. But why? What did it mean?

The thought plagued her the rest of the day. Feeling suddenly restless, she stood up and began walking up and down the streets, streets Alejandro Valverde had walked on over a hundred years ago. Had he stopped at the Boone Store? Played cards at the Sawdust Corner Saloon? Wandered the streets of Chinatown?

Later, she sat on the hillside, watching the other tourists, contemplating the changing shadows of daylight as the sun moved across the sky. The setting sun cast shimmering orange highlights on the buildings, making them look as though they were on fire.

Finally, it was six forty-five. Rising, she dusted off her shorts and started walking down the hill to meet Clark McDonald.

Chapter Three

Shaye was back at the museum a few minutes before seven. Clark McDonald was waiting for her out on the broadwalk.

"You're early," he remarked.

"So are you."

"Well, there's a good reason for that," he said, revealing a dimple in his left cheek. "After all, it's not every day that I get to have dinner with a pretty tourist."

Shaye laughed self-consciously. She had never thought of herself as pretty. She wasn't ugly by any means, but she wasn't sure she qualified as pretty. Her shoulder-length hair was an unremarkable shade of brown. Her eyes were green. Her figure was okay, perhaps a little on the skinny side. She had nice legs, though. Long, slender, and tan. They were, she thought, her only vanity.

"It must have been quite a long day for you," Clark remarked as they walked through the now deserted ghost town. "Once you've toured the town, there's not much else to do."

She hesitated before replying. "It was an interesting day."

He looked at her askance a moment, but she wasn't ready yet to discuss what she had seen, or thought she had seen, at the jail.

"I noticed one of the houses is called the McDonald house," Shaye remarked. "Any relation?"

"No, 'fraid not."

They walked down Green Street, past Main, and made a right turn on Wood Street. They passed several houses until they came to one with a wooden sign on the side that said *Nolan House—Employee Residence*. Like all the other houses in Bodie, it was made of time-weathered wood. The picket fence sagged, the gate hung from one hinge, the stairs were crooked.

"Is this where you live?" Shaye asked dubiously.

Clark chuckled. "I admit, it doesn't look like much on the outside, but I assure you the inside is a lot more modern."

She followed him through the rickety gate, climbed the three stairs to the porch, and stood to one side while he unlocked the door, then held it open for her. "Come on in."

Shaye crossed the threshold and found herself in an average-size living room, furnished with a green and tan plaid sofa, a dark green easy chair, and a couple of mahogany end tables. The walls were painted off-white, there were a couple of colorful throw rugs on the floor, an old-fashioned-looking clock hung on the wall over the brick fireplace.

McDonald closed the door behind her. "Would you like to take a look around?"

"Sure."

"Here, let me take that." Clark took her backpack and set it on a ladder-back chair beside the front door.

"Well, this is the living room," Clark said, and went on to explain that the shell of the house was original but the inside had been modernized to accommodate the employees who lived there. It was a large house: living room, kitchen, bathroom, and two fair-size bedrooms.

"Do the park rangers live here year round?" Shaye asked.

"Only a couple of us stay all year. I'm one of them. The winters can be rough, and we don't get many tourists. Do you want to keep me company while I fix dinner?"

"I'm not much of a cook, but I'll be glad to help, if you like."

"Sure."

She followed him into the kitchen. "What do you want me to do?"

"I've got some steaks in the fridge. Think you could fix us a salad while I put the steaks on the grill?"

"That I can do."

*   *   *

Clark McDonald proved to be an amiable dinner companion. He told her he had been employed at the park for the last four years. The summers were hot, he said, the winters downright frigid, but there was something about the place that kept him there year after year. Talk of the present day inevitably led to talk of the past. Clark had done a great deal of research on the town and its people.

He smiled at her. "Helps to pass the time when the snow's fifteen or twenty feet deep and the wind's howling. Sometimes I think I missed my calling. I think I should have been a history teacher. The past really intrigues me, though I'm not sure why."

"I never cared much for history in school," Shaye remarked, "but ghost towns have always fascinated me. Durango, Silverton, Jerome. Oh! And Virginia City in Montana. There's a candy store there that has the best saltwater taffy I've ever tasted." She grinned at him. "I guess I know what you mean about the past, though. I can't quite put my finger on it, but there's something about walking down the streets of one of those old towns. I don't know what it is . . ."

"Yeah, I know what you mean. Gives me the feeling of . . . shoot, I don't know . . ."

"Of connecting to the past?"

Clark nodded. "I guess that's it. I'm pretty rootless at the moment, and being here, I guess it gives me a sense of . . ." He shrugged. "A sense of where I came from. Hell, I can't explain it."

"You don't have to. I know what you mean. I did

a little reading about the town last night. It must have been pretty wild in its day."

"Oh, it was that, all right. Gold was discovered here in eighteen fifty-nine, but it was another twenty years before the boom began. In June of eighteenth seventy-eight there was a big strike up at the Bodie Mine. Ore was assayed at a thousand dollars a ton. In six weeks, the Bodie Mine shipped a million dollars' worth of gold bullion, and the rush was on."

"That's amazing," Shaye exclaimed. "All that wealth buried under those barren brown hills."

Clark nodded. "By the end of the year, there were more than six hundred buildings. The winter of seventy-eight was reported to be one of the worst. There were thousands of people living here then. Housing was poor. Food was scarce. Nothing much to do except hang out at the saloons and get drunk. Men gambled and fought. Hundreds of them died from exposure and disease.

"In the spring of seventy-nine, gold-hungry men and women were pouring into town as fast as they could get here. Buildings were going up everywhere. Nearly everybody had a claim or stock in one of the mines. The men had money, and they were anxious to spend it."

Shaye nodded. It was easy to imagine how it must have been back then. Even now, Bodie was in a remote area. In the 1800's, the area had been sparsely settled. There had been no government and practically no law, making the town a haven for con men and prostitutes. There were no modern conveniences.

Housing had been poor, the climate harsh both summer and winter. Only the saloons and gambling dens, the dance halls and cribs, provided warmth and entertainment.

Once again, she was glad she had not lived back then, when the only lights were coal-oil lamps and candles. How had people managed with no running water, no gas, no electricity, no hospitals, no theaters, no entertainment of any kind suitable for a decent woman except picnics and an occasional dance? They hadn't even had a church until the late 1800's. Of course, women had very little spare time in those days, when practically everything had to be done by hand and made from scratch. She would have made a lousy pioneer. She couldn't sew, hated to cook, couldn't imagine scrubbing laundry in a tub or hanging clothes on a line to dry.

"Well," Clark said, "I guess I've bored you long enough. I'll get that book."

Shaye smiled. Rising, she started to clear the table.

"Leave it," Clark said.

"I don't mind. Really."

"I'll do them later." He smiled at her. "You're a guest, after all."

With a shrug, Shaye followed him into the living room. Clark went to a bookcase and took a small, leather-bound book from the second shelf. Opening the book, he pulled out a square white envelope and offered it to her.

Shaye took a deep breath, knowing, in that moment, that her life was about to change forever, change in ways she could not fathom.

With a hand that trembled, she opened the envelope and withdrew a small picture. She turned it over and found herself looking at the face of the man she had seen in the jail, the man she had been searching for in her dream. Alejandro Valverde. It was him. There was no doubt in her mind. None at all.

"Miss Montgomery?"

She looked up, her gaze meeting his.

"It's him, isn't it?" Clark asked. "The man you saw in the jail."

"Oh, yes." She sat down on a chair near the book-case. "It's him." It was a face she would never forget. She looked at the photograph again. "When was this taken?"

"I'm not sure."

"But it's here, in Bodie?"

"Yes. I think maybe it was taken in front of one of the saloons. See here—" He pointed at the top right corner of the photo. "This looks like the edge of a sign. And this"—his finger moved down a little— "looks like it might be an I and an E. I thinks he's standing in front of the Queen of Bodie saloon, maybe the day it opened."

Shaye took a deep breath. "I saw him again today."

"You did?"

She nodded.

Clark sat down on the sofa. "Where did you see him this time?"

"In the jail again. It only lasted a few moments, but it was so real."

"What happened?" He leaned forward, his elbows resting on his knees, his gaze intent upon her face. "Did he see you? Did he say anything?"

"It happened so fast. I looked in the window, and suddenly he was there. He didn't say anything, but he looked at me . . ." She glanced down at the photograph in her hand, remembering the impact of his gaze meeting hers. "I felt what he was feeling."

Clark shook his head. "Amazing," he murmured. "Simply amazing." He studied her a moment. "But why you?"

"I don't know."

"I tried to contact him again after I saw him that first time, but I never could. I even got a medium out here one night," he admitted, looking somewhat sheepish. "Nothing."

Shaye didn't know what to say, so she gestured at the book in his hand. "Did he write that?"

"What? Oh, no. It's a diary, written by the woman he was supposed to have killed."

"May I see it?"

"Of course."

Shaye placed the photograph on the end table, face up, as Clark offered her the book.

"I could use a cup of coffee," he said. "How about you?"

"Yes, please."

The cover of the diary was brown leather; the pages were old and brittle, yellow around the edges. She opened the book carefully, her gaze skimming the first page. *Diary of Daisy Joanna Sullivan, commenced this 1st day of January in the year of our Lord, 1879.*

Shaye thumbed through the book, skimming over the entries, until she came to a page dated April 2nd.

I started work at the Velvet Rose today. It is a much Nicer place than my old crib on Maiden Lane. The girls are friendly and my room is nice, although there is dust everywhere. I can't believe I've been in Bodie almost a Year. I've never worked a mining town before. The traffick in the streets is never-ending. Huge wagons arrive carrying freight from the railroad. They are pulled by teams of twenty horses, sometimes more. Ore wagons come down from the mines, and there are wood carts and hay wagons and lumber wagons. Stage Coaches, too. One of the coaches was robbed today.

April 3rd. I had eight customers today. I love this town. All the men are rich. And generous. And Madame Louisa lets me keep half of what I make. If this Keeps up, I'll be able to save enough money to go back home.

April 4th. This town never closes. There isn't much Law here. The sheriff lives in the County Seat, which is twelve Miles away. Killings are frequent, especially in Chinatown. I guess that is to be expected, since all the men carry guns.

April 5th. One of the girls who worked at one

of the other saloons killed herself last night. Her body was found in a ditch two miles south of town.

April 6th. I met someone tonight. His name is Alejandro Valverde. He is a gambler, and a good One, too. I took him a drink, and he asked me to stay. I sat beside him for an hour, and he won over a thousand dollars. When he was ready to leave, he gave me a hundred dollars! He said it was because I'd brought him luck.

April 7th. He came into the Rose again tonight and asked me to sit beside him. For luck, he said. He is a most Handsome man. And Kind. He treats me like I was a lady of quality. He won again tonight, and gave me another hundred dollars.

"Coffee?"

Shaye looked up, startled. "Yes, thank you."

Clark handed her a mug, then sat down on the sofa. "Lose yourself in the Old West, did you?"

"Yes, I'm afraid so. How was Daisy killed?"

"She was shot in the head. They found her body in the bedroom of her house."

Shaye took a sip of coffee, her gaze falling on the photo on the table. It was a strong, handsome face, but it was his eyes that held her attention. They were vibrant and alive, even in a photograph that had been taken over a hundred years ago. Alejandro Valverde. "You said he swore he was innocent. Weren't there any other suspects?"

"Dade McCrory was questioned."

"McCrory?"

"He was Daisy's partner in a saloon. In her diary, she mentioned that she thought McCrory was stealing from the till. Apparently, they had several fights about it."

Shaye nodded. "Go on."

"Like I said, McCrory was questioned, but according to an old newspaper article, he had an alibi." Clark grunted. "Claimed he spent the night with one of the girls at the Rose. And the girl backed him up; swore he'd been there the whole night."

"Why did they think Valverde did it?"

Clark blew out a deep breath. "He used to carry a hideout gun. They found it beside her body."

"What about fingerprints . . . oh, I guess they didn't do that back then, did they?"

"No. Too bad."

"Do you really think he was innocent?"

"I think he was capable of violence, but not murder."

Shaye glanced at her watch. As much as she wanted to stay and hear more, as anxious as she was to read the rest of the diary, it was after nine, and she had a long drive ahead of her. "I'd best be going. Thank you so much for dinner, and everything."

"It's late," Clark remarked. "Maybe you should spend the night. I hate to think of you bouncing over that road at this time of night."

"Oh, no, I couldn't."

"I'd feel better if you did. My roommate's on vacation. He won't be back until next week. You can use his room."

"Well . . ." It was tempting. She looked at her watch again. If she left now, she wouldn't get to Reno until midnight. Besides, how many tourists had a chance to spend the night in Bodie?

"I wish you would. It's a bad road. What if you got a flat? You wouldn't want to be stuck out there in the middle of the night, would you?"

He had a point, she thought, but she really needed to be on her way. She was about to refuse when her glance fell on Valverde's photograph. She didn't really want to leave, she thought, at least not until she'd read the rest of Daisy's diary. "I think I will stay. I'll just run up to my car and get my overnight bag."

"I'll go with you."

"That's not necessary. I'll be fine."

"You're sure?"

She laughed softly. "Of course."

Some of Shaye's confidence waned as she left the house behind. The town was dark, lit only by a full moon and a dark sky filled with glittering stars. She hadn't realized how far away the Nolan House was from the parking area until she had to walk it in the dark.

She was a little breathless by the time she reached her car, the only one left in the lot. Unlocking the rear hatch, she grabbed her overnight bag, which held her cosmetics and toothbrush, pulled a change of clothes, socks, underwear, and her nightshirt out of her suitcase and jammed them into the overnight case, then closed and locked the door of the Rover.

She stood at the top of the path a moment, looking down at the sleeping town, trying to imagine what it would have looked like in its heyday, the streets crowded with wagons and people. A cold chill slid down her spine. In the drifting shadows of the night, it did indeed look like a town inhabited by ghosts. Wispy white clouds appeared over the hills, moving slowly across the indigo sky, playing peekaboo with the moon.

"There are no such things as ghosts, Shaye Montgomery," she muttered. "No matter what you think you've seen, there are no such things as ghosts. Or goblins. Or things that go bump in the night."

She repeated the words over and over again as she walked down the path and turned left on Green Street. Yet even as she told herself she didn't believe, she knew in her heart of hearts that what she had seen was real.

A cool breeze seemed to follow her down the street, stirring small dust devils, carrying the echoes of voices long dead. The childish voice of the Angel of Bodie. The sultry laughter of the ladies of the evening. A slow, deep voice that she knew was his.

She wanted to run, but something slowed her steps.

She passed the Methodist Church, and the notes of an old hymn seemed to whisper to the wind. She heard the clanging of a blacksmith's hammer and the whinny of a horse as she passed the old barn; the caching of a cash register as she neared the Boone Store; the faint sound of weeping as she passed the

49

morgue; the ringing of a school bell; the sound of children reciting their lessons as she approached Main Street.

When she reached the schoolhouse, she glanced in the window, and the inside of the building seemed to light up. She could see two dozen boys and girls sitting at their desks, see the schoolteacher standing at the head of the classroom, a long pointer in her hand. She stared, transfixed, thinking it looked like a scene out of the Haunted Mansion at Disneyland.

What would she see if she went to the jail?

The soft summer breeze kissed her cheek as she reversed her direction. She turned right on Main Street, her steps quickening as she made her way through the darkness toward the jail.

As she passed the Kirkwood Stable, she caught the pungent odor of manure, the sweet scent of hay, and then she was standing in front of the jail, her body trembling, her heart pounding wildly.

Step by slow step, she moved closer to the iron-barred window. Took a deep breath. Looked inside.

In the flickering light of an oil lamp, she saw Alejandro Valverde stretched out on a narrow cot. One arm was folded behind his head; his ankles were crossed. A thin plume of smoke rose from the cigarette he held in his left hand. She glanced quickly around the room. A square table and two chairs stood in the opposite corner. A black coat was folded over the back of one of the chairs. She could hear snoring coming from the sheriff's office adjacent to the jail.

Valverde took a deep drag on the cigarette. Sitting

up, he dropped the butt on the floor, ground it out with his boot heel. He sat there a moment, and then he stood up and began to pace the floor, his long legs carrying him quickly from one side of the room to the other.

He didn't look like a ghost at all. He had form and substance. She could smell the smoke from his cigarette, hear the sound of his footsteps as he paced the floor, see his shadow move across the wall.

Shaye watched as though mesmerized. She saw him so clearly. He wore black wool trousers, a white shirt, a black vest embroidered with tiny gold fleurs-de-lis, black boots. The candlelight cast red highlights in his hair, which was long and black with no hint of a wave. His brows were straight, his nose was sharply defined, his jaw was firm and shadowed by the beginnings of a beard.

And his eyes were brown. A deep, dark brown. She saw them clearly when he came to stare out the window.

She started to back away, then realized there was nothing to fear. He couldn't see her. She probably wasn't really seeing him. It was probably just an illusion, or maybe she was dreaming. Of course, that was it. She wasn't really here at all. She was asleep back in the Nolan House . . .

And then his gaze settled on her face, and for one heart-stopping, soul-shattering moment, she would have sworn that Alejandro Valverde was alive, that he was looking at her, seeing her. He was close, so close she could see the tiny lines that fanned out

51

around his eyes, the faint white scar near his hairline. So close.

Overcome by a sudden, inexplicable need to touch him, she lifted her hand, her heart pounding fiercely as she reached toward him . . .

And the moment was gone. The cell was dark and empty, and she was alone save for the sighing of the wind that had suddenly turned brisk and cold.

Hugging her overnight bag to her chest, she turned and ran down Main Street and didn't stop running until she reached the Nolan House.

Clark was standing on the porch. "I was beginning to worry about you," he said. "Hey, are you all right? You look like you've seen a . . ."

"A ghost? I have." She moved past him into the house, stood shivering in the middle of the room, her overnight case clutched to her chest.

Clark shut and locked the door. He pried the bag from her arms, urged her to sit down on the sofa, draped a thick red wool blanket around her shoulders. He left the room for a moment, came back carrying a glass which he thrust into her hand. "Here, drink this."

She took a sip, gasped as the liquid burned a path down her throat. "It's whiskey!"

"Drink it," he said, "All of it."

She coughed, then drained the glass, grateful for the warmth that engulfed her. "It was so real," she said. "So real."

Clark smiled sympathetically as he sat down at the opposite end of the sofa. "Bodie has its share of ghost stories. Some of the workers have claimed to see lights going on and off in some of the buildings—"

"I did," Shaye said, her voice rising with nervous excitement. "I saw lights tonight. In the schoolhouse."

"Really? My roommate swears he heard piano music coming from the old Sawdust Corner Saloon last year, but no one I know has ever seen anything."

"I heard music, too, coming from the church."

Clark shook his head. "One of the park employees was living in the old Mendocini house a while back. He was having lasagna for dinner one night, disappointed because he didn't have any garlic. He said all of a sudden his eyes began to water and he started sneezing. He went outside for some fresh air, and when he went back inside, the whole house reeked of fresh-cut garlic."

Shaye grinned, amused in spite of herself. "I've never believed in ghosts."

"Until now?"

She couldn't say it out loud. If she admitted it, it would make it true somehow. "I think I'd better get ready for bed."

Clark nodded. "Sleep as long as you want. I don't have to go in until ten tomorrow, so I'll probably sleep late. If you get up before I do, help yourself to something to eat. There's coffee in the cupboard."

"Thank you." She pointed to the diary on the table. "Is it all right if I finish reading that before I go to bed?"

"Sure."

Picking up her overnight bag and the book, Shaye

followed Clark down a narrow hall into a small square bedroom furnished with a double bed and a chest of drawers. There was a pair of well-worn sneakers in the corner; a Dodgers baseball jacket hung from an old-fashioned brass hook on the back of the door.

"There's an extra blanket on the shelf in the closet if you get cold." Clark lifted his hand in a gesture that took in the whole room. "Make yourself at home. There's plenty of hot water if you want to take a shower."

"Thank you."

"If I don't see you in the morning, it was nice spending the evening with you."

"Thank you. I enjoyed spending the evening with you, too. Good night, Clark."

"Good night."

Shaye closed the door behind him. With a sigh, she dropped her overnight case on the bed, popped the lid, and took out her nightshirt and toothbrush. She felt a little self-conscious about taking a shower in the house of a man she had just met, but a hot shower was just what she needed to relax her.

She showered quickly, slipped into her nightshirt, brushed her teeth, and hurried back to her room. Closing the door, she picked up the diary and slipped into bed.

She turned the pages carefully, skimming over the entries, pausing to read whenever she saw Alejandro Valverde's name. As the days went by, he was mentioned more and more frequently. Strangely, they were never intimate, yet Daisy's feelings for him were obviously very deep. He continued to visit the Velvet Rose saloon and give her money, and in a short time, Daisy had saved enough to quit.

The entry for May 5th read:

I can't believe it. Rio and I are partners. Our new saloon will open next week. We're going to call it the Bodie Belle. Instead of being one of the girls, I will be the hostess. It's like a dream come true. The only men I'll have to share my bed with will be those of my own choosing, and I won't have to charge them. Best of all, I'll get to see Alejandro every night. I love him so much. I wonder if he knows. I wish he felt the same . . .

The new saloon appeared to be a success. Of course, in a town of ten thousand, that was no surprise. Daisy talked of having money for the first time in her life, of ordering clothes from New York City and Paris, of trying to become a lady so Alejandro would notice her.

She had drawn flowers around the borders of the page dated June 3rd.

Today is my nineteenth birthday. The girls made me a cake. Celeste gave me some perfumed soap. It smells divine. Bethie gave me a silk kimono. But, best of all is the gold locket from Rio. Maybe he does care.

Nineteen, Shaye thought, and already a seasoned prostitute. She tried to imagine such a life, tried to imagine what it would have been like to work in a smoky saloon, to sell her body to any man who had the price. She remembered reading about some of the whores in one of the books she had bought. One, named Eleanor Dumont, had lived in Bodie. According to the book, she had been a pretty young French girl with a flair for gambling. Female gamblers had been rare in those days, and the men had been fascinated by her. She had spent twenty years following gold strikes from Idaho to South Dakota. When her luck was bad, she turned to prostitution. As she grew older, Dumont was dubbed Madame Moustache due to a thin line of dark hair above her upper lip. In 1879, Dumont was residing in Bodie. In September of that year, she borrowed three hundred dollars, which she lost gambling. Leaving town on foot, she went out into the desert and swallowed poison. She was buried in the outcast cemetery in an unmarked grave.

There were others: French Joe, Nellie Monroe, Emma Goldsmith. And Lottie Johl, who had once been a whore but gained respectability with her painting, and by marrying the local butcher.

Shaye glanced at her watch. It was after midnight. One more entry, she thought, one more page. But she couldn't stop reading.

In July, Daisy bought a house, and for the next month most of the entries were about the house and the fun she had furnishing it.

But mostly Daisy wrote about Alejandro. It reminded Shaye of her own first schoolgirl crush, of the diary she had kept, when every entry was about Steve Adams and how cute he was. Shaye had written practically every word he had said to her, what he wore to school, how jealous she was when he ate lunch with Sherri Bensal. Daisy had recorded the same kinds of things about Alejandro, and Shaye realized that, for all Daisy's "experience" with men, she was very naïve and very innocent.

In early August, jealousy reared its ugly head. Alejandro hired a new girl to work in the saloon. An entry dated October 8th read: *I hate her! Why doesn't he look at me the way he looks at Maddy Brown?*

Shaye sighed as she read on. Every entry was tinged with jealousy. Some of the pages were tear-stained, the words blurred and illegible.

She read on, unable to stop. There were fights and harsh words through a long, cold fall. It culminated in mid-December. The entry for the 15th was stained with tears:

Rio told me today that he sold his half of the Belle to Dade McCrory. I can't believe he would do such a thing without discussing it with me first. He said he doesn't like owning a saloon, that it involves too much responsibility. He said he talked to Rojas over at the Queen of Bodie, and he's going to start dealing there tomorrow night. Well, he can just take Maddy Brown with him, because tomorrow she'll be out of a job!

. . . Maybe I'm being too hasty. If I keep Maddy here, maybe he'll come back to see her . . .

The next few pages were tear-stained, filled with the pain and heartache that only the very young can feel.

The entry for January 1st, 1880, read: *A New Year. I wonder what it will hold for me.*

The entry for January 31st was only four words that conveyed a world of sadness: *Will winter never end?*

Shaye quickly read the succeeding entries, which talked about Daisy's new partner. As Clark had said, Daisy wrote that she was certain McCrory was skimming the profits. In February, she started drinking with the customers, something she had apparently never done before. By March, she had graduated to whiskey. In April, she was taking men to her bed again, sometimes for money, sometimes for "love." In May and June, there were more references to McCrory.

It was in June that she found the nerve to confront McCrory. The entry for the 7th read:

He can deny it all he likes, but I know he is Stealing money from the cash drawer. We have more customers than ever and should be making a bigger profit. Dade said it was my fault, that I was drinking up our profits. The Bastard. I told him if it didn't stop, I was going to ask Rio for help.

June 20th. I went to see Rio this morning. I

wore my new dress. I didn't have anything to drink last night. I was very nervous about seeing him again, but he was very Kind and Gentle-manly. I told him that I was sure Dade is cheat-ing me, and he said he would have a talk with Dade. He said he was sorry things hadn't worked out better with Dade, and that he would take care of everything. And then he told me how pretty I looked, and I threw myself in his arms and told him I loved him. I begged him to come back to the saloon, to give me another chance. He smiled down at me, not with love, but with Pity in his eyes. How could I have done such a thing? I have never been so mortified in my Life.

There were several other entries. She mentioned a new shipment of crystal glasses from New York City, a letter from her sister informing her that her mother had died.

The entry for the 30th took Shaye completely by surprise.

I can't believe it! Dade asked me to Marry him! He went down on his knee and declared he loved me. I didn't know whether to laugh or cry. I told him I couldn't marry him, that I didn't love him. He told me I was a fool, that Rio would never marry a girl like me, and stormed out of the house.

And then, abruptly, the entries stopped. The last one, dated July 4th, 1880, read:

I can't stop loving him, but I know he will never love me. I don't want to go on living without him.

With a sigh, Shaye closed the diary and put it on the table beside the bed, then turned out the light. She couldn't think of any reason why Valverde would have killed Daisy. McCrory seemed to be the only one with a motive.

Slipping under the covers, she closed her eyes. Love, she thought. Was there really such a thing? And did it ever last?

Chapter Four

It was a typical Old West saloon, as big as a barn. The bar was to the left of the swinging doors and ran the length of the building. The obligatory picture of a nude hung over the bar. The woman in this one was plump, with long, red-gold hair that fell over her ample breasts. Across the room from the bar was a short-order restaurant with a long counter and a number of stools. The rest of the room was filled with gambling tables. Most of them seemed to be for faro games. Grim-faced dealers sat behind the tables. She stared at the stacks of gold and silver piled on the tables. Hundreds and hundreds of dollars' worth, she thought, or maybe thousands.

Miners in faded red shirts, canvas pants, and high black boots rubbed shoulders with dapper gamblers clad in white linen shirts, silk cravats, and black city suits. The smell of cigar smoke, unwashed bodies, and cheap perfume mingled with the scent of bacon and onions.

She moved slowly through the crowd, and then she saw him. He was sitting at a poker table with four other men, his expression bland, his eyes narrowed as he opened a fresh deck, shuffled the cards, and dealt a hand. She couldn't draw her gaze from his face. His skin was innately dark. His hair was thick and black and fell past his shoulders. He had a proud nose, a firm jaw, straight black brows. His lips were full, sensual. He grinned at something one of the men said, and she saw the hint of a dimple in his cheek.

A woman walked over to the table, her hips swaying in bold invitation as she went to stand behind him. She laid a hand on his shoulder in a gesture that managed to be both casual and possessive as she bent over to whisper something in his ear, revealing a generous expanse of powdered flesh.

He laughed and waved the woman away. Then he looked up, and his gaze met hers. There was a flicker of recognition, of disbelief. He spoke to one of the men, then laid his cards face down on the table. Rising, he walked toward her, a predatory gleam in his dark, dark eyes.

Shaye's heart began to pound with fear, trepidation, excitement . . .

"Shaye, if you're awake, breakfast is almost ready."

The soft-spoken words woke her with a start. She

closed her eyes, wanting to go back to the dream, but it was gone.

With a sigh, she sat up. "Thanks, Clark, I'll be right out."

She dressed quickly in a pair of white shorts and a black Jekyll and Hyde tee shirt, brushed her teeth, stuffed her dirty clothes in her overnight bag, made the bed, then went into the kitchen. A glance out the window showed it was going to be a beautiful day.

"Morning," Clark said. "I hope you're hungry."

She didn't usually eat breakfast, but today she was starving. "I am. Anything I can do to help?"

He shook his head. "Want some coffee?"

"Please."

She sat down, thinking how nice it was to have a man wait on her. Josh wouldn't have thought of fixing her breakfast any more than he would have thought of making the bed. She had always wondered why making the bed was her job. After all, he had slept in it, too. She pushed his memory from her mind. It was over and done. She was never going to give a man the power to hurt her again.

"Hey?"

She looked up. "I'm sorry, did you say something?"

He laughed softly. "Your breakfast is getting cold."

"What?" She looked down at the plate in front of her. "I'm sorry."

"Where were you this time? Back in the past again?"

"Yes," she admitted. "But this time it was my past."

He grunted softly. "Do you want to talk about it?"

"Not really."

"I'm a good listener."

Suddenly, she did want to talk about it. "Are you married?"

"Not anymore."

"Divorced?"

Clark nodded. "Three years."

"Me, too. I guess no one stays married anymore. Why did you get divorced?"

"No reason. Lots of reasons. Heck, I don't know. We got along fine until we got married, and then it was just one fight after another. We split up for a while and found out we were both happier that way, so . . ." He shook his head. "I guess some people just can't live together."

"I'm sorry."

"What about you?"

"I was away on an assignment. I came home early and found him in bed with a friend of mine."

"That's rough."

She shrugged, as if it weren't important. "It was my own fault. I should have seen it coming. He hated my job. He wanted me to quit. He thought I should stay home and be a housewife, like his mother."

Clark sat back, his expression thoughtful. "No, I can't picture you doing that."

"I couldn't either."

"So you divorced him?"

She nodded. "He married her a week after the divorce was final. They had a baby six months later."

"Are you sorry you left him?"

"No!" She stared down at the eggs, now cold, on her plate. She wasn't sorry she had left Josh. She could never stay with a man who had been unfaithful to her. And contrary to what Josh had believed, she did want a home and a family. But they had both been young. She hadn't wanted to get pregnant until she could stay home with the baby, and she hadn't been ready to quit her job. It was fun, exciting work, and she loved it. Maybe she had loved it too much. Maybe she hadn't loved Josh enough. "I don't know," she said with a sigh. "Maybe it was my fault."

"If I've learned anything, it's that it takes two to make a marriage," he remarked.

"I suppose."

"Do you want me to warm those eggs up for you?"

"No, thank you. I guess I'm not as hungry as I thought."

"The least I can do is warm up your coffee." He stood up and got the coffee pot.

It was nice to be waited on, Shaye thought, nice to have a man who thought of her needs, too, instead of just his own. She drank her coffee, accepted a refill.

"I guess you'll be leaving today," Clark said.

She nodded. "I'm on my way to Plumas Pines."

"Pretty place," he said. "My folks used to take me there in the summer. I haven't been there in years. Good fishing, as I recall."

"The best," she said with a sigh. "I should probably be on my way."

He nodded, but neither of them moved.

Shaye looked out the window. "Maybe I'll spend another day here," she remarked. Maybe she really would write that book. The longer she stayed here, the more fascinated she was by the town, by the story of Alejandro Valverde.

"Well, I've got to get going." Rising, Clark carried his plate to the sink and rinsed it off. "If you decide to stay another day, you're welcome to stay here. I'll be at the museum the rest of the day. If you decide to go, try and stop by before you leave."

"I will."

"If I don't see you before you leave, have a safe trip."

"Thank you. Now that I know where you live, maybe I'll send you a postcard."

"I'd like that. Lock up when you leave, will you? And don't worry about the dishes. I'll do them later."

Shaye stood up. "Thanks for everything, Clark."

"My pleasure."

They stood a few feet apart, not quite friends but no longer strangers.

"Well," Clark said, "I'd better go." He closed the distance between them, started to take her hand, and then gave her a quick hug instead. "Maybe you'll stop by on your way home."

"Maybe. Thanks again, for everything."

He nodded, then grabbed his hat and left the house. Shaye stared after him. She thought about Clark as she filled the sink with hot water and washed their few dishes. He was a nice man. If she'd had time, and if he lived closer to Los Angeles, she might have liked to get to know him better, she thought, and then shook her head. No way. She didn't need another man in her life. At least not now.

She dried the dishes and put them away, grabbed her overnight bag and her backpack, and left the house, being careful to lock the door.

It was time to get back to the real world, time to forget about ghosts and Alejandro Valverde. She was a newspaper reporter. She didn't have time to write a novel. She was on vacation, obviously a much-needed vacation. It was time to get on with it.

She didn't see any other tourists as she walked down the dusty road. She thought that was odd, but maybe not. Clark had said there were days when hardly anyone came through.

It struck her suddenly how quiet it was. Not even a breeze stirred the air. It was as if the whole town were holding its breath. In spite of the sun's heat, she felt suddenly cold.

She had an inexplicable urge to glance over her shoulder, and an equally strong urge to run away just as fast as she could.

"You've been here too long," she muttered.

When she reached the corner of Green and Main, the wind began to blow. She shivered, overcome by the strangest feeling that she had never felt a wind quite like this one before. The sky turned suddenly dark. Blowing sand stung her eyes and she squeezed them shut, wondering if there was a storm coming.

And then, as quickly as it had begun, the wind stilled. She adjusted her grip on her overnight bag and stepped into the intersection. It was then she heard it, the sound of a piano. It wasn't her imagination this time. She took a few steps down Main Street, and the music grew louder.

She paused a moment, and then continued on. She stopped in front of a two-story building on the left side of the street. A weathered sign proclaimed it was the Queen of Bodie saloon. The music was coming from inside.

Shaye frowned. She didn't remember seeing this place before, and she had walked through the town at least three times in the last couple of days. The Queen of Bodie. Suddenly, the name rang a bell. Of course! It was one of the saloons that Daisy had mentioned in her diary.

Wondering how she had missed it on her earlier excursions, Shaye stepped up on the wooden sidewalk, surprised that the swinging doors weren't locked. Only a few of the buildings were open to the public.

She could hear voices now, a woman's laughter. With a shrug, Shaye pushed her way through the doors.

The saloon was crowded with people, mostly men. Men dressed in faded red shirts and tall black boots. Smoke hung over the room like a thick gray shroud. She could hear the whir of a wheel of fortune, the click of dice, the solid clink of gold and silver coins.

Unforgettable

A long bar stretched away from the door. There was a restaurant across from the bar, every stool occupied. She frowned, thinking the place felt vaguely familiar, and then shook the feeling off.

She stared at the scene before her, her mind racing. Her first thought was that they were shooting a movie, but there were no lights, no cameras, and then she realized it had to be some sort of Old West reenactment. She wondered briefly why Clark hadn't mentioned it to her, and why it was being held on a day when she seemed to be the only tourist in the park.

Still, it was a once-in-a-lifetime opportunity, and she decided to make the best of it while she was there. Tucking her overnight bag under one arm, she worked her way through the crowd, wondering if it was okay to take pictures. Several of the men stared at her legs as she passed by, but she was used to that. She had nice legs.

Voices rose over the din. Male voices. Angry voices.

"You damned cheat!"

There was a sudden silence, as if someone had turned off the sound.

The crowd before her parted, giving her a clear view of the confrontation at the poker table in the back of the room.

A miner pushed away from the table and stood up, his body tense, as he glared at the man across from him. His face was almost as red as his shirt as he shouted, "Damn you, Valverde, that card came off the bottom!"

Shaye's heart slammed against her rib cage. Valverde.

The gambler stood up, his movements slow, graceful, deliberate. He wore black trousers, a white shirt, a black broadcloth coat, which he swept out of the way, revealing a black gun belt and a holster. "I don't have to cheat, Syler. You're a piss-poor card player if I ever saw one."

The miner's face turned even redder. His hand hovered over the gun on his hip.

Another man, also wearing a red shirt, laid a hand on Syler's arm. "Fred, don't. He'll kill you."

"I ain't afraid of him," Syler retorted, yet even as he spoke, his hand fell away from his gun and he was backing away from the table.

She stared at the scene before her. It was familiar somehow, yet she knew she had never been there before. Slowly, afraid of what she might see, she glanced to the left, her gaze drawn to the picture over the bar. A shiver slid down her spine. She recognized the place and the buxom nude all too well. It was the saloon from her dream.

And the man at the table, the one slowly turning in her direction, was a dead ringer for Alejandro Valverde.

Her blood ran cold, then hot, then cold again as his gaze met hers. She felt suddenly light-headed. She closed her eyes a moment, and when she opened them, she seemed to see everything through a blue-gray haze. A loud buzzing filled her ears, she felt herself falling, watched helplessly as the floor rushed up to meet her, and then everything went black.

Chapter Five

Alejandro darted forward and caught the woman just before she hit the floor. Swinging her into his arms, he headed for the stairway. "Rosa, bring her bag."

He took the stairs two at a time. In his room, he laid the woman on his bed, then stood staring down at her.

"I've never seen a woman dressed like that," Rosa said. "Who is she?"

"Damned if I know," Alejandro replied, but he couldn't shake the feeling that he had seen her somewhere before.

"Well, *hombre,* holler if you need anything else," Rosa said. She dropped the woman's valise on the floor near the door, then flashed him a sultry smile. "Anything at all."

Alejandro grinned as she sashayed out of the room

and quietly closed the door. Of all the doves at the Queen, Rosa was his favorite.

He frowned as he turned his attention back to the woman in his bed. Who was she? And why did she look so familiar? And why was she dressed so strangely? She wore some sort of sleeveless black shirt with writing across the front and a pair of white trousers cut well above the knee. Her feet were encased in a pair of short black stockings and blue and white shoes unlike any he had ever seen. He eased her out of the odd-looking pack on her back and dumped it on the floor near her valise.

He stared at her shirt, at the strange drawing of two faces, one white, one red, beneath the words Jekyll and Hyde, also written in red and white. But it was the woman herself who held his attention. Her skin was nicely tanned, smooth and clear. She had a lovely mouth with a full lower lip, a softly rounded jaw, a nice nose, delicate brows, thick lashes. He knew somehow that her eyes were green . . .

And even as the thought crossed his mind, her eyelids fluttered open and she was staring at him. "What happened?"

He shrugged. "You fainted."

She shook her head. "Don't be ridiculous. I've never fainted in my life."

He shrugged again. "First time for everything, I reckon."

Her gaze moved over him. Dark skin, long black hair, dark brown eyes, high cheekbones. Sort of a cross between David Duchovny and Antonio Banderas. Not a bad combination, she mused.

"Where am I?" she asked, glancing around.

"My room. I keep one here in the saloon."

Her mouth went dry. "Did you bring me here?"

He nodded.

"Why?

A faint smile curved his lips. "I guess I could have left you on the floor."

"Who are you?"

"Alejandro Valverde."

. "No, I mean who are you, really."

He lifted one black brow. "Alejandro Valverde."

"You don't understand—"

"I think it is you who do not understand."

"I know you're playing him, but what's your real name?"

He frowned. "Playing?"

Shaye sat up, and the room seemed to spin. The man was instantly beside her, his hand on her shoulder, steadying her. It was a large hand. Heat suffused her, his touch making her skin tingle, his nearness making her heart pound.

"All right. Stay in character. I've got to go."

He looked at her through narrowed eyes. "Are you sure you're all right?"

"Yes, I'm fine. Or I will be. I've got to go." She couldn't stay there, couldn't think with him staring at her like that. His resemblance to Alejandro Valverde was uncanny, which was no doubt why he'd got the part. She stood up, swaying, and again felt his hand on her shoulder as he steadied her.

"Sit," he said. "I'll get you something to drink."

She started to protest, but he gave her a gentle push, easing her backward until she sat down on the edge of the bed.

"Stay there."

Something in his tone warned her not to move.

He regarded her a moment, then left the room.

Shaye tapped her foot impatiently for a few moments, then stood up. The chair in the corner looked like one her grandmother used to have. She moved toward the dresser across from the bed, ran her hand over the top. She had seen similar looking pieces in her mom's antique shop. She opened the top drawer. Inside, she found a white shirt, neatly folded. She ran her hand over the material, frowned as she felt something hard beneath the cloth. Moving the shirt aside, she discovered a small revolver and three boxes of ammunition.

Curious, she picked up the weapon and turned it over in her hand. It was heavier than she'd expected for such a small weapon, and looked very real. The initials AV were worked into the design on the butt of the gun.

"I'd be careful with that if I were you. It's loaded."

Startled, she almost dropped the gun. He was beside her in a heartbeat. Taking the derringer from her hand, he put it back in the drawer and slid it shut.

"Here." He handed her a glass filled with dark red liquid. "This will calm your nerves."

"What is it?"

"Wine. It's good for the blood." He lifted one brow. "I assure you it's not poisoned."

She took a drink, relaxing a little as she sipped the warmed wine.

Head tilted to one side, his gaze ran over her in a long assessing glance. "What's that getup you're wearing?" he asked.

"What do you mean?"

He made a gesture that encompassed her tee shirt and shorts. "I've never seen a lady dressed in such revealing attire."

"Revealing?" Shaye glanced down at her outfit and frowned. A sleeveless shirt and a pair of walking shorts were hardly revealing.

"Your arms and legs are . . . exposed."

"Exposed?" She started to laugh, then realized he was quite serious. "You really have buried yourself in the part, haven't you?"

He frowned at her again. "Part? What part? What the hell are you talking about?" He shook his head. "You are obviously addle-brained. Maybe I'd better send Rosa for the doctor."

Shaye thrust the glass into his hand and stood up. "I am not addle-brained, and I don't need a doctor. Now, get out of my way. I'm leaving."

She pushed past him, grabbed her overnight bag and her backpack, and made her way down the stairs, careful to keep hold of the banister. Several men turned to stare at her as she made her way to the door. She came to an abrupt stop as the doors swung closed behind her.

Where there had once been only a few scattered buildings decayed by weather and time, there now stood hundreds of buildings, most of them whitewashed. The street was clogged with people and wagons. The air was thick with dust. She could hear hammering from nearby, the chiming of a clock as it struck the hour, the crack of a whip, and a low roaring sound she didn't recognize, which seemed to come from the mines up on the hill.

She was suddenly aware of a presence beside her. Turning her head, she saw the man claiming to be Alejandro Valverde.

She looked up at him, looked deep into his eyes, felt the spark of recognition clear down to her toes.

She stared at him, her mind refusing to accept what she knew to be true. He wasn't a man playing a part. He really was Alejandro Valverde. Alive. In the flesh.

She glanced at the scene before her again, and felt fear's cold fingers slide down her spine. It wasn't possible.

"Do you have a place to stay?" he asked.

She shook her head as the world spun out of focus and she fell into darkness once more.

When she came to, she was on a bed in a room. A different room. She lay there a moment, staring at the whitewashed ceiling. She had never fainted in her whole life, and now it had happened twice in one day. Of course, if what she suspected was true, she had a good reason.

She sat up, her back braced on a pillow propped

against the brass headboard, and surveyed the room. It was square, about ten by ten, simply furnished with a double bed, a tall, four-drawer chest made of dark oak and topped with an oval mirror, and the round table beside the bed. There was a folded newspaper on the table, as well as an oil lamp. White lace curtains covered the room's single window. A couple of suit coats hung from pegs along one wall; two pairs of boots, one pair black, one brown, stood neatly side by side.

It was his room. She knew it as surely as she knew her name. The other one was probably a place where he stayed from time to time, but he lived here.

Overcome by a sudden, nameless fear, she stood up. She had to get out of here. Right now. Before it was too late. Before . . .

Before what, she didn't know. She was trembling all over as she opened the door and stepped into a dimly lit, narrow corridor. The walls were covered with flowered paper. A dark green runner muted her footsteps. She glanced up and down, then walked toward what looked like an exit at the far end of the hallway.

The door opened onto a narrow wooden staircase that led into an alley. She hurried down the stairs and around the side of the building. It took her a few minutes to find Green Street, and then she was running, not caring that people stared at her, not caring about anything but reaching her car and going home. She knew a moment of panic when she realized she had left her backpack and her keys behind, quickly followed by a wave of relief when she remembered that she had an extra key hidden under the left front fender of the Rover for just such an emergency.

She paused when she reached the corner of Green and Fuller where the Methodist Church should have been. Had she gone the wrong way? But no, there was the barn, looking new now. A man stood outside, currying a horse, while two other men looked on. She could hear the ring of a blacksmith's hammer from somewhere in the distance.

She waited for a break in the seemingly endless flow of wagons and carts, then darted across the street.

She started running again, faster now, turning up the hill that led to the parking lot. Soon, she thought, soon she'd be safe in her car and this nightmare would be over.

Only the parking lot was gone. The blacktop was gone. Her Rover was gone. There was nothing there but dirt and sagebrush and the backs of several buildings that hadn't been there before.

She shook her head. "No. No. This can't be true!" She turned around, looked down at the town below, at the flood of wagons in the street, at the hundreds of people milling about. She heard what sounded like an explosion, the echo of gunshots, which didn't sound nearly as loud as they did in the movies, the clang of a blacksmith's hammer, the rumble of ore carts carrying ore to the mill. Dozens of men in red shirts could be seen scurrying over the hillsides. She knew then why the church wasn't there. It hadn't been built yet, hadn't been built until 1882.

It wasn't a dream. It wasn't a nightmare. It was real, and she was part of it. Part of a boomtown that had been dead for over a hundred years.

Chapter Six

Alejandro stared at the empty bed, wondering where the woman had gone. Not far, he mused, since she had left her belongings behind.

He stared at the strange dark green cloth bag she had worn on her back. Curious, he picked it up, looking for an opening, but found none. He ran his finger over a thin strip of metal, toyed with the small bit of metal dangling at the end. He took hold of it, wondering what it was. He wiggled it back and forth, surprised when, with a faint ripping sound, it made a small opening. Lifting one brow, he drew the tab back further, still further, disclosing the inside of the bag.

Sitting down on the foot of the bed, he dumped the contents onto the mattress, only to stare at them in complete bafflement. The only things he recognized were a ring of what he thought might be keys, although they were much smaller than any he had ever seen before, a comb made of some strange slick material, and a bright red hairbrush. He had never seen a hairbrush that color, never seen a brush made of anything but wood and boar bristles. There was a small round tube of something called Wine With Everything, a boxlike thing with a tiny glass window showing the number four, a small gray canister, three containers with blue, white, and pink labels that said Evian Natural Spring Water. From the French Alps. He tapped on one container. It was clear, like glass, but it wasn't glass. He picked it up and turned it around in his hands.

Sodium Free. Bottled by S. A. Evian Co. at Evian 74503 France. He frowned, wondering if she was French. There was some other writing, some numbers, an odd-looking symbol. *Recyclable. Check to see if facilities exist in your area.* He shook his head. "What the deuce does that mean?"

He put the container down and examined the other items. There was a pair of spectacles with blue frames and dark gray lenses. There was also a small purple object with the word *Nokia* across the top and buttons numbered one through zero, and other buttons labeled *Pwr, Send*, and *End.*

He tossed each item on the bed after he inspected it, then picked up a leather wallet unlike any he had ever seen. Inside, he found several small cards made of some strange hard paper. He pulled one out of its slot. It had the woman's photograph in one corner. The word *California* was printed across the top in large blue letters. Below that he read *Driver License Class C* and below that, some numbers. A line printed in red ink said *Expires 03–19–04,* and, in very small print he read, *This license is issued as a license to drive a motor vehicle. It does not establish eligibility for employment, voter registration, or public benefits.* Below that was a name, *Shaye Montgomery*, and an address of some kind. And below that, two more lines of print:

Sex: F	Hair: Brn	Eyes: Blu
Ht: 5-05	WT: 130	DOB: 03-19-73

He grunted softly, wondering what the words and numbers and letters meant. There were more cards made of the strange hard paper, each emblazoned with names that meant nothing to him: *America OnLine Platinum VISA; Automobile Club of Southern California; Robinsons May; Nordstrom.* They all had numbers on them, and the name *Shaye Montgomery*. Anther section held greenbacks of some kind, but they were smaller than any he had ever seen. There were several small photographs encased in some kind of clear . . . he shrugged, having no name for it.

He looked through the pictures. One was of the woman, Shaye, holding a child on her lap. One was of Shaye with an older couple. Her parents, he guessed, for there was a remarkable resemblance between the two women. There were other photographs. A little boy holding a baby, a young woman.

He glanced at the items, puzzled. Putting them all

back inside the pack, he stood up, wondering where the woman had gone. Wondering if he should go look for her. She was obviously a stranger in town. Remembering how she had fainted, not once but twice, he began to worry about her health.

He glanced at the other bag sitting on the floor near the door, wondering what strange things it might hold, but worry for the woman overrode his curiosity.

Damn. She hadn't gone out the front door. He would have seen her. The back door?

Leaving his room, he went out the back door. Standing on the landing, he glanced up and down the alley that ran behind the hotel. Paddy Sullivan, one of the town's two blacksmiths, was shoeing a horse across the way.

"Hey, Paddy," he called, leaning over the railing, "did you see a woman leave the hotel?"

Paddy nodded. "About half an hour ago, Rio. Who was she?"

"I'm not sure."

"Odd attire she was wearin'. Never seen anything like it."

"Which way did she go?"

Paddy jerked a finger over his shoulder. "That way. And she was in an itching hurry." Paddy grinned. "Never seen a woman running *away* from you."

Muttering an oath, Rio descended the stairs and made his way around to the front of the building. Which way would she have gone?

"Hey, Rio, honey, when are you coming to see me again?"

Madeline Baker

He looked up, grinning at the girl hanging over the balcony of the adjoining hotel. Her hair, waist length and dyed red, fell over her shoulders. "Not right now," he replied. "I'm looking for someone."

She pouted prettily. "Another woman, I'll bet."

He grinned. "She's not near as pretty as you are, Frenchy."

"Then why are you looking for her?"

"Because she's lost, darlin'."

Frenchy batted her eyelashes at him. "If I was lost, would you come looking for me?"

"You know I would."

"Then maybe I'll have to get lost," she replied with a laugh. "So who's the lucky girl?"

"I'm not sure. But you'd know if you'd seen her."

"Oh, that one!" Frenchy exclaimed, pointing down the street. "She went that way."

"Thanks, Frenchy." He pulled a silver dollar from his pocket and tossed it to her.

She caught it and waved her fist in the air. "Thanks, Rio."

He winked at her and continued down Green Street, making inquiries as he went. Everyone who had seen her remembered her.

A short time later, he passed the sawmill. Pausing, he glanced around. She was nowhere in sight. He rounded a curve in the road, and then he saw her, standing on the rise at the head of the path that led to Miller's Stable.

With a shake of his head, he climbed the hill.

*   *   *

Shaye blew out a breath as she watched Alejandro Valverde approach. He moved effortlessly, she thought, and was struck again by his rugged good looks, and by his resemblance to Antonio Banderas a la *Desperado*. He wasn't wearing a coat now, and she couldn't help noticing the way his white shirt empha- sized his dark good looks, or the way the material stretched across his broad shoulders.

"What are you doing up here?" he asked curtly.

"Looking for a way home."

"The stage depot is that way," he said, jerking his thumb over his shoulder. "but there aren't any stages leaving today. Where's home?"

"Los Angeles. And I wasn't planning to take a stagecoach."

"No?" He lifted one brow. "You weren't thinking of walking?"

"Of course not."

"Well, the stable's at the other end of town."

"I don't need a horse. I've got a car."

"Car?"

She shook her head at his look of confusion. "Never mind." She laughed abruptly. "Doesn't look like I'm going anywhere." She stared down at the town. What was she doing here? More importantly, how was she going to get back where she belonged? And where was she going to stay until she figured it out?

"It's about time for supper," Alejandro remarked. "Let's go get something to eat."

She didn't want to go anywhere with him. He

scared her in ways she didn't want to explore. She was about to say she wasn't hungry, thank you, when her stomach growled. And as much as she hated to share a meal with him, she didn't see as how she had much choice. Her money probably wouldn't be accepted any more than her credit cards.

"Shaye? That is your name, isn't it?"

"Yes. How did you know?"

He shrugged. "I saw something with your name on it."

"Did you go through my things?" she asked indignantly. "You did, didn't you?"

"Yes, and maybe after we've had something to eat, you will explain them to me."

He took her to the U.S. Hotel on Main Street for dinner. It was a large two-story building with a peaked roof and a railed balcony upstairs. Shaye was acutely conscious of the stares she received as they entered the dining room and took a table near the window. Every table was occupied, most with red-shirted miners discussing the day's events, speculating on the new mine that had just opened, the new mill being built.

Alejandro leaned back in his chair. "So, how long are you planing to stay in Bodie?"

"I don't know."

"Where are you staying?"

"I don't know."

He grunted softly. "You don't know much, do you?"

"I used to," Shaye muttered.

"You're welcome to stay in my room at the hotel." He grinned at her. "Unless you'd rather stay at the saloon."

"No, thank you, I'll find a place of my own."

"Use my room at the hotel," he said. "I'll stay over at the Queen."

She wanted to refuse, but she needed a place to stay and she wasn't likely to find another. "Thank you."

A waitress came to take their order. There were two choices: steak and potatoes or chicken and dumplings. Alejandro ordered steak, Shaye opted for chicken.

She tried not to stare at him, but her gaze was drawn to his face again and again. He was quite a handsome man. Not smooth and pretty like so many of the men of her day, but rugged. Wild and untamed. And utterly male. She pushed such thoughts from her mind. She didn't want a man in her life again. Didn't need a man in her life. *A woman without a man is like a fish without a bicycle.* She had read that somewhere and used it as a mantra whenever she was tempted. She had been badly burned once; she didn't intend to subject herself to that kind of agony again. But she couldn't stop looking at Alejandro, couldn't deny the attraction she felt for him. Couldn't keep from wondering . . .

Alejandro returned her gaze, one black brow arched. "Something wrong?"

"No. Why?"

"You look at me as if you've never seen a man before."

A faint smile tugged at Shaye's lips. "Well, I've never seen one like you, that's for certain."

"Like me? What the hell does that mean, like me? A man's a man."

She couldn't help it. She laughed. "You'd be surprised."

"What's that mean?" he asked, pointing at her shirt. "Jekyll and Hyde."

"It's the name of a play. You know, a theatrical production."

Their food came then. Shaye turned her attention to the meal, glad to have something to focus on besides Alejandro Valverde.

When dinner was over, Alejandro paid the check and they left the restaurant. The streets were as crowded at night as they had been during the day.

"Nice night for a walk," Alejandro said.

"Yes." It was warm and clear. A million stars twinkled against the dark blanket of the sky.

They passed a casino at the corner of Main and Green Streets. Music and laughter poured out of the swinging doors. It seemed every other building was a saloon, and they were all running at full steam.

"It's a hell of a town," Alejandro remarked.

"How long have you been here?"

"A year, more or less."

"How long are you going to stay?" she asked, then bit down on her lower lip. She knew how long he would be here. Knew he would never leave.

Alejandro shrugged. "Until the mines play out, I guess. Must be close to thirty mining properties here, and new ones opening every day. Men getting rich practically overnight."

"But you're a gambler, not a miner."

He laughed softly. "Mining is hard work. Those men work twelve-hour shifts six days a week. And for what? Four bucks a day. Hell, the chief engineer only gets six dollars." He shook his head. "It's a hell of a lot easier to take the gold after it's been dug out of the ground."

"Yes, I guess so."

"You don't approve?"

"It's none of my business."

"Here we are," he said.

Shaye stopped beside him. A large sign proclaimed they were at the Palace Hotel. "Ah," she murmured. "Home sweet home."

"I'll walk you up," he said.

She was going to tell him there was no need, but it was, after all, his room. Without his generosity, she would have had no place to spend the night.

Alejandro held the door for her and they crossed the lobby to the staircase. When they reached his room, he pulled a key from his pocket. Unlocking the door, he opened it for her, then handed her the key.

His fingers brushed hers, sending a little frisson of heated awareness skittering up her arm. Her gaze flew to his, and he grinned at her.

"Why do you look so surprised, darlin'?" he asked.

His question, and her unexpected response to his touch, left her speechless. Not knowing what to say, she slipped the key into her pocket, turned, and went into the room, felt her heart skip a beat when he followed her.

"What do you want?" she asked.

"I told you," he said, gesturing at her backpack. "I want to know what those things in your bag are."

"I don't have to tell you anything," she retorted.

"I reckon not, but you will."

She started to protest, then shrugged. She couldn't blame him for being curious. Sitting down on the bed, she reached into her backpack and withdrew the first thing her hand touched. "This is a lipstick." Opening it, she applied it to her lips, then dropped it on the bed. "This is a hairbrush." She held it up, then dropped it beside the lipstick. "This is my wallet. This is bottled water . . ."

He reached out and tapped the bottle. "It doesn't feel like any bottle I've ever seen."

"It's made out of plastic." She put it aside and picked up the small gray container. "This is an extra roll of film." She put it down, pointing at other items as she identified them. "This is sun screen. This is a cell phone, like a telephone, only portable." She stared at it a minute, wondering if anyone would answer if she dialed the operator. She swallowed the bubble of hysterical laughter that rose in her throat as she imagined dialing 911 and asking for directions back to the twenty-first century. "Anything else you want to know?"

He stared at the small purple contraption in her hand. He knew what a telephone was. He had seen one back East, but it hadn't looked anything like what she was holding. The one he had seen had been big and made of wood and hung on the wall. With a shake of his head, he picked up her wallet and removed her driver's license and her credit cards. "What are these?"

She plucked her driver's license out of his hand. "This says I can drive a car." She took her credit cards from him, one by one. "These say that my credit is good."

He shook his head, clearly not understanding.

"A car is an automobile. A . . . a horseless carriage. Well, anyway, it's something you drive, and you need a license to do it. And credit cards can be used instead of cash to buy clothes and food and anything else you can think of."

She blew out a sigh of exasperation. From his expression, she knew he was more convinced than ever that she was crazy.

He gestured at the credit cards. "What kind of paper is that?"

"It's plastic."

"Plastic?" He glanced at the bottle of Evian. She could almost see his mind working, trying to figure out how two such diverse things could be made of the same material.

She withdrew the last item from her pack. "And this is my camera."

Alejandro laughed at that. He knew what cameras looked like. They were large, bulky, black boxes made of wood that sometimes took two men to carry and operate, not little things like the one in her hand.

She lifted the camera in front of her face and said, "Smile."

He jumped as a burst of light exploded in his face. "What the hell?"

"It's just the flash."

He frowned. There had been no little poof of smoke. He glowered at her when she laughed.

Shaye put the camera on the bed, wondering if a twentieth-century camera could capture the image of a nineteenth-century chauvinist.

"Why are you dressed like that?" he asked. "Is that how women dress in Los Angeles?"

"Yes, and it's not considered immodest by any means."

He ran a hand across his jaw. "Well, it's downright scandalous here in Bodie. No lady would dream of showing off her arms and legs in such a brazen manner."

"Maybe I'm not a lady," Shaye retorted.

Arching a brow, he glanced at the bed. It wasn't difficult for her to guess what he was thinking. There were only two kinds of women in Bodie. If she wasn't a lady, then she must be a whore. For a fleeting moment, she wondered if she would have to fight him off, although she knew instinctively that he would never force a woman. With that face, that lazy velvet voice, he wouldn't have to.

He shoved his hands in his pants pockets and rocked back on his heels. "Tell me who you are."

"You know who I am. Shaye Montgomery."

He studied her face intently, his probing gaze making her uncomfortable. Why on earth was he looking at her like that?

"Have we met?" he asked. "You look familiar."

She felt her heart skip a beat. "Do I?" Was it possible he really had seen her that night at the jail?

He nodded slowly. "I'd bet my last dollar that I've seen you before."

Shaye shook her head. "That's impossible. I've never been here before. Never." *At least not in this century,* she added silently.

"Yeah, well, I never forget a face." His gaze moved over her again, a long, slow look that made her blood flow hot in her veins even as it made her heart beat faster. He had beautiful eyes, deep, dark brown eyes that seemed to penetrate her very soul.

He lifted one hand and cupped her cheek, his thumb making lazy circles on her skin. "Especially a face as beautiful as this."

It felt as if all the air had been suddenly sucked out of the room. She felt a rush of heat climb her neck and suffuse her cheeks, and she looked away, overcome by the fluttery feeling in her stomach. She had never been one to melt at the sight of a handsome man, never turned to mush over a few meaningless compliments.

She had been flattered before, by sweet-talking playboys and an occasional celebrity, but none of them had ever had such an effect on her. She had always laughed such praises off, knowing they were just empty words. She wasn't beautiful, and she knew it. But when Alejandro Valverde said it, she almost believed it was true.

For one brief, crazy moment she thought he was going to kiss her. And what was even crazier, she wanted him to. She looked up at him, waiting, wondering . . . and then, with a shake of her head, she turned away. What was she thinking? Instead of mooning over some nineteenth-century gambling man, she should be trying to figure out how to get back to the twenty-first century, where she belonged.

Alejandro grunted softly and then, without a word, he left the room, quietly closing the door behind him.

Chapter Seven

Alejandro stood in the corridor a moment; then, with a shake of his head, he left the hotel. Strange woman, he mused as he crossed the street and headed for the Queen of Bodie. Mighty strange, with her water in a . . . the frowned, what was the word? Plastic. A plastic bottle. Plastic paper. Carriages without horses. He swore under his breath, wondering if she had escaped from a lunatic asylum somewhere. But even if that was true, it didn't explain the peculiar things in her peculiar bag.

He grinned, wondering if everything was made of plastic where she came from, and then shook his head. He had been to Los Angeles last year, and he hadn't seen any horseless carriages, or plastic bottles of water. Los Angeles. Was that where he had seen her? Dammit, why couldn't he remember?

He shook his head again. He had done a lot of traveling in the last ten years. He could have met her in any one of a dozen boomtowns, and yet he couldn't shake the feeling that he had seen her here, in Bodie. But when? And where?

He shouldered his way through the crowd in the saloon, heading for his usual table at the back of the room. He had done James Rojas a favor a few months back. In return, Rojas let Alejandro have a table of his own for no charge. Five nights a week, Alejandro played poker with his own money. What he lost, he lost; what he won, he kept. On the other two nights, he dealt for the house. On those nights, Rojas covered Alejandro's losses, which were few, and took a hundred percent of his winnings. It was a deal that profited both of them.

Alejandro smiled at the doves as he moved through the room: Rosa, with her dark knowing eyes; Frenchy, with her dyed red hair and fake accent: Sally, with her porcelain skin and pouty pink lips; Lucy, with her perfect figure; Alice, who had the face of an angel and the vocabulary of a mule skinner.

He took his seat at the table, his back to the wall. Opening a fresh deck of cards, he spread them, fan-like, on the table, indicating he was ready for business. In minutes, four men joined him and the night's work had begun.

He looked up as Nellie came to stand beside him. She was a new girl, probably the youngest dove in the place. She was a pretty thing, with curly yellow hair and dark blue eyes. She smiled at him and he smiled back. Nellie thought she was in love with him, but he was used to that. He'd always had a way with the doves, probably because he treated them like ladies instead of whores, and because he never bedded any of the women where he worked.

"How about getting me a drink?" he asked, squeezing Nellie's hand.

"Whiskey?" She smiled at him again, her eyes glowing as she ran her hand over his shoulder.

"Thanks, darlin'." He winked at her, then turned his attention back to the game. "Cards, gents?"

As the night wore on, he found his mind drifting all too frequently to Shaye Montgomery. Strange woman, that one, with her odd clothing and belongings. Pretty, though, with her deep green eyes and delicate features. And those long, long legs . . .

He shook her image from his mind when he lost the third hand in a row. He couldn't concentrate on the cards and think about her at the same time.

Tired but not sleepy, Shaye wandered around the small room. There were a comb and bristle brush on top of the dresser, a couple of poker chips, a deck of cards. Crossing the floor, she ran her fingers over one of his coats, impulsively slipped it on. And had the strange feeling that his arms were around her. Shaking her head at such foolishness, she took it off and hung it back up. Maybe Alejandro was right. Maybe she was addle-brained.

Sitting on the edge of the bed, she took off her shoes and socks, wiggled her toes. This couldn't be happening, she thought; it had to be a dream. It had to be. She glanced at the newspaper on the bedside table. Feeling as though she were moving in slow motion, she picked it up. Opened it. Searched for the date. Tuesday, June 17, 1880.

She stared at the date, ran her hand over the paper, stared at the faint black smudge on her thumb. It wasn't a copy, but the genuine article.

So it was true. Somehow she had been transported into the past. But why? She had never been susceptible to suggestion, had never possessed any psychic abilities. She didn't know when the phone was going to ring, or who would be on the line when she answered. She didn't have hunches or "feelings." She had always been grounded in reality, so why had she been thrust back in time? It should be Clark McDonald sitting here, she thought. He was the one who had done research on Alejandro. Heck, he was even related to the man. So why had the Fates chosen her?

She glanced around the room again. His room. Picking up her camera, she crossed the floor and opened the window. Pushing the curtains aside, she took a couple of pictures of the activity in the street below, then turned and took a picture of the room.

Placing the camera on the dresser, she removed the rubber band from her braid, ran her fingers through her hair. She took off her tee shirt and shorts and slipped into her nightshirt, wishing she had brought something more substantial to sleep in, but then, she had never expected to find herself spending her nights in the homes of strangers. Folding her clothes, she put them on the bedside table.

Feeling chilly, she went to the dresser and opened the drawers, one by one, until she found an old flannel shirt that looked soft and comfy. She slipped it on and then crawled under the covers, turned onto her stomach, and closed her eyes. His scent clung to the blankets, the pillow, his shirt. Surrounding her. Alejandro Valverde. She fell asleep with his image in her mind.

It was well after midnight when Alejandro returned to the hotel. He'd had every intention of spending the night at the Queen, but Fate and Rojas had conspired against him.

The woman was asleep in his bed. She had left the lamp burning, and the light fell across her cheek and cast gold highlights in her hair, tempting his touch. He moved quietly across the room and stood looking down at her, again overcome by the certainty that he had seen her before.

With a shake of his head, he sat down on the chair and removed his boots. It would come to him, sooner or later. He never forgot a face, especially one like that. He unbuckled his gun belt and placed it on top of the dresser, shrugged off his coat, removed his shirt. It had been a long but profitable night, once he'd got his mind off the woman and back on the cards where it belonged.

He started to shuck his trousers, then thought better of it. Putting out the light, he slid into bed, acutely aware of the woman sleeping beside him. Muttering an oath, he put his back to her and closed his eyes.

Sleep was a long time coming.

Shaye woke slowly, reluctant to leave the dream behind. Reluctant to leave the man behind. It had been so real, the feel of his arms around her, the warmth of his breath on her skin, so real she could feel it, even now . . .

With a start, her eyes flew open. "You! What are you doing in my bed?"

His gaze moved over her, heating her skin wherever it touched. Oh, Lord, what if her dream had been reality? What if it had been his breath on her skin, his lips on hers?

His smile was slow and devastating. "It is *you* who are in *my* bed, *querida*."

She started to deny it, then felt a flush heat her cheeks as she remembered where she was. "But . . . but I . . . you said you had a room at the saloon. I thought . . ."

"Rojas hired a new dove last night. I had to move out."

"A new dove?"

"A new saloon girl."

"Oh." He was too close. And too handsome. She stared at his shoulders, visible above the blanket, and wondered if he was naked from the waist down, too.

"You have beautiful eyes," he murmured.

"Thank you."

"Soft skin."

Mesmerized, she watched his hand move toward her, felt her heart skip a beat as his fingertips stroked her cheek. She should tell him to stop, she thought, but couldn't seem to find the words. His hand was big and brown, yet his touch was gentle.

"So soft," he repeated, and before she knew quite how it happened, she was in his arms and he was kissing her.

Her eyelids fluttered down as heat flowed from his lips to hers, spreading through her like liquid sunshine, warming every place it touched. She put her hands on his chest, intending to push him away. Instead, her fingers drifted slowly over his skin, sliding up over his shoulders and down his arms, settling on his biceps. She had always had a weakness for well-muscled arms, and his were firm and solid.

She was breathless when he took his mouth from hers. Breathless and aching for more and terribly afraid that what little resistance she possessed would vanish if he kissed her again. She was grateful for the two layers of clothing that kept her modesty intact.

He cupped the back of her head in his hand, his eyes dark with desire.

"What do you think you're doing?" she gasped.

"This," he replied softly, and kissed her again.

His second kiss was as soul-shattering as the first. She might have melted into his arms, might have done any number of foolish things, if the sound of gunshots hadn't jolted her back to reality. With a gasp, she pushed Alejandro away and scrambled out of bed.

She stared down at him, the reality of where she

was washing over her and with it the knowledge that, in another few minutes, she would have let him make love to her.

She turned away from him, stunned by what had almost happened. She hadn't let a man get close to her since her divorce. Walking to the window, she stared down into the street. A look at her watch showed it was barely seven-thirty, yet the streets were already crowded. Wagon wheels churned the dust. She saw a woman clad in a red silk wrapper leaning over the balcony of the saloon across the street.

She wondered where the shots she'd heard earlier had come from, and even as the thought crossed her mind, she saw three men carrying a body out of the saloon.

"Another man for breakfast," Alejandro drawled.

Shaye glanced over her shoulder. "What?"

He grinned. "Bodie has a man for breakfast just about every day."

"I hardly think it's anything to laugh about."

"Sometimes it's more than one."

Shaye blew out a breath. In a town where ten thousand men had access to guns and booze and women twenty-four hours a day, she supposed it wasn't surprising that there would be arguments that ended in gunplay.

"Why don't you come back to bed?" Alejandro suggested.

It was tempting. He was tempting. Far too tempting, with his broad shoulders and muscular arms and roguish grin. Her gaze moved over him. He was lying on his side, his elbow bent, his head resting on his hand. Long black hair framed the most handsome face she had ever seen; his deep brown eyes held the promise of ecstasy.

She shook her head. "No. I need to . . ." To what? Find her way back to her own time? Find a place to stay until she did? She needed to find a job, since her credit cards wouldn't do her any good. And clothes, she thought. She definitely needed a change of clothes so she wouldn't stand out from everyone else.

Alejandro sat up, stretching, and she looked away. The man had far too much sex appeal for his own good or her peace of mind.

She didn't hear him move, but suddenly he was standing behind her. She went rigid as his arms slid around her waist. "We've met before, haven't we?" he asked.

"No. No, we haven't."

"I've seen you somewhere before. I'd bet my last dollar on it."

What would he say if she told him the truth? Would he think her insane? Addle-brained, he had called her before. Telling him she had come here from the future would only convince him she was one brick short of a load. He would never believe it. She didn't want to believe it, either.

She moved out of his arms, ran a hand through her hair. "Mr. Valverde—"

"We just spent the night together," he said with a wry grin. "I think you can call me Rio."

"We did not spend the night together. I mean . . . never mind. I need to . . . to . . ."

He lifted one brow. "To?"

"I need an . . . an outhouse."

"There's a chamber pot under the bed."

"No, thanks."

He grinned at her. "Down the back stairs. Turn right."

She muttered a quick thank you and left the room, only then wondering what people in the past had used for toilet paper.

The visit to the outhouse made her long for home as nothing else had. She had done a lot of traveling for the newspaper, but she had never encountered such crude facilities. The smell alone almost made her decide to find a nice clean bush somewhere, but, clad only in what she had slept in, she decided she'd better stay close to the hotel. And pages from an old mail order catalog were a poor excuse for toilet paper.

When she returned to the room, Alejandro was standing in front of the dresser, shaving. She felt a ripple of pleasure as she watched him drag the razor over his jaw. There was something terribly intimate about watching a man shave. Especially when that man wasn't wearing a shirt. Especially when he had a muscular chest sprinkled with curly black hair.

His gaze met hers in the mirror, and he smiled. It was a decidedly knowing smile. She had a sudden, overwhelming urge to stick her tongue out at him.

"You hungry?" he asked.

Shaye nodded. She was starved, she thought. But not for food.

"I'll be finished here in a minute."

She nodded again, mesmerized by the sight of the razor moving over his skin. It was a wicked-looking blade. Josh had used an electric razor. She had never seen him shave, though. He hadn't liked her to be in the bathroom when he was there.

Alejandro wiped the remaining lather from his face with a towel, which he then tossed on the chair. Pulling a dark blue shirt from the second drawer, he slipped it on, tucked it into his pants, buckled on his gun belt, reached for his coat. "I'll wait in the hall while you dress," he said, and then, catching sight of her shirt and shorts on the table, he shook his head. "You can't go out in those."

"Well," she said, tugging on the hem of his shirt, "I can't go out in this, either."

"I'll be right back," he said, and left the room.

She picked up the hairbrush, wondering where he had gone while she ran it through her hair, remembering how she had stood staring at him while he shaved, watching like some idiot schoolgirl who had never seen a man without a shirt before. In all fairness, she had to admit she had never seen a man quite like this one before.

Putting the brush aside, she washed her face with the water left in the pitcher. If she ever got back home, she would never again take flush toilets and hot running water for granted.

He returned about ten minutes later. "Here," he said, "this should fit you."

Shaye took the dress from his hand. It was a garish orange and yellow stripe, with a low-cut bodice. "Where did you get this?"

A smile twitched his lips. "It belongs to one of the doves over at the Queen."

"I see." Interesting, she mused, that wearing a prostitute's borrowed dress was more acceptable than her own shorts and shirt. She waited for him to leave the room, then shook her head. "Would you mind waiting outside?"

"Oh, right."

She took off his flannel shirt and put it back in the drawer, pulled her nightshirt over her head, and put on her bra, grimacing when she stepped into the panties she had worn the night before. She slipped the dress on over her head and smoothed it over her hips. It fit her like a second skin, revealing every curve, and more cleavage than she was comfortable with. The only good thing about it was that it was long enough to hide her shoes.

She took a look in the mirror and shook her head. Even if he hadn't told her, she would have known where the dress came from. "People will think *I'm* a hooker," she muttered. "But at least my arms and legs are covered up."

Sitting on the bed, she pulled on her Nikes and laced them up. She started to reach for her backpack, then realized there was nothing in it that would be of use to her here.

Taking a deep breath, she stood up and left the room.

Alejandro was waiting for her in the corridor. His eyes widened when he saw her. "Ready?"

"I guess so. And stop looking at me like that."

"Like what?" he asked innocently.

"Never mind," she muttered, "let's go."

On the street, men and women alike stared at Shaye. "I've got to get a change of clothes," she muttered.

"I'll take you to the dry goods store after we eat," Alejandro offered.

"It won't do any good. I don't have any money."

"I do."

She started to refuse, then thought better of it. No one would take her seriously or give her a job until she had some decent clothes to wear. And he could afford it. She remembered the entries in Daisy's diary where it stated he had given Daisy a hundred dollars on two separate occasions. "Thank you. I'll pay you back."

"Afraid to be beholden to me, are you?"

"I prefer to pay my own way."

His gaze moved over her, hot and slow, like warm molasses. "I can think of a way for you to repay me. Won't cost you a cent."

Shaye glared at him, wishing the offer weren't quite so tempting.

Alejandro tipped his hat as a woman clad in a white shirtwaist, green skirt and straw bonnet approached.

The woman offered him her hand and he bowed over it. *"Buenos dias,* Miss Lottie."

"Good morning to you, Alejandro." The woman looked Shaye up and down. "Who's your friend?"

"Miss Lottie, this is Miss Shaye Montgomery. Shaye, this is Lottie Johl."

Lottie extended a gloved hand. "Any friend of Rio's is a friend of mine."

"I'm pleased to meet you, Miss Johl," Shaye replied. The name rang a bell in the back of her mind.

"Will we see you at the Fourth of July dance, Rio?"

Alejandro smiled. "I'm afraid I'll be working at the Queen that night," he replied.

Lottie pouted prettily. "And I was so looking forward to dancing with you."

"Another time," Alejandro said gallantly.

"I'll hold you to that, Rio. It was a pleasure to meet you, Miss Montgomery."

Shaye nodded. She glanced over her shoulder as the woman swept past. "Lottie Johl . . . isn't she a . . . never mind."

Alejandro chuckled. "She was indeed, but she's a respectable woman now. She's achieved some recognition as an artist." He looked at her speculatively. "How did you know?"

"I . . . um, someone mentioned it to me."

"Uh-huh. Well, here we are," he said. Moving ahead of her, he opened the restaurant door for her. Even at this early hour, the restaurant was crowded. Harried-looking waitresses moved from table to table, taking orders, refilling coffee cups, clearing away dirty dishes.

She felt more conspicuous in the gaudy dress than she had in her tee shirt and shorts, but no one paid her any mind as she followed Alejandro to a table near the window. A few of the men spoke to Alejandro. Several of them smiled at her. Dressed as she was, they probably thought she was a new saloon girl. Alejandro held her chair for her. Removing his hat, he hung it from a hook on the wall, then took the seat across the table from her.

A young woman with a wealth of curly red hair, dark green eyes, and a sprinkling of freckles across her nose and cheeks made a beeline for their table, effectively cutting off another waitress headed in their direction.

"Good morning, Rio," she said brightly. "What'll you be having this fine day?"

"Ham and eggs and fried potatoes, Lily, my darlin'. And lots of coffee, hot and black."

Lily smiled expansively. "And you, miss?" she asked, though her gaze was still on Alejandro.

"The same," Shaye replied. She would have preferred a bowl of cereal and a glass of orange juice, but she doubted it was on the menu. "Oh, and could I have decaf, please?"

Lily stared at her. "De-what?"

"De . . . never mind."

Lily looked at Alejandro, shrugged, and left the table.

"What's de-caf?" he asked.

"It's a kind of coffee that's popular where I come from."

"In Los Angeles?"

"Yes."

"Uh-huh."

Lily returned moments later with two cups of coffee. "If you need anything else, Rio," she said huskily, "just holler."

Alejandro winked at Lily. "Thanks, darlin'."

Shaye blew out an exasperated sigh. The man had enough charm for a dozen men. If she could find a way to bottle it, she could probably make a million dollars in no time at all.

"Why do people call you Rio?"

He shrugged. "An old friend of mine once remarked that I had a temper as slow as the Rio Grande in summer and a draw faster than a flash flood, and it stuck."

"You don't like it?"

Picking up his coffee cup, he grinned at her. "I've got more important things to worry about than a silly name."

"Like what?" She grimaced as she took a sip of her coffee. It didn't taste anything like what she was used to.

"Like whether Fred Syler will show up at the Queen tonight."

Shaye added a generous amount of milk and sugar to her coffee. "Why? You're not afraid of him, are you?"

He laughed. "No, I'm not afraid of him, but he

always brings trouble with him. One of these days he won't back down, and I'll have to kill him.

"You wouldn't!"

"I will if he doesn't give me any other choice."

She pondered that a moment, weighing the implications. "Have you killed many men?"

"A few."

She regarded him a moment. She had never known anyone who had taken a life. "How many is a few?"

"Three."

"You've killed three men?"

"Gambling's a dangerous game, especially in a boomtown. Too many men. Too much booze. Not enough law." He shrugged. "They were all fair fights." He grunted softly. "What's the matter? I know they have guns in Los Angeles. Don't tell me no one ever gets shot."

She had to laugh at that. You couldn't pick up a newspaper or turn on the TV without hearing about some nut who'd grabbed a pistol or an assault weapon and gone on a rampage, killing innocent women and children, and often killing themselves as well.

"Did I say something funny?"

"Not really."

"Here you go, Rio. Ham and eggs, just the way you like 'em."

"*Gracias*, Lily, my darlin'."

Shaye murmured her own thanks as Lily set a plate in front of her, noticing as she did so that there were three extra slices of ham on Alejandro's plate, and two extra biscuits.

"Anything else I can get for you, Rio?" Lily asked. "Anything at all?"

Alejandro held up his empty cup. "More coffee?"

"Coming right up. I just made a fresh pot."

Alejandro looked at Shaye, one brow raised. "What's wrong?" he asked when Lily moved away from the table.

"Nothing. I'm just surprised she didn't offer to feed you, that's all."

A broad grin spread over his face. "You jealous?"

"Don't be absurd!"

"Hey, can I help it if she likes me?"

"Likes you! That's putting it mildly."

Alejandro chuckled. She was mighty pretty when her color was up. And even when it wasn't. The borrowed dress outlined every curve. It was a shame to cover up those long legs, he thought. Last night, he had dreamed of having them wrapped around his waist.

With a sigh of exasperation, Shaye turned her attention to her breakfast, which was surprisingly good. She refused to meet Alejandro's gaze, but she could feel him watching her, could just imagine the smug expression on his handsome face.

Lily came by twice to refill his coffee cup, and once apparently just to run her hand over his shoulder and give him a smile.

Shaye looked up when she finished eating to find him watching her. "What?"

"Nothing. You ready to go?"

"Yes, if you can tear yourself away."

He laughed as he stood up and reached for his hat. He settled it on his head, then dropped a couple of silver dollars on the table.

Muttering under her breath, Shaye followed him out of the restaurant. Why was she letting him get to her? What difference did it make if women found him irresistible? Or if he took advantage of it?

He took her arm as they threaded their way through the crowded boardwalk. Men outnumbered the women about a hundred to one. Bodie was quite a melting pot, she mused as she overheard men speaking in Italian and French, caught the sound of a heavy Irish brogue. She saw a slender Chinaman dressed in baggy trousers pulling a cart filled with vegetables. Dust tickled her nostrils, and she sneezed and sneezed again.

A huge wagon loaded with pipe and drawn by a team of six tired-looking horses rumbled past, followed by a stagecoach, which raised even more dust.

She stopped when he squeezed her arm.

"You should be able to find something to wear in here," Alejandro said.

Shaye glanced at the building. The words "Madame Sophie's Creations" were painted on the window in flowing white script over a bright red rose. "This doesn't look like the dry goods store," she remarked.

"Changed my mind," he said with a wink. Opening the door, he poked his head inside. "Hey, Sophie, give Shaye here anything she wants and send me the bill."

There was a muffled reply which Shaye assumed was assent.

"Sophie'll take good care of you," he said.

"Another admirer?" Shaye asked.

Alejandro grinned at her. "I can't help it, darlin'. Can you find your way back to the hotel?"

"I think so," she replied curtly.

The sound of Alejandro's laughter followed her as she stepped into the shop. Annoyed, she slammed the door, which set the bell to ringing violently.

A small, slender woman with orange hair and rouged cheeks emerged from a curtained-off area at the back of the shop.

"Something troubles you, *chérie*?" she remarked. "Well, you have come to the right place. There is nothing like the new ensemble to put the world to rights, no?" She beamed at Shaye. "I am Sophie. Welcome to my salon." Sophie looked her up and down. "*Chérie*, what is that you are wearing?" She shook her head. "We must get you out of that *inmediatemente!*"

Sophie tapped a finger to her lips as she studied Shaye's measurements. "Giselle, bring me the striped taffeta skirt and matching shirtwaist, the green crepe de chine, and the burgundy challis."

Before she quite knew how it happened, Shaye found herself in a dressing room, stripped to the skin.

Sophie held up Shaye's bra, frowning. "Never have I seen anything like this. Or these," she said, pointing at Shaye's Nikes.

"Well, they're all the rage where I come from," Shaye replied.

With a shake of her head, Sophie dropped the bra on the top of Shaye's dress.

Shaye had always wondered what women in the Old West had worn under their voluminous dresses, and she soon found out. A camisole, white cotton stockings, pantaloons that tied just below the knee, a corset, a corset cover, a bustle, an organdy petticoat, and lastly, a linen underskirt lined with cotton. She lifted her arms as Madame Sophie dropped an over-skirt of brown, green, and white striped taffeta over her head, then helped her into a long-sleeved blouse of the same material. A pair of brown kid half boots completed the outfit.

Sophie stood back, her gaze critical. "Giselle, bring my pins."

Moments later, Shaye's hair was pinned up and she was wearing a dainty bonnet with green and white streamers. White gloves came next. And then a parasol.

"Magnifique!" Sophie said, and turned Shaye around so she could see herself in the full-length mirror.

A stranger stared back at her.

Sophie nodded, obviously pleased with her handiwork. *"Très belle!"* she declared. "You are beautiful, no?"

"I am beautiful, yes," Shaye murmured as she turned this way and that. The full skirt made her waist seem incredibly small. The colors in the blouse complemented her hair and eyes. Though she had never cared much for hats, she had to admit that the bonnet added the perfect touch.

Sophie smiled. "I am pleased that you are pleased," she said. "Alejandro will also be pleased, I think."

Shaye nodded. He probably wouldn't recognize her. She hardly recognized herself.

Sophie insisted she try on the other two dresses, declared them a perfect fit, then suggested a few other dresses for everyday—a blue gingham, a pink muslin, a dark green calico, as well as a frilly white blouse and a wine red skirt. Then Sophie added a white cotton nightgown with dainty pink roses embroidered across the bodice, a robe, a change of undergarments, and several pairs of stockings, both white and black, both cotton and silk. Shaye was amazed when Sophie included a pair of red stockings to match one of her petticoats. Lastly came the *pièce de résistance*, a gown of deep green watered silk with a slim skirt and a modest bustle covered with tiny pink silk roses. The green in the dress deepened the color of Shaye's eyes to dark emerald.

Three hours later, Shaye left the shop attired in the striped taffeta, parasol in hand. Sophie had assured her she would send the rest of her wardrobe to the hotel later in the day. The bill would be sent to Alejandro.

Shaye felt like a different woman as she walked down the street. Men smiled at her, bowed at her, bade her good day. Women nodded at her; a few smiled.

She was perspiring when she reached the hotel.

Whatever possessed women to bury themselves under so many layers of clothing? She was surprised they didn't all faint from heat prostration!

She saw Alejandro the minute she entered the hotel. He was sitting on one of the curved sofas, talking to another man. Alejandro looked up as she drew near, smiled, and returned his attention to the other man. And then, very slowly, he looked up at her again. Stunned was the only word to describe his expression.

"Shaye."

"Good afternoon, Mr. Valverde," she replied in her most ladylike voice.

The man sitting beside Alejandro punched him on the arm. "Valverde, introduce me to this lovely creature."

"Philo, this is Miss Montgomery. Shaye, this is Philo Richardson. He's the editor of the *Bodie Gazette*."

Philo stood up and removed his hat. She had noticed that all the men wore hats. Philo Richardson wore a brown bowler; Alejandro wore a black Stetson.

"My pleasure, Miss Montgomery," Philo said.

Remembering her meeting with Lottie Johl, Shaye extended a gloved hand. "I'm pleased to make your acquaintance, Mr. Richardson."

Philo bowed over her hand. "You must be new in town."

"Yes, I've only been here a short while."

He rocked back on his heels. He was a head shorter

than Alejandro, with dark brown hair just turning gray, and twinkling brown eyes. He wore a brown suit with a garish red and orange striped vest.

"Can I hope your visit will be an extended one?" he asked.

She smiled at him. "I'm not sure yet," she replied.

"If there's anything I can do," Philo said gallantly, "you have only to let me know."

"Thank you. That's very kind."

Alejandro had been staring at her. Rising, he moved to stand beside Shaye. "That's enough, Philo. If Miss Montgomery needs anything, I'll take care of it."

"Ah," Philo drawled, glancing at Shaye and then back at Alejandro. "That's the way it is."

Shaye flushed.

Alejandro grinned.

Shaye's hand tightened on the handle of her parasol as she resisted the urge to strike Alejandro over the head with it. The nerve of the man!

"It was a pleasure to meet you, Miss Montgomery. I hope to see you again, soon."

"Thank you."

She waited until Philo left the hotel, then turned on Alejandro. "How dare you!"

"How dare I what?"

"I saw the way he looked at you. He thinks I'm your . . . that we're . . ."

Alejandro grinned at her, obviously amused by her anger. "What does he think?"

"You know very well what he thinks."

"It's for your own good. There aren't many single women in town, and most of those are saloon girls. It's better if the men think you're spoken for."

"I can assure you I'm quite capable of taking care of myself."

"Is that right?"

"Yes. I don't know about the women in Bodie, but I'm not some helpless female, and I won't be treated like one."

Alejandro raised his hands in a gesture of surrender. "All right, all right, I'm sorry." His gaze moved over her in blatant male approval as he offered her his arm. "I don't have to be at work for another couple of hours, Miss Montgomery. Would you care to go into the dining room and have some pie and coffee?"

Shaye smiled at him. Wearing nineteenth-century clothing made her feel as if she were someone else, as if she were playacting. To her amazement, she found herself batting her lashes a little as she said, "Why, thank you, Mr. Valverde, I'd love to."

He looked at her a moment, clearly astonished by her abrupt change of mood, and then he threw back his head and laughed. It was the most masculine, sexy laugh she had ever heard, and it filled her with a sudden burst of happiness that quickly turned to sadness when she remembered that he had only a few months to live.

Chapter Eight

Shaye pushed the thought of Alejandro's demise to the back of her mind as they entered the restaurant. His fate had been decided over a century ago and there was nothing she could do about it, though she couldn't help wondering if it was possible to change his destiny. If she warned Alejandro of what was to happen, would he be able to avoid it? Or was his fate already sealed? And if it was possible to change his fate, what would the repercussions be? Could changing one man's fate alter the future course of history?

"Penny for your thoughts?"

"What? Oh, I was just wondering . . . wondering what kind of pie to have."

"Well, there's usually only two choices," Alejandro replied with a grin. "Apple or apple."

She pushed her fears for his future to the back of

her mind as she grinned back at him. "Then I think I'll have apple."

As usual, they got immediate service, large slices of pie, and lots of coffee. She was surprised he wasn't as fat as a pig, the way the waitresses fawned over him, giving him generous servings of whatever he ordered.

She heard a clock chime the hour. "What time do you have to be at work?"

"Rojas is expecting me around eight, I think. Why?"

"I'd like to see the Bodie Belle."

Alejandro lifted one brow. "Is that so?"

Shaye nodded, though it wasn't the saloon she really wanted to see, but Daisy Sullivan. "Would it be all right?"

"Sure, darlin'."

He paid the check and they left the restaurant.

The Bodie Belle was decorated in red and black. The colors were striking, if a little loud, but then, Shaye thought, maybe that was the idea. Between the colors and the noise, she was pretty sure no one ever fell asleep over his cards.

The place was crowded, but Shaye was getting used to that wherever they went. As luck would have it, several miners vacated a table as they passed by, and Alejandro grabbed it for the two of them.

A short time later, a pretty girl with waist-length blond hair and gray eyes approached their table. In keeping with the room's color scheme, she wore a short red dress, black stockings, and red high-heeled shoes.

"Rio, honey!" she exclaimed. "It's been ages."

"Hi, Maddy. How's life treating you?"

"A lot better than Daisy is," she replied with a grimace.

"She's not still giving you a bad time?"

"Oh, isn't she?"

"I'm sorry, Maddy, darlin'."

She shrugged. "So what'll you have?"

"The usual for me. Shaye?"

"Beer." Shaye stared at the girl. Maddy. It had to be the same girl mentioned in Daisy's diary, the one Daisy had been so jealous of.

"Something wrong?" Alejandro asked.

"No. Why?"

"You were giving Maddy the once-over like maybe you thought you knew her."

"Oh, no. I was just . . . just admiring her hair. It's lovely."

Alejandro nodded, but she wasn't sure he was convinced.

Maddy returned a short time later with a shot of whiskey and a glass of beer. She placed the drinks on the table, then leaned toward Alejandro, giving him a clear view of her cleavage, which was quite spectacular. "You don't work here anymore," she said in a sultry voice. "And I'll be home by midnight."

Alejandro caught Shaye's amused expression and gave a slight shrug, as if to say, what can I do?

She might have told him if another woman hadn't

come storming up to the table, eyes narrowed, mouth drawn in a tight, angry line. Shaye knew immediately that it had to be Daisy Sullivan. She was short and slender, with a wealth of black hair, an olive complexion, and blue eyes. She wore an expensive-looking low-cut wine red dress and matching slippers. A gold locket nestled in the hollow of her throat. Shaye wondered if it was the one mentioned in Daisy's diary, the one Alejandro had given her for her birthday.

"I'm not paying you to throw yourself in the customers' arms, Maddy Brown," the woman said.

Maddy looked over her shoulder. "Funny, I thought you were. Or maybe it's just this customer you don't want me throwing myself at."

An angry flush swept into the other woman's cheeks. "Get out."

Alejandro stood up. "Now wait a minute, Daisy—"

"You're no longer the boss here, Rio," Daisy said, eyes flashing. "Get out, Maddy. I should have fired you long ago. Go on, get!"

Alejandro laid a hand on Maddy's arm. "Pete's looking for girls over at the Number Six. Tell him I sent you."

"Thanks, Rio." Maddy gave Daisy a smug look, then smiled up at Rio. "See you soon, Rio, honey."

Alejandro nodded. He waited until Maddy was out of sight, then turned to Daisy. "That was uncalled for."

"It's none of your business what I do."

"That's right, it isn't. Good afternoon."

"Rio! Rio, wait. I'm sorry."

Daisy reached for him, but he shook off her hand. "Let's go, Shaye."

"Rio!"

Alejandro took Shaye's arm and they left the saloon.

Outside, Alejandro took a deep breath. "I'm sorry about that."

"It's okay."

"I should have known better than to go in there, but I thought . . . oh, hell, it doesn't matter. Come on, I'll walk you back to the hotel."

Alejandro left her at the door. Shaye watched him walk away, then went inside and shut the door. Sitting down on the edge of the bed, she took off her boots and stockings. The half boots were kind of cute, but you just couldn't beat a good pair of tennis shoes for comfort. She sat there a minute, wiggling her toes. Ah, but that felt good. She shook her head, amused and amazed that she was actually living in the past. With a sigh, she fell back on the mattress and closed her eyes.

Alejandro's image immediately sprang to mind. He could be a poster boy for tall, dark, and handsome, she mused. He had the most beautiful eyes. They were a deep, dark brown, fringed with short, stubby, black lashes. When he looked at her, she felt it clear down to her toes. She liked everything about him, she mused, from the coppery color of his skin to the sometimes sardonic look in his eyes that told her he was no stranger to the darker side of life. Like it or not, she was attracted to him. When she was with him, everything else seemed to fly right out of her mind. He was far and away too handsome and much too charming for his own good, she thought, and for hers, too.

With a sigh, she rolled onto her side, her head pillowed on her hand. He was just a man, she told herself, no different from any other, but she didn't believe it for a minute. She had never felt like this before, all shivery and excited inside, as if she were on the brink of some marvelous discovery. And even as the thought crossed her mind, she wondered just what it was she was feeling. Why, of all the people who had come through Bodie in the last hundred years, was she the one who had seen the ghost of Alejandro Valverde in the jail, felt his thoughts, his anguish? Why . . . ?

She woke to the sound of a clock chiming the hour. For a moment, she thought she was at home, but the bed felt unfamiliar, and when she opened her eyes, the ceiling was the wrong color.

Sitting up, she glanced around the room—his room. From outside came the sound of wagon wheels and men's voices, a muffled explosion from one of the mines, the reverberation of a gunshot, the constant sound of the stamp mill. How did people ever get used to the noise? Maybe it was like living close to the railroad tracks, she mused. After a while, you didn't hear the trains anymore.

A knock at the door brought her to her feet. "Who is it?" she called.

"Delivery for Miss Montgomery from Madame Sophie's."

"Oh." Crossing the room, she opened the door.

Two teenage boys, their arms laden with packages, stood in the hallway. "Evening, ma'am," said the taller of the two.

"Hi. Come on in." She stepped back so they could enter the room. "Just put all that stuff on the bed, I guess."

They did as she asked, then stood there, shuffling their feet.

"Oh, a tip!" Shaye exclaimed. "I'm sorry, I don't have any money. But I'll see that you're taken care of."

"Yes, ma'am."

"Thank you, ma'am."

Shaye smiled as she walked them to the door. "Thanks, fellas."

When they were gone, she turned around and regarded the pile of packages on the bed, wondering where she was going to put everything. She really needed to get her own room, she thought. She couldn't stay here, with him. She had to find her way back to her own time . . . but how? And what was she going to do until then?

Sitting on the edge of the bed, she pulled on her Nikes. Her skirt brushed the floor, so she figured no one would see her shoes anyway. She reached for her gloves, decided against wearing them, and then, with a sigh, she put them on. It was appalling, the hundred and one little things expected of a nineteenth-century lady, like wearing gloves and a hat and a dozen petticoats when it was eighty degrees outside.

With a huff of resignation, she smoothed her skirt, then slipped her camera into the cute little drawstring bag she had picked out at the dress shop. A reticule, Madame Sophie had called it.

Feeling as though she were wearing enough clothes for at least three women, she left the hotel, certain that a twenty-first-century female had no place in nineteenth-century Bodie. Maybe if she went back to the Queen of Bodie saloon, she would be transported back to her own time where she belonged.

She paused at the corner to take a couple of pictures, ignoring the strange looks she received from passersby.

The Queen was filled almost to overflowing. Someone was pounding out "I'll Take You Home Again, Kathleen" on the piano.

Taking a deep breath, she put her hands on the swinging doors and entered the room. Too late, she remembered that decent women didn't frequent saloons.

She stood there, just inside the doors. Tense. Waiting. But nothing happened. And then, as had happened before, the crowd parted and she was staring at Alejandro Valverde. He looked just as he had in her dream; just as he had the first time she had seen him in here.

As though feeling her gaze, he turned his head,

recognition flickering in his eyes, a faint smile touching his lips as he picked up his cards and walked toward her.

Her heart was racing like a runaway freight train as he closed the distance between them.

"Shaye, what are you doing here?"

She shook her head, unable to speak as the truth speared through her. She hadn't come here hoping to go back to her own time. She had come here to see him, to be with him. Incredible as it seemed, she was falling in love with a ghost.

"Shaye?"

"I . . . I was lonely and . . ." She shrugged.

"You don't belong in here."

"I know."

His smile caressed her. "But as long as you're here, come and keep me company."

She followed him back to the table. There were three men sitting there, and they all stood up as she approached.

"Henry, Spooner, Digger, this is Miss Shaye Montgomery. She's a friend of mine, and she's a lady, so watch your language while she's here."

The men all bobbed their heads in agreement and remained standing until she had taken the empty chair next to Alejandro's.

"Pot's light," Henry said. "You in or out, Rio?"

Alejandro tossed a double eagle into the center of the table. "In." He put his hand aside and picked up the deck. "Cards, gents?"

"One for me," Henry said.

Spooner took two.

"I'll play these," Digger said.

"Dealer takes one."

Shaye looked at Alejandro, wondering what kind of hand he had. Catching her gaze, he picked up his cards and showed them to her. A full house. Queens over tens. She started to smile, but caught herself just in time.

"Spooner?"

"Bet five dollars. Say, where's Shep tonight?"

"I'll see that five," Digger said, "and raise you five."

"Henry?"

"Too rich for my blood." Henry threw his cards face down on the table. "Shep's over at the Opera House."

Alejandro just called.

Spooner spread his cards on the table, revealing three jacks, a nine, and a deuce.

Digger blew out a sigh of exasperation. "Beats me," he muttered sourly.

Spooner looked at Alejandro. "Well?"

"Full house," he declared, and spread his cards on the table.

"Damn!" Spooner exclaimed. "I swan, if I didn't know you was honest as the day is long . . ." He shook his head ruefully.

Alejandro looked over at Shaye and grinned as he raked in the pot. "Would you like to sit in?"

"Me?" She couldn't have been more surprised if he had asked her to stand up on the table and strip.

129

"Sure. I'll stake you." Alejandro glanced at the other men at the table. "You gents don't mind if the lady joins us, do you?"

"Hell . . . uh, heck, no," Digger said.

"All right by me," Spooner said. "Nice to have something pretty to look at while I'm losin'."

Henry laughed. "Be glad to take your money, Miss Montgomery."

Alejandro divided the cash stacked in front of him and pushed half of it in front of Shaye. He tossed a double eagle into the pot for himself, and another for her.

Shaye stared at the money he had given her. Silver dollars. Gold coins. Greenbacks. A rough count put it at close to five hundred dollars. She picked up a ten-dollar bill. "This note is legal tender for ten dollars" was written across the top. "Will pay the bearer ten dollars" was printed across the middle. There was a picture of a man in the lower left corner, and what looked like some sort of historical scene in the lower right.

She felt a surge of excitement as she watched Alejandro deal the cards. She had never been much of a gambler. She enjoyed playing the slot machines in Vegas, but quickly grew bored with it. Blackjack was her favorite game, but it was too expensive for her taste now that it was almost impossible to find a dollar table. Craps looked like fun, but she had never been able to figure it out.

Removing her gloves, she picked up her cards one by one. Jack of spades, queen of spades, nine of spades, three of diamonds, eight of spades.

Alejandro picked up his cards, looked them over, removed two, and placed them face down on the table, then picked up the deck again. "How many, Digger?"

Digger took three, Henry took two, Spooner took one.

Shaye asked for one. She tossed the three of diamonds on the table and picked up her new card, gasped when she realized what she had. What were the odds? she thought.

"I'd say she got the card she needed," Spooner remarked dryly.

Digger laughed.

Henry nodded.

Alejandro smiled at her, his eyes twinkling. "I can see we need to work on your poker face," he drawled.

Warmth filled her heart and spread to her cheeks. "Maybe I'm bluffing now," she said tartly.

Digger tossed a double eagle in the pot, Henry raised him ten dollars, Spooner upped the ante another five dollars. Alejandro saw his raise and raised it five more.

"So it'll cost me forty dollars to stay in?" Shaye asked dubiously.

Alejandro nodded. "That's right, darlin'. Unless you want to raise the stakes." She had never bet more than five dollars on the turn of a card in her life. "No." Taking a deep breath, she added her money to the pot.

Alejandro grinned at her. "All right, darlin', let's see what you're holding."

Her heart was beating wildly as she put her cards on the table, face up, one at a time. Ten of spades, jack of spades, queen of spades, nine of spades, eight of spades. A straight flush.

Alejandro leaned over and kissed her on the cheek. "That's my girl," he murmured.

"Beginner's luck," Digger muttered. "Damn, I had a good hand, too. Best one I've had all night." He tossed his cards on the table. "Full house, kings and tens."

"Hell . . . er, heck, Digger, I had four of a kind!"

"Doesn't matter what you had," Alejandro said, chuckling, "it wasn't good enough. The lady wins. Rake it in, darlin', it's all yours."

"Well, actually, it's yours," Shaye replied.

"Keep it."

"No, I couldn't."

"We'll settle it later." He gathered the cards and began to shuffle them.

Shaye was about to insist she couldn't keep it when one of the saloon girls sashayed up to the table. She wore a low-cut red dress, a pure, lustful shade of red that was guaranteed to draw every man's eye, black net stockings, and high-heeled slippers. "Drinks, gents?"

"'Bout time you got over this way, Ginny girl," Digger said. "Bring me a whiskey. And make sure it's the good stuff and not that rotgut Rojas keeps under the bar."

"You buyin'?" Spooner asked.

"Sure," Digger said.

"I'll have the same then," Spooner said. "And make it a double."

"What'll you have, Rio, honey?"

"Whiskey's fine with me. Shaye, do you want anything?"

She wasn't much of a drinker. On those occasions when she did drink, she usually ordered a Singapore Sling, or Seven and Seven on the rocks. She was about to order the latter when it occurred to her that the bartender would have no idea what she was talking about, and that Seven-Up hadn't even been invented yet.

"Shaye?"

"Nothing, thank you."

"You sure? Digger doesn't buy often," Alejandro said with a grin. "Better take advantage of it while you can."

"Could I get a glass of wine?"

"Wine?" Ginny said with a look of disdain. "This is a saloon, honey. We've got whiskey, bourbon, and beer."

"The lady wants wine, Ginny." Alejandro handed the woman a couple of greenbacks. "Send someone over to The Occidental. Tell Floyd it's for me."

"Alejandro, there's no need—"

"Wine you want, wine you get," he said with a wink. "Right, Ginny?"

Ginny glared briefly at Shaye, then looked at Alejandro. "Sure, Rio," she said. "Whatever you want."

The saloon girl smiled at Alejandro, a come-hither smile if Shaye had ever seen one. Then, bold as brass, she bent over, giving him a clear view of her ample cleavage. "I'll be waiting for you later," she whispered, just loud enough for Shaye to hear. Then, smiling smugly, she moved away from the table, her hips swaying seductively.

Alejandro looked at Shaye. She was watching him, one brow arched in wry amusement.

Digger and Spooner exchanged knowing grins. Alejandro shuffled the cards, then slid the deck in front of Digger for the cut.

Shaye picked up her cards as they were dealt, but for a moment, they meant nothing to her. All she could see was Ginny bending toward Alejandro, offering him a clear view of her cleavage and the delights that were his for the taking. Would he go to her later?

"Shaye, are you in?"

Alejandro's voice drew her back to the game at hand. She glanced quickly at her cards. A pair of queens, an ace, a four, and a seven. "Yes." She picked up a double eagle and tossed it into the center of the table.

"Cards?" Alejandro asked when the pot was right.

Digger took two, Spooner took one, Henry took one, Shaye asked for three, and Alejandro took two.

Shaye picked up her new cards, kept her face carefully blank as she added them to her hand: a pair of kings and a trey. Two pair. Not bad.

"Shaye, it's up to you."

She hesitated a moment, then put five dollars in the pot.

Digger, Spooner, and Henry folded.

"I'm gonna see your five," Alejandro said, "and raise you ten."

A thrill of excitement spiraled through her. "I'll see your ten and raise you ten more."

Alejandro regarded her for a long moment, so long she felt her cheeks grow hot.

"The pot's yours," he said at last.

"Two pair," she said, and placed her cards on the table, face up.

"I'll be . . . Are you sure you haven't played before?"

"What were you holding, Rio?" Digger asked.

"Three aces," Alejandro replied dryly.

Shaye couldn't help it. She burst out laughing.

She lost track of the time. She kept telling herself just one more hand and then she would go back to the hotel, but she couldn't bring herself to leave. She enjoyed bantering with Digger and Spooner and Henry. Flirting with Alejandro. Several times, the play was just between the two of them. She never beat him again, though, and as the night wore on, she began to wonder if he had let her win the first time.

She loved to watch him shuffle and deal the cards. It was almost as if he caressed each one. More than once, she found herself wondering what it would be like to feel those long, bronze fingers moving over her skin, delving into her hair. Once, his gaze met hers and the attraction between them sizzled like summer lightning. For a moment, it was as if they were alone in the room, just the two of them. She could almost feel his hands sliding around her waist, pulling her close; feel his breath on her face, his lips moving over the sensitive skin just behind her ear; hear his voice, low and husky with desire as he whispered her name. The heat of his eyes caused a seductive warmth to spread through her, and she wished they were alone, wished she could crawl onto his lap, feel his arms around her, his mouth on hers. . . .

A raucous shout from the next table broke the spell between them. Shaye looked away, afraid everything she had been thinking was clearly visible on her face.

A short time later, Digger decided to call it a night. Spooner and Henry agreed it was time to quit, and the three men gathered up their money. They bade Alejandro good night, assured Shaye she was welcome to join them any time, and left the table.

Alejandro smiled at her. "Tired?"

She shook her head. "Not really."

"Care to take a walk around town before turning in?"

"Isn't Ginny expecting you?"

He laughed softly. "No, darlin', not tonight or any other night. Now, how about that walk?"

"Yes, I'd like that." She looked at the greenbacks and silver in front of her. "Thanks for the loan."

"Keep it."

"No, I couldn't."

"Have you got any money?"

"No."

He winked at her. "Then keep it." He held up a hand, staying her protest. "You can pay me back later if it'll make you feel better."

"All right. Thank you." She picked up her gloves and slipped them into her skirt pocket. "You're very kind."

"Kind? Me?" He laughed at that as he began to gather up his cash. "My winnings in the left pocket, yours in the right," he said. He grabbed his hat, settled it on his head, then offered her his hand.

His fingers were long and warm and strong as they folded over her own. Mesmerized by his nearness, by his touch, she was hardly aware of leaving the saloon.

Outside, the air seemed unusually fresh after the stale, smoky atmosphere of the saloon, giving her a new appreciation for the No Smoking laws in California in the twenty-first century. All that smoke, combined with dozens of unwashed bodies and the cheap, cloying perfume the saloon girls wore had given her a headache.

Hand in hand, they walked away from the town, leaving the noise and confusion behind. The sky was clear, peppered with a million twinkling stars. A butter-yellow moon hung low on the horizon.

Shaye felt a shiver of nervous tension, an awareness of the man walking beside her. She hadn't realized how tall he was, how broad his shoulders were, until now. An aura of self-confidence surrounded him. He was a man who knew who he was, a man comfortable in his own skin.

They walked until they had left the town far behind, until they were surrounded only by the sheltering darkness and the vast indigo vault of the sky.

They walked in silence, the tension thick between them. Nervous, she cast about for something to say. "I don't recall seeing any opera house in town," she remarked, remembering that Henry had said Shep was there.

Alejandro laughed softly. "The Opera House is a dance hall. It backs up to Bonanza Street."

Shaye frowned, then nodded. Bonanza Street was where the doves plied their trade.

"It's a popular place."

"What's it like inside?"

Alejandro shrugged. "Just a big building with a pine floor. Men go there and buy tickets to dance."

"Oh."

They walked on, the silence between them thick enough to cut, and when at last he stopped, she knew he was going to kiss her.

"Shaye." She heard the confusion in his voice, knew he was just as disconcerted by the attraction between them as she was. "We've met before, haven't we?"

"No, not really."

"Dammit, I know that I know you. I've seen you before, haven't I?"

"No." She shook her head. "It's impossible."

"So is what I'm feeling right now," he muttered, and sweeping her into his arms, he kissed her.

It sent every rational thought out of her mind, left her drowning in a tidal wave of sensation. His lips were warm and firm and tasted faintly of whiskey. His arms were strong around her, familiar somehow, even though that was impossible. She moved closer, and closer still, until her body was molded to his, until his hard masculine length was pressed intimately against her body from shoulder to thigh, until she couldn't tell where he ended and she began.

No one had ever kissed her like this, made her feel like this. The tip of his tongue was like a flame dancing over her lips. She opened to him with a sigh, and the flame became an inferno.

It was a moment that seemed to last an eternity, yet ended all too quickly.

Breathless, they stared at each other.

She was twenty-eight years old, she had been married and divorced, yet he made her feel young and giddy, like a schoolgirl with her first crush.

She looked up at him and whispered, "More," felt herself falling into the same pool of sensation as his lips claimed hers once again.

She was standing on the brink of a bottomless pit. One more kiss, one more caress, would send her plummeting into the abyss. *Oh, Lord, please don't let me fall in love.*

Love! She'd been down that road before; she didn't intend to open herself to that kind of hurt again. With an effort, she put some distance between herself and Alejandro. Took a deep breath. *He's not real,* she told herself. *None of this is real.*

"It's late," she said.

"Yeah, must be all of eleven o'clock."

"Well, it's been a long day. I'm tired."

He nodded, his gaze intent upon her face, his dark eyes all too wise. "Come on," he said, taking her by the hand. "I'll walk you back."

Chapter Nine

Shaye felt as though a vast gulf had opened between them as they walked back to the hotel. Try as she might, she couldn't think of a single thing to say. She had to find her way back home, she thought desperately, had to get out of here before she did something incredibly stupid.

When they reached the hotel, Alejandro walked her up the stairs, waited while she unlocked the door.

"Thank you for dinner," she said.

"You're welcome."

"Good night."

"Shaye?"

She looked up at him, mute, every fiber of her being yearning toward him.

"What did I do wrong?" he asked quietly.

"Nothing," she said quickly. Too quickly. "Everything's fine. I'm just tired, that's all."

He reached for her, and she backed away.

"Dammit, Shaye, what's wrong?"

She shook her head, wishing she could explain, wishing she could tell him the truth, that she didn't belong here, that some quirk had sent her through time and space and dropped her in an unfamiliar world, but she was certain he would never believe her. Even now, she could hardly believe it herself.

"All right, darlin'," he said softly. "Good night."

"Good night." She started to turn away, then paused when he called her name.

"Here," he said, reaching into his coat pocket. "You forgot something."

He pulled her share of the winnings from his pocket and placed the money into her cupped hands. Her skin tingled when his fingers brushed against hers.

"Where will you spend the night?" she asked, and then thought what a silly question that was. There were probably any number of women who would welcome him at any time of the day or night.

"Don't worry about me, darlin'. I'll find a place."

His gaze, dark and smoldering, caressed her like summer heat, and then he turned and walked away, leaving her feeling cold and empty and aching deep inside.

Shaye rose early after a restless sleep that had been plagued with nightmares she could not now recall.

She looked at Alejandro's side of the bed, and wondered where he had spent the night.

A short time later, after washing her hands and face in a bowl of cool water and drying with a coarse cotton towel, she dressed and went downstairs in search of breakfast. She was acutely conscious of the layers of ruffled petticoats and the long calico skirt swirling around her ankles. Her white blouse—it was called a shirtwaist—had long, poofy sleeves that narrowed at the wrists. She had shunned the corset and pantalets in favor of her bra and bikini briefs, which she had rinsed out the night before. The half boots were far more comfortable than they looked, but she would have preferred pantyhose or even a pair of socks to the long cotton stockings. She wore a straw bonnet that tied under her chin. Her reticule, which held her camera and some of the money she had won in the poker game, dangled from her wrist.

Feeling as if she were playing dress-up in her great-grandmother's clothes, she entered the hotel dining room. It was crowded with miners, all eating with gusto and talking about the latest strike in one of the mines.

"Hit a rich vein this time!"

"Ore's top grade, too!"

"I knew I should have bought some stock in that damn mine."

Shaye hurried across the room toward an empty table and sat down. Two waitresses threaded their way around the tables, taking orders, filling coffee cups.

She sat there a good fifteen minutes before a short, plump waitress wearing a harried expression stopped by her table. "What'll you have, honey?"

"What's good?"

The woman brushed a lock of limp brown hair from her forehead. "Honey, if you're hungry enough, it's all good."

"A stack of hot cakes and a cup of coffee."

With a nod, the waitress wrote it down, then moved to the next table.

Shaye removed her gloves and slipped them into her skirt pocket. Looking out the window, she saw the ever-present flood of miners and wagons that clogged the boardwalks and the streets. The shouts of teamsters, the rumble of wagon wheels, the distant sound of blasting from one of the mines, the whinny of a horse, the chiming of a clock, the sound of a blacksmith's hammer, all combined to fill the air with discordant music. Added to this was the constant noise of the Standard stamp mill, which ran twenty-four hours a day, six days a week. A thick haze of dust hung over the town, churned up by wagon wheels and the hooves of horses and mules.

She shook her head. She had only been here two days and she was already growing accustomed to the noise and the dust. Outhouses, however, were something she would never get used to. If she ever went time traveling again, she was going to be sure to pack some toilet paper!

She smiled as the waitress returned with her breakfast.

The pancakes were some of the best Shaye had ever eaten. The coffee was the strongest she had ever tasted. Even adding a generous amount of milk and sugar didn't help much.

She was on her second cup of coffee when she felt a tingle along her spine. Glancing toward the entrance, she saw Alejandro striding toward her, felt her whole body react to the sight of him. She licked her lips, remembering the way he had kissed her the night before and her response to it.

He winked at her as he slid into the chair across from hers. "I thought I might find you here."

"Did you?"

The waitress appeared at their table, her brown eyes shining as she smiled at Alejandro. "Morning, Rio," she said, handing him a cup of coffee. "The usual?"

He nodded. "*Gracias*, Addy Mae."

Cheeks flushed, Addy Mae practically floated away from the table. It was obvious the girl, who didn't look like she was more than seventeen or eighteen, had a crush on him.

"Why were you looking for me?" Shaye asked. Seeing the look in his eyes, she felt her own cheeks grow warm with the knowledge that he, too, was remembering the kisses they had shared the night before.

"I wanted to let you know I took another room at the hotel."

"Oh, good." It was for the best, of course, but she couldn't help feeling bereft somehow, and ridiculously relieved that he hadn't spent the night with someone else. "I'd hate to think of you sleeping in the street."

He grinned at her, and she knew they were both thinking that he would never have any trouble finding a bed to sleep in, or a woman to share it with.

"That wasn't the only reason I wanted to see you," he said.

"Oh? Is something wrong?"

"No. I was hoping to spend the day with you."

Her heartbeat speeded up just a little. "Were you?"

"If you don't mind, darlin'."

Mind? Was he crazy? "I'd like that."

"I was hopin' you would," he drawled softly.

Oh, Lord, she was going to fall and fall hard, she thought frantically. Just the sound of his voice made her heart race like chain lightning across dry grass. She had never fallen head over heels in love. It had come slowly with Josh, and even then, it had never been wild and spontaneous, it had just happened. Maybe she had never really loved Josh at all. Heaven knew she had never felt this way about him. His voice had never made her heart pound. Of course, it had been just an ordinary voice, not low and sexy like Alejandro's. Josh's kisses had never spread through her like wildfire. They had given her pleasure, aroused her, but never made her feel as if she were drowning in honey.

Oh, Lord, this couldn't be happening.

"What . . ." Her voice came out in a high-pitched squeak. "What did you want to do?"

"Anything you like."

146

Visions of cool sheets and hot kisses flooded her mind. She could feel herself blushing furiously.

"Well, I've never seen a gold mine," she said. She had never wanted to, either, but it was the first thing that came to mind.

His gaze trapped hers. "Is that what you want to see, darlin'?"

Addy Mae arrived with his breakfast then, sparing Shaye the necessity of answering. "Anything else I can get for you, Rio?"

He smiled up at her. "No, Addy, this looks fine."

Shaye stared at the plate the waitress put in front of him. It was piled high with pancakes, eggs, sausage, and fried potatoes. It was a wonder he didn't weigh three hundred pounds.

"Could I get another cup of coffee?" Shaye asked.

"Coming right up," Addy Mae replied.

The waitress returned in a few minutes. "Everything all right, Rio?" she asked as she filled Shaye's cup.

"As always," he replied.

Shaye sipped her coffee while he ate, only vaguely aware of the other people in the room. All she could see was Alejandro. His long black hair, the bronze of his skin, the way his fingers curled around his cup, his deep brown eyes, the way his gaze moved over the room. He seemed relaxed, yet she had the feeling he was aware of everyone in the place.

He finished his coffee and put the cup on the table. "Ready?"

She nodded, slipping on her gloves while he

dropped a couple of greenbacks on the table. He was, she thought, a generous tipper.

Rising, he pulled out her chair, then took her hand. Gallant, she thought, and tried to remember the last time a man had done the little things once so common in everyday society. How times have changed, she mused. Men rarely held a door for a woman anymore, or helped her on with her coat. Women in her time had to pump their own gas and pretty much look out for themselves. And while she was perfectly capable of opening a door and filling her own gas tank, it was nice to be treated like a lady for a change.

Alejandro held the door for her. Outside, he took her arm, and they walked down the boardwalk. "So you want to see a gold mine, do you?"

"Not really."

"Well, there's not much to do in Bodie this time of day," he remarked with a grin. "It's a little too early for poker, and I'm not much for drinking before noon. I guess that leaves digging for gold."

"You're kidding, aren't you? I'm hardly dressed to go tromping around in a mine."

He laughed softly. "Have you ever been in a gold mine?

"No."

"Come along, then," he said, and led her across the street and up the side of a hill.

"Where are we going?"

"To the Robison mine."

"Will they let us go in?"

"Sure, darlin'. The foreman's a friend of mine."

Darlin'. Never in her life had she heard anyone caress that endearment the way he did. "Must be a female," Shaye muttered.

"What?

"Nothing." She lifted her long skirts to keep them out of the dirt and to keep from tripping over the hem. It had been a lot easier to climb the hill in her shorts and tennis shoes.

It was a bleak land, she mused as they neared the mine. There were no green fields, no trees, no birds. Just barren hills that housed mines with fanciful names: the Oro, the Champion, the Noonday, the Red Cloud. And acres and acres of sagebrush. Wood was freighted in, or brought in by burro from the Mono Mill. She seemed to remember reading in one of the books that Bodie went through 100,000 cords of wood a year.

She stopped several times on the way up the hill to take pictures of the mine and the countryside, wondering as she did so if she would ever get back to her own time to get them developed, and if there would be anything on the film when she did. She took pictures of Alejandro, too, amused by the expression on his face.

"There was no flash this time," he remarked.

"I don't need a flash in the daytime," she explained. "Would you like to take one?"

"Sure."

"What do you want to take a picture of?"

"You, of course."

She showed him how the camera worked, smiled

as he took the picture. "Come here," she said. "We'll take one of us together."

"How can you do that?"

"I'll show you. Stand here." She checked the shot in the viewfinder, set the timer, put the camera on a post, then went to stand beside Alejandro. A moment later, the camera took the picture.

"Amazing," Alejandro muttered.

"Isn't it, though?"

She knew a moment of hesitation when they reached the entrance and she looked down into what seemed to be a bottomless hole in the ground. Thoughts of cave-ins flashed across her mind.

A small cage hung suspended over the pit. Shaye looked at the man who operated the hoist. "Are you sure this is safe?"

"Safe as anything can be," the man replied with a grin that did little to reassure her.

Alejandro lifted the bar and stepped inside, then held out his hand. "You coming?"

Shaye took a deep breath, and nodded.

The operator rang a bell, there was a lurch, and the cage began its descent into the shaft.

Darkness soon closed around them, held at bay only by the dim yellow glow of the lantern.

"You all right?" Alejandro asked as the cage plunged downward.

"Yes," she replied, but her heart was pounding. She had never realized she was afraid of narrow, dark places until now. She remembered an old Andy Griffith show where Andy and Helen had gone exploring and been trapped in a cave-in. If anything happened now, there was no Barney Fife to launch a rescue effort.

"You sure?" he asked.

"Yes. Why?"

" 'Cause I've lost the feeling in my hand," he replied, his voice filled with suppressed laughter.

Muttering, "Sorry," Shaye instantly loosened her grip.

"Don't worry, darlin'. They hoist loads of up to nine hundred pounds in this thing." He grinned at her. "And you don't look like you weigh near that much."

"Very funny," Shaye retorted.

Moments later, she forgot her fear. "Oh, my," she murmured, "will you look at that?" In the lanternlight, flecks of gold and silver glittered from the cave walls. "How far down are we going?"

"I think they're at eight hundred feet."

Eight hundred feet! She looked up, felt her heart begin to pound when all she saw was darkness.

A short time later, the cage landed with a dull thud. A tunnel stretched out ahead of them, illuminated in the glow of the lanterns strung overhead. The sound of metal striking rock echoed off the walls.

"Hey, Rio, is that you?"

"How ya doing, Moose?" Alejandro lifted the bar and stepped out of the cage. Turning, he offered Shaye his hand.

"Who's that you've got with you?"

"This here's Miss Shaye Montgomery. She's never been in a mine before."

"Well, bring her on down. We hit a rich vein yesterday morning."

They walked down the tunnel, careful to avoid the tracks. She could hear the rumble of an ore cart in the distance.

Moose was aptly named. He was far and away the biggest man Shaye had ever met. Solid and square, he was well over six feet tall. Sweat gleamed on his chest; his biceps were bigger than her thighs. He had long blond hair; a faded red bandana was tied around his forehead to keep his hair out of his face. There was a snake tattooed on his left shoulder.

"Miz Montgomery, welcome to the Robison mine." His voice was as big as he was, and echoed off the walls.

"Thank you." She glanced around, feeling uneasy. The tunnel was about seven feet high and five feet wide. Here and there, she could see huge timbers shoring up the ceiling. Wooden planks had been placed against one wall. The precautions should have made her feel better, but somehow they only made her more nervous. A few feet behind Moose, she could see a wooden ladder leading up to another level.

"All right if we look around?" Alejandro asked.

"Sure. We're not doing any more blasting today." Moose reached into his pocket. "Ever seen raw gold, Miss Montgomery?"

"No."

"Here ya go." He handed her a lump of gold the size of a marble. "Found that in some clay this morning."

When she started to give it back to him, he shook his head. "Keep it."

"Really? Thank you."

"Well, come along." Moose said, moving down the tunnel. He pointed at the wall on the left. "Vein starts here. Don't know how we missed it the first time. The face of this here drift assayed at three thousand a ton; some prime samples went over four grand."

Alejandro whistled. "Guess I should have bought some stock."

"I told you so," Moose said. "It's nigh on to seventeen dollars a share."

Alejandro laughed. "That you did! Well," he said, slapping Moose on the back, "I'll get my share one way or the other."

Moose laughed, too. "I reckon you will, at that. They hit a new vein over to the Standard, too."

Alejandro nodded. "I heard Jim Mason struck it rich, too."

"Yep. Ole Jim, he bought stock in the Standard when it was forty cents a share. Hear he made more than six thousand dollars. I remember a few years back when a couple miners bought a claim for nine hundred fifty dollars. They brung out thirty-seven thousand in gold, then sold the mine for sixty-five thousand."

Shaye's eyes widened. Sixty-five thousand dollars was a pile of money; in this day and age, when you could buy three pounds of salt pork for ten cents and a man could buy a pocket watch for a dollar, it must have seemed like a million.

"I heard about a couple of miners at the Bodie who found a pocket of rich ore a while back," Alejandro remarked. "They asked for shares instead of wages, then told the owners about their strike."

"Yeah, I recollect that. Stock went up to fifty-five bucks a share. Pretty soon those two were earnin' near 'bout nine hundred dollars a day."

Shaye pressed against the wall as a tall man pushing an ore cart moved down the tunnel toward the hoist.

"Moose, dammit, if you don't light a fire under Tolley, I'm gonna whip his ass. I swan, he—"

"Hey, watch your language, Dave, we got comp'ny," Moose said.

Dave's eyes widened when he saw Shaye. "My apologies, ma'am. I didn't mean no disrespect. Howdy, Rio."

"Hey, Dave," Alejandro said. "How are you doing, *amigo*?"

"Same as always, Rio," Dave replied with a grin. "Counting the hours until shift change."

Shaye could understand that. She was anxious to get out of the mine herself. She knew it was just her imagination, but she felt as if the walls were closing in on her. How did the miners spend twelve hours a day down here? She edged closer to Alejandro, finding comfort in his nearness.

"How did William Bodey happen to find gold here?" she asked, hoping to take her mind off her growing claustrophobia.

Moose rubbed a hand over his jaw. "Well, according to the story I heard, he was huntin' his dinner and he shot hisself a rabbit. Didn't kill it, though. He followed the rabbit to its den and while he was digging down, trying to get the dang thing, he hit pay dirt. Thing is, he never got to spend any of it 'cause he froze to death that winter."

"That's so sad," Shaye remarked.

"Reckon so," Moose agreed.

"Thanks for letting us look around, Moose," Alejandro said. He looked at Shaye. "You ready to go back up?"

"More than ready."

"Come back any time," Moose said. "A pretty girl is always welcome."

"Thank you, but I think once is enough."

"Well, if you change your mind, come see us again. I'll walk you back."

"No need," Alejandro said. He took Shaye's hand in his and they started walking back toward the shaft.

Shaye frowned as she heard a dull roaring sound. "I thought Moose said they weren't doing any more blasting today."

"Yeah." His hand tightened around hers as the ground beneath them shuddered. Muttering an oath, he pulled her into a passageway that led off the main tunnel. She stared ahead into the darkness, wondering where it led.

Alejandro dropped to his knees, pulling her with him. "Shit! Get down!"

Before Shaye had time to wonder what was happening, she was facedown in the dirt with Alejandro lying across her, his big body shielding hers. There was a low rumble, like distant thunder, a shriek that sounded eerily like a woman's scream. The ground beneath her shifted, heaving violently. Clods of dirt rained down around them.

Being a California girl, her first thought was that it was an earthquake. And then she heard the faint wail of a siren from above ground, the cries and screams of frightened men, and she knew it wasn't an earthquake.

The mine had caved in.

Chapter Ten

Shaye released a breath she hadn't realized she was holding when the earth beneath her stopped trembling. There was a pain in her left cheek; her reticule was an uncomfortable lump under her left arm.

A moment later, Alejandro rolled off her. She felt a rush of panic as she opened her eyes to utter blackness. She knew he was there, but she couldn't see him, couldn't see anything.

"Rio?"

"I'm right here."

His hand brushed her shoulder, slid down her arm, closed around her fingers. "Are you all right?"

"Yes, I think so." She sat up. Lifting one hand to her cheek, she felt a warm stickiness on her fingertips.

Alejandro helped her to her feet. "Guess I picked a bad day to show you the mine," he muttered wryly.

"Yes, I guess so."

"Don't worry. I'm sure help's on the way."

She nodded; then, realizing he couldn't see her, she said, "I hope so." She clung to his hand, her heart pounding like a jackhammer. The mine had caved in. But maybe they weren't in any danger. Alejandro had pulled her into an offshoot of the main tunnel. Maybe it led to the outside.

She took a deep breath. "This leads outside, right?"

"No. It's just a tunnel where the vein played out."

She tried not to think of what would happen if this section of the mine collapsed, too, or if they ran out of air before someone came to rescue them. Buried alive . . . she clung tighter to Alejandro's hand.

"Moose!" she exclaimed. "What happened to him?"

"I don't know. Moose!" Alejandro shouted. "Moose, can you hear me?"

There was no answer.

She didn't want to think about Moose and the other men buried beneath tons of dirt and rock, and she shook the thought away. She and Alejandro were still alive. Maybe Moose and the others were, too.

He gave a tug on her hand. "Come on, let's see how far back this goes. Maybe it leads up to the next level."

She followed him down the narrow passageway. The blind leading the blind, she thought. He was right in front of her, yet she couldn't see a thing.

They hadn't gone far when he swore under his breath.

"What's wrong?" she asked anxiously.

"It's a dead end."

"Are you sure?"

"Yeah."

She didn't want to believe it. There had to be a way out, if they could just see it. Her camera! Why hadn't she thought of it sooner? Reaching into her reticule, she pulled out her camera. Easing to Alejandro's left, she took a picture. In the light of the flash, she saw that he was right.

"Handy," Alejandro remarked as she took another photo.

She shivered as she tucked the camera into her reticule again. She couldn't help wondering if she was going to die down here. Alejandro would probably survive, she thought, since history said he had been hanged on August twelfth, but what if her journey into the past had changed history? If not for her, he wouldn't be down here now. Today was the twenty-sixth of June. Had she robbed him of forty-seven days of life? If he died and she made it back to her own time, would Bodie's history books now say he had died in a cave-in?

He turned and drew her into his arms. She was shivering uncontrollably. "It'll be all right," he said, his voice low and soothing. "Trust me. Hear that?"

She cocked her head to the side as she heard the faint wail of a siren from up above. "Yes."

"They know what to do. They'll have us out of here as soon as possible."

She slipped her arms around his waist and held on

tight. She couldn't seem to stop shaking. "How long do you think it will take?"

"I don't know, darlin'."

"Maybe we could dig our way out."

"With what? Our bare hands?"

The idea was ludicrous, but at the moment she was willing to try anything. "Maybe we could find a piece of wood. Or a . . . a, I don't know, a rock."

"They know we're down here. They'll come for us." His lips brushed the top of her head; she felt it down to her toes. "We might as well sit down while we're waiting," he suggested. "It might take them a while to dig us out."

What if no one knew they were here? What if the man who let them down in the hoist didn't remember them? What if . . . she pushed the morbid thoughts from her mind. Someone would find them. She had to believe that.

He sat down, and she sat close beside him, grateful for his arm around her shoulders.

"How long will the air last?"

"Long enough," he said reassuringly.

"Do you think . . . do you think that Moose and the others are dead?"

She felt him shrug. "Damned if I know."

Her gaze moved through the darkness, seeing nothing. She couldn't remember ever being in total darkness before. It was oddly disorienting, and more than a little frightening.

They sat in silence for several minutes, the only sound that of dirt trickling down from overhead. She didn't know what Alejandro was thinking about, but all she could think about was the fact that there were tons and tons of dirt overhead that could come crashing down on them at any second.

She couldn't remember ever being so afraid, or so close to death. She wasn't ready to die, she thought frantically. Not now. She took several deep breaths, willing herself to stay calm.

"You all right, darlin'?" he asked.

"I guess so. What did you do before you came to Bodie?" she asked. Maybe, if she could get him talking, it would take her mind off how afraid she was.

"Same thing I do here."

"Gamble?"

"Seems to be my chosen profession. It's the one thing I'm good at."

"So you've always been a gambler?"

"No, not always."

He drew her closer. His nearness was warm and comforting.

"I worked on a ranch in Montana for a while, breaking horses. It was steady work. Fair pay." He laughed softly. "But the real money was gambling with the other hands on Saturday night. I made more playing poker in one night than I made in wages."

"Why did you leave?"

"I took the foreman for three hundred dollars one night. He accused me of cheating, called me a couple of names a lady shouldn't hear. I was young and hot headed, and I laid into him. Broke his nose and a couple of ribs. I left before he could fire me."

"How old were you?"

"Nineteen."

"And you've been earning your living gambling ever since?"

"Yeah. I guess it ain't much of a life, but I've seen a lot of country, and just about every boomtown in the West. I reckon this one'll go bust, too, sooner or later. They all do."

It was on the tip of her tongue to tell him that by next year, only six mines would still be operating. Instead, she asked him if he had ever lived with his mother's people.

"I spent my summers in the Black Hills when I was young," he said. "My old man had a small ranch near Deadwood. My mother and I went to see her people during the Sun Dance. Those were good days. I miss them."

"I've read about the Sun Dance. It always seemed like such a barbaric custom. Did you ever—"

"No. My mother died when I was nine. A Pawnee raiding party burned our house down the following year. My old man packed us up and we moved back East to take care of his sister, who was ailing. I didn't like city life, not after growing up wild. Seems like I was always in trouble of one kind or another. By the time I was sixteen, my old man and I were hardly speaking to each other. We had a big blow-up one night, and I left."

He'd never had a place to call home since then. He had slept in the open when he was broke, in hotels when he was flush, gradually coming to the realization that it wasn't the place that made a house a home, but the people in it. He wondered briefly what it would be like to be married to Shaye, then shrugged the idea aside. She was a lady through and through, far too good for the likes of him.

"What did you and your father fight about?" Shaye asked.

"Everything. I didn't like school and I didn't go much. I was keeping company with a pretty wild bunch. Drinking." He grunted softly. "Gambling. Anyway, one thing led to another. We both said some things we shouldn't have, but I was just as stubborn as he was, and I refused to back down." He blew out a deep breath. "I never went back," he said softly, and she heard the regret in his voice. "Two years later I got a letter from my aunt telling me he was dead."

"I'm sorry, Rio."

"Yeah," he said softly. "Me, too, but it was a long time ago. Hell, that's enough about me. What about you?"

"My life is much less exciting. I lived my whole life in the same house until I got married—"

"You're married!"

"Not anymore."

His hand squeezed her shoulder. "I'm sorry for your loss."

Shaye frowned, then realized he thought her husband was dead. "We're divorced," she said, and then wondered if being divorced was still as scandalous as it had once been.

"I've never met a divorced woman," he remarked.

"Can't say I'm sorry your marriage didn't work out, though, 'cause if it had, you probably wouldn't be here now, with me." He laughed softly. "Of course, I don't imagine you're too happy about that at the moment, all things considered."

She had to laugh at that. All things considered, she was still glad to be here, with him.

"Go on," he urged.

"There's really nothing to tell. I grew up, got a job, got married, got divorced." Except for a couple of high-profile news stories she had covered early in her career, being trapped in a mine in a ghost town that had been dead for over a hundred years was the most exciting, and frightening, experience she'd ever had. And Alejandro Valverde was definitely the most exciting man she had ever met. She shrugged. "That about sums it up."

"I have a feeling there's a lot more to you than that."

"Well, I was just giving you the *Reader's Digest* version."

"What the deuce is that?"

She grinned. "It's like a synopsis. The short version as opposed to the long, boring one."

"I doubt if you could ever be boring, darlin'."

Silence fell between them for a long while. The darkness seemed heavy, overpowering. She shifted her weight, and the movement dislodged a trickle of dirt. She felt it against her cheek, reminding her that there were several tons of earth just overhead. She clenched her hands, shivering as fear crawled over her skin again. What if this tunnel collapsed, too? What if they were never found?

"Talk to me, Rio."

"What about, darlin'?"

"Anything. Anything at all." She needed the sound of his voice to distract her. He had a beautiful voice, soft and low and sexy, blatantly male. Blatantly intimate. Like black velvet.

Alejandro thought a minute. "I remember my grandmother telling me how light came into the world," he began. "Long ago, in the time before time, the People lived in the underworld. There was no sun or moon or stars, no light at all, except the light cast by the eagle feathers that the People carried. After a time, the wise men of the tribe got together to see if they could find a way to make more light. One of the wise men decided they should make a sun and a moon, and so they found a piece of round hide and painted it yellow and placed it in the sky. This sun did not give much light, and the next day, they took it down and made it larger and brighter. Four times the sun rose and set and was made larger, until it was very large and very bright.

"There lived with the People a witch and a wizard who were angry with what the wise men had done, and they tried to destroy the sun and the moon. This frightened the sun and the moon, and they fled the underworld and escaped to the heavens."

"That's a wonderful story," Shaye said. "How long do you think we've been down here?"

"I don't know. A couple of hours, maybe more."

165

It seemed like forever. How long would it take for the miners who were topside to dig them out? Hours? Days? She posed the question to Alejandro, dreading the answer.

"It's hard to say," he replied. "Depends on how much dirt they have to dig through to get to us, and whether the shaft is still clear."

"It might be days, then?"

"Shaye—"

"Tell me the truth."

"It's a possibility, but I wouldn't worry about it. The miners have dealt with cave-ins before. They know what to do."

Yes, she thought, shivering, but would they be able to do it in time?

"Shaye, it'll be all right, trust me."

"I can't help it, I'm scared."

Alejandro blew out a breath. He didn't blame her for being scared. He was a mite unsettled himself. It was true there had been cave-ins before; he'd seen the bodies carried out of the mines, heard the sobs of the widows and children.

"It'll be all right," he said again.

Shaye laughed softly. "Who are you trying to convince?"

He laughed, too, his arm tightening around her shoulders, and suddenly neither of them was laughing.

"Shaye . . ."

She couldn't see him in the darkness, but she could feel the heat of his body next to hers, his thigh pressed against her own. It was suddenly hard to breathe, hard to think of anything but the man beside her.

She wanted him, she thought, wanted him to hold her, to kiss her. To make love to her. Oh, but it was crazy. She hardly knew him, yet there was no denying the attraction that hummed between them whenever their eyes met. And in the back of her mind was the thought, what if? What if they were going to die here? Alejandro might live. Maybe her being here wouldn't change his fate, but that didn't mean she would get out alive. . . .

She felt his breath on her face, and then his lips claimed hers and drove every other thought from her mind. Heat spiraled through her as his tongue caressed her lower lip, tasting her. He turned toward her, and she melted into his embrace, all her fears forgotten. His arms were strong around her; surely he would keep her safe. His hand stroked her back, his touch light, sending shivers of pleasure down her spine. And his mouth . . . she closed her eyes, lost in the wonder of his kiss. Her hands clutched his shoulders, drifted down his arms, curving over his biceps to lightly knead the muscles there.

She fit in his arms so perfectly . . . was he aware of it, too?

She moaned softly, heard the sharp intake of his breath as she leaned into him, wanting to be closer, closer, cursing the voluminous skirt and petticoats that bunched between them.

He murmured her name, then kissed her again, and yet again. And somehow they were lying side by side in an intimate tangle of arms and legs. She didn't know if it was the darkness or the man, but her every sense seemed heightened, her every nerve attuned to his nearness. Her skin came alive at his touch, tingling with need, burning with awareness. She tugged off her gloves, her fingertips moving over the face she could not see, tracing the shape of his nose, his jaw, lingering over his lips.

With a low growl, he opened his mouth, capturing her finger, sucking lightly.

Her breath escaped in a long, husky sigh. A kiss, a touch, and she was on fire for him, filled with a longing she had never known before.

"Shaye . . ."

She heard her own longing reflected in his voice.

He rained kisses over her face, his touch incredibly gentle, so filled with tenderness it brought an ache to her heart and tears to her eyes. Since her divorce, it had been easy to keep men at arm's length. Hurt and disillusioned, she had been certain she would never trust another man, never want another man in her life. But she wanted Alejandro Valverde with her whole heart and soul.

She was about to tell him so when she realized he had gone suddenly still. "Listen!" he exclaimed softly. "Did you hear that?"

"What? I don't hear any—"

And then she heard it, a man's voice. "Hey! Anybody alive down there?"

Alejandro sat up. "Yes!" he shouted. "We're here!"

"Sit tight. We'll have you out of there in no time at all."

They were, Shaye thought, the sweetest words she had ever heard. And even as the thought crossed her mind, she couldn't help wishing their rescuers had waited another hour, or maybe two.

The man was as good as his word. A short time later, they could hear the sound of men digging, and in less than an hour, she was above ground again. Hundreds of people were gathered at the mine entrance. They cheered as Shaye and Alejandro emerged. Shaye took a deep breath, filling her lungs with fresh air. It was, she thought, almost like being reborn.

The doctor came forward to check them over. He examined the cut on Shaye's cheek, applied some sort of antiseptic that hurt worse than the cut itself, and pronounced both her and Alejandro in good health.

Several women surged forward, offering them cake, sandwiches, coffee, and lemonade.

Lily and Addy Mae and a dark-eyed girl Shaye didn't recognize hovered over Alejandro, touching his arm, his shoulder, his cheek, expressing their relief that he was all right.

"We were so worried," Addy Mae said, and the other two girls nodded.

Alejandro looked at Shaye over their heads, and shrugged.

Shaye accepted a roast beef sandwich and a glass of lemonade from one of the townswomen. "Do they know if the others are all right?"

169

The woman shook her head. "No word yet. The cave-in wasn't so bad where you were. From what my Harlan said, the worst of it was farther down the tunnel. They're still digging down there."

Shaye took a drink, trying not to think of Moose and the other men buried beneath tons of dirt.

Around her, men and women talked in subdued voices punctuated by the whine of the hoist as dirt was lifted from the mine.

"Too bad," a grizzled veteran said.

"Bound to happen sooner or later."

"Yup. Mining's a dangerous business. Could just as easily have been a fire."

"Or an explosion. Remember when the powder magazine blew up at the Old Rough and Ready? In all my born days, I never heard such an awful sound."

"Terrible, just terrible. I thought the whole house was gonna come down around us."

"Yeah, I recollect that. Thought we was havin' an earthquake."

"Blew the boardinghouse next to the mine to smithereens."

"Yep. Danged explosion rained rocks down on Main Street. Lucky more folks weren't hurt."

"Killed seven men in the mine."

"Heard tell folks felt the blast clear to Bridgeport."

And on and on it went, with the bystanders recalling other misfortunes and catastrophes while a new tragedy was being played out in front of them.

Shaye had just finished her sandwich when Alejandro came for her. "You look all done in," he said,

taking her by the arm. "Come on, I'll take you back
to the hotel."

"What about Moose and the others?"

"There's nothing we can do for them. Come on,
let's go get cleaned up."

She was too tired to argue. Alejandro had borrowed
a buggy from one of the townspeople. He helped her
in, then took his seat. Picking up the reins, he clucked
to the team.

"They're dead, aren't they?"

"I reckon."

"What a horrible way to die."

"There aren't many good ways that I know of,"
Alejandro replied.

"No, I guess not."

And hanging had to be one of the worst, she
thought, and wondered if there was some way to
change his fate, and if there was, what the conse-
quences would be.

When they reached the hotel, Alejandro helped her
from the carriage. Inside, he asked the clerk to send
some hot water up to her room right away. Shaye was
all too conscious of the speculation in the clerk's eyes
as she followed Alejandro up the stairs. She could
almost read the man's thoughts, knew he was wondering what their relationship was, but she was too
drained, physically and emotionally, to worry about
it.

She unlocked the door and Alejandro followed her
inside. She stood there, too weary to move, to think,
while he lit the lamp.

"Here, now." He took her reticule and placed it on top of the dresser. "Sit down before you fall down."

She sat down in the chair, startled when he dropped to his knees, lifted her skirt, and began to unlace her shoes. He removed them one by one, peeled off her long cotton stockings, and then he began to massage her foot.

"Rio . . . ?"

He looked up at her, head cocked to one side. "Don't you like it?"

She shrugged, keenly aware of his hands moving over her foot. His skin was very dark compared to her own. His touch made her skin tingle.

"Should I stop?"

She shook her head, felt her heart skip a beat as his hands moved up her leg, gently massaging her calf. No one had ever done such a thing for her before. She had never realized how sensual such a thing could be, to have a man kneeling at her feet, massaging her foot, her leg.

His gaze held hers as he lowered her foot, then cradled the other one in his lap. His hands were big and strong, yet so gentle.

She looked at him, and she wanted him. Even now, she could remember the taste of his kisses, the way her body had molded so perfectly to his. She had come so close, she thought, so close to surrendering her heart and soul into his keeping. Oh, yes, she wanted him desperately. Even now, covered with dirt and emotionally and physically exhausted, she wanted to feel his mouth on hers again, to hear his voice call her darlin' as only he could, to feel his weight pressing her down . . .

And he wanted her. She could feel it in his touch, read it in the depths of his eyes, those dark dark eyes that seemed to know her better than she knew herself.

"Shaye?"

She shook her head. She couldn't, wouldn't, let herself love him. She didn't belong here, didn't know when she might find herself back in her own time. How could she hope to survive in the future if she left her heart in the past?

He didn't argue, didn't force the issue. Instead, he stood up. "I'm going back to the mine to see if I can help."

"All right."

"Good night, Shaye."

"Good night. Alejandro? Be careful."

He looked at her a moment; then, reaching down, he took hold of her shoulders and pulled her to her feet. And kissed her.

She was breathless when he let her go.

His knuckles skimmed her check. "Enjoy your bath," he said, and left the room.

She stared after him, her fingertips pressed against her lips, and knew she had lost the battle, and her heart, as well.

Chapter Eleven

Shaye pulled a chair over in front of the window, grabbed a blanket off the bed and wrapped it around her shoulders, then sat down, staring into the distance. She had bathed and washed her hair, had tried to sleep, but sleep wouldn't come. Every time she closed her eyes, she saw Moose being buried beneath tons of rock and earth. It could so easily have been her and Alejandro. The thought made her shiver, and she drew the blanket she had wrapped around her shoulders tighter.

The hours passed slowly. Lights shone like tiny beacons on the hill near the Robison mine. She thought about the men who had been killed, about their families huddled together near the mine entrance, waiting, their hopes dimming as each body was brought to the surface. She wondered if Moose had a wife, children, who were waiting, praying.

She wondered what drove a man to work in the mines. It was a hard life, working twelve hours a day, six days a week, for a paltry four dollars a day, yet men from all over the world had traveled here. Mexicans and Swedes, Italians and Irishmen had all come here, some bringing their families with them.

She remembered reading somewhere about three park aides who worked in Bodie. They had gone hiking at dusk and stopped at one of the abandoned mines. They were tossing rocks down the twelve-hundred-foot shaft when they reported hearing a voice calmly call out, "Hey, you." They said the voice seemed to come from the pit's opening. The depth of the shaft, together with the fact that it had been caved in for years, seemed to rule out any human presence, but they swore they had heard a voice. Had it been the Robinson mine? Shaye wondered. Had the voice belonged to one of the miners who had been killed there this night? There was a time when she would have dismissed such a tale as nonsense, but not anymore.

Dawn was lighting the sky when Alejandro returned. One look at his face confirmed her worst fears.

"All of them?" she asked.

He nodded. "We brought the last body out just a few minutes ago."

"You must be exhausted."

"I am that. It's been a hell of a night."

She tossed the blanket aside, only then remembering that she was in her nightgown. Not that it revealed anything, she thought. Made of heavy white cotton, it covered her completely from her neck to her ankles.

Rising, Shaye went to him and helped him out of his coat. She tossed it on top of her skirt and shirt waist. All were in need of a good cleaning.

"Here," she said. "Sit down before you fall down."

He grinned faintly, recognizing the words he had said to her earlier. Sitting down on the chair, he put his head back and closed his eyes. She filled the basin with water, wishing it wasn't so cold, and washed the dirt from his hands and face; then, kneeling in front of him, she removed his boots and socks. Lifting his left foot into her lap, she began to massage it.

He looked at her through half-lowered lids. "What are you doing?"

"Returning a favor."

He made a soft sound of pleasure and closed his eyes again.

It was, Shaye thought, remarkably satisfying to sit there and massage his foot. She couldn't remember ever having done it for anyone else. She did his other foot, then pulled him to his feet and helped him remove his shirt. She wasn't willing to go further than that, and he didn't seem to care.

She drew back the covers on the bed, then turned away so he could remove his trousers. She heard the whisper of cloth over skin, the creak of the mattress as it took his weight. She gave him a minute to cover himself before she turned around.

He was already asleep, sprawled facedown on the bed. On top of the blankets.

Unable to help herself, she stood there, her gaze moving over his broad back and shoulders, noting the indentation at the base of his spine. He should be doing ads for Jockey shorts, she thought, with those long legs and that tight butt.

With a sigh, she tugged the covers out from under him, pulled them up over his shoulders, and then slid under the blankets, staying as close to the edge of the bed as she could without falling off the mattress.

She closed her eyes and tried not to think of him lying less than an arm's length away, tried not to remember how potent his kisses were, the way her body had felt next to his. The way his hands had felt moving over her skin.

Gradually, she drifted off to sleep, and in her dreams, he fulfilled her every wish, every desire.

It was, she thought, the best dream she had ever had, better even than the one where Harrison Ford, Mel Gibson, and Brad Pitt were all fighting over her. She sighed as Alejandro's lips slanted over hers, warm and firm, his tongue like teasing fire. And his hands . . . oh, those big brown hands. They moved sensuously over her skin, stroking, caressing, arousing. His breath was hot when he pressed his mouth to her breast; his long dark hair tickled her cheek.

As from a great distance, she heard a door slam, the rumble of wagon wheels, the crack of a bullwhip, but she wasn't ready to wake up, not now. Not when he was kissing her again. A kiss to take her breath away.

She ran her hands over his chest, his shoulders, down his arms, loving the feel of his skin against her palms, the way the muscles in his arms bunched and relaxed. She loved his arms . . .

"Shaye."

His voice, that wonderful sexy voice, deep and husky, filled with want and desire.

"Shaye . . . darlin', tell me to stop before it's too late."

Stop? Why on earth would she want him to stop? She couldn't love him in the cold light of day, in the harsh realm of reality. But here, safe within her dreams, anything was possible.

"Don't stop," she murmured. "Oh, Lord, don't ever stop."

The bed creaked as he shifted on the mattress. She felt a whisper of cool air as he gently tugged her nightgown over her head.

In her dream, she opened her eyes . . . and realized with sudden, startling clarity that she wasn't dreaming at all, and that her nightgown was now on the floor.

And Alejandro was poised over her, his dark eyes smoldering.

For a moment, she couldn't speak, couldn't breathe, could only stare at him. He was every woman's fantasy, she thought, a man without equal. His hair fell over his shoulders, thick and black. His skin was the color of burnished copper, every muscle taut with desire.

She tried to find her voice as he lowered himself over her, but she seemed to have lost the power of

· speech. She had to stop him before it was too late. But it was already too late. His mouth covered hers, hot and hungry, coaxing and sweet, so sweet.

She moaned softly as she drew him closer, her hands sliding restlessly over his back. Right or wrong, she wanted this moment, and she meant to have it before it was too late, before she was zapped back to the present, before he met his Fate . . .

An image of Alejandro being led to the gallows, his hands tied behind his back, flashed through her mind in vivid detail. With a strangled sob, she burst into tears.

"I guess you changed your mind," he muttered ruefully.

She shook her head. "No . . . no . . . you don't understand. I . . . you . . ."

"Shaye, what's wrong? You can tell me."

"Nothing," she said, and sobbed harder.

"Dammit, Shaye, why are you crying?" He rolled off her and sat up, his back against the headboard. "I thought that you . . . that we . . ." He ran a hand through his hair. "Whatever I did, I'm sorry."

"You . . . you . . . haven't done . . . anything," she sobbed. Grabbing the covers, she drew them over her.

"Then why are you crying?"

"Because you . . . you're . . ."

"I'm what?"

"You're going to die!"

"Darlin', we're all gonna die."

She sat up, drawing the covers up to her chin. "Oh,

179

you don't understand! I know *when* you're going to die."

He stared at her, one brow arched. "The only way you could know that is if you're planning to kill me," he mused. "Are you?"

"Of course not!"

Alejandro shook his head. "Don't tell me you're a fortune-teller?"

"No. Oh, you'll never believe me!"

"Try me and see."

"I know because I came here from the future."

"The future?"

She nodded, sniffling. "From the year two thousand. I was born March nineteenth, nineteen hundred and seventy-three in Los Angeles, California."

Alejandro grunted softly. He'd suspected it from the very beginning. She was addle-brained, there was no doubt about it now.

"It's true! You saw my driver's license. It expires in two thousand and four, one hundred and twenty-four years from now."

"It's not possible."

"I know that. Don't you think I know that? I didn't believe it either at first, but it's true."

"I've heard some tall tales in my day," he muttered, "but this one beats them all to hell."

"If it's not true, how do you explain the things in my backpack?"

"I don't know." He ran a hand over his jaw. "I reckon there are lots of newfangled things being invented in the big cities back East that we haven't heard about yet."

Shaye let out an exasperated sigh. "What about my watch? And my shoes? What about my camera? And my phone? And my water bottle?"

He shook his head, clearly unconvinced. "For all I know, those things are common as warts in Los Angeles and New York City."

"Your mother was an Indian. Her name was Lark or Dove. Your father was Irish and Spanish. You were born in the Black Hills. You came to Bodie in eighteen seventy-nine."

"Her name was White Eagle Woman," Alejandro replied. He studied her a moment, his expression wary, then thoughtful. "So tell me, when am I going to die?"

"This year. You're going to be hanged on August twelfth."

"Hanged! *Maldición!* Why?"

"You were convicted of killing Daisy Sullivan."

He swore again, in English and Spanish. "Supposing I was to believe you, how do you know so much about me?"

"I met a relative of yours. In Bodie. In the year two thousand. He told me. I also read Daisy's diary."

"How do you know about her diary?" he asked sharply. "I'm the only one who knows about that, and she never lets anyone read it. Not even me."

"Well, I read it."

It was impossible, preposterous, and yet he was beginning to believe her. "What's the town like in your time? In . . ." He swore softly. "In two thousand."

"It's a ghost town. By eighteen eighty-two, only six mines were still in operation. By the eighteen nineties, the population was less than a thousand. In nineteen thirty-two, a little boy started a fire behind the Sawdust Corner Saloon. It wiped out more than half of the town."

Alejandro shook his head. It couldn't be true. No matter how plausible she made it sound, no one could travel from the future into the past. But if it was true, it would explain so many things, like the strange outfit she had been wearing when he'd first met her, the peculiar objects in her peculiar pack, the odd words that occasionally cropped up in her speech.

Damn, what if it was true? He rubbed his hand over his jaw again, remembering how she had kept asking him who he really was the day they met.

"So," he asked, "how did you travel through time? And why did you come here?"

"I don't know. I came to the ghost town to look around, and I heard music coming out of the saloon." She shrugged. "Whatever happened, happened when I went into the Queen of Bodie saloon. It wasn't there when I walked through the town the first time, I'm sure of it." She bit down on her lower lip. "I'd seen a picture of you the night before. And I . . . I had dreamed about you."

"Oh?"

She nodded. "In my dream, you were in a saloon, playing cards. It was the Queen of Bodie."

He grunted softly. "So you dreamed of me, and now you're here?"

"There's more."

Something in her voice sent a shiver down his spine. "Go on."

"I saw you. Before I saw you in my dream."

The air seemed to spark between them. Alejandro stared at her, felt the hair raise along his arms. His mouth felt suddenly dry. Everything else faded into the distance as he waited for her to go on.

"When I was walking through the town the first day I got there, I stopped at the jail." She took a deep breath. "When I looked in the window, I saw you. And later that night, I saw you in the jail again. You were wearing a pair of black pants and a white shirt and a black vest embroidered with little gold fleurs-de-lis."

Alejandro swore. He had ordered the vest she described from San Francisco a month ago. He hadn't received it yet; there was no way she could possibly know about it. Yet she did.

"You came to stand at the window of the cell, and even though it was impossible, I had the feeling you saw me."

He stared at her a moment and then, too agitated to sit still, he stood up. Unmindful of his nudity, he crossed the floor to stare out the window. He had always been certain he had seen her somewhere before. Of course, it had never occurred to him that he might have been a ghost at the time. He shook his head. How could he remember something that hadn't even happened yet? It was preposterous.

"You believe me, don't you?"

"I don't know."

"I'm telling the truth! You've got to believe me. You've got to leave town before it's too late."

"I like it here."

"Are you crazy?" she exclaimed, her voice rising. "If you stay, they'll hang you."

"I don't have any reason to kill Daisy."

"Well, they convicted you of her murder just the same."

He turned to face her. "Even if what you say is true, it's Daisy who has to leave town. Not me."

Shaye nodded. He was right, of course. Getting Daisy out of town would solve everything. "How will we convince her to go?"

"I don't know. I guess you could try talking to her."

Shaye blew out a sigh. "She probably won't believe me any more than you do."

"I'm sorry, darlin', but it's just too far-fetched."

"Even if you don't believe me, promise me you'll leave town before August the ninth."

"Why? What happens then?"

"You'll be arrested. Please promise me. At least promise me you'll think about it."

A knock on the door put an end to their conversation.

"Who is it?" Alejandro called.

"It's me, Rio. I need to see you."

Alejandro glanced at Shaye, a wry smile curving

184

his lips. "Sounds like Fate's come knocking at the door."

He reached for a pair of trousers hanging on one of the hooks and pulled them on. He smoothed his hair back with his hands, then opened the door. "Mornin' Daisy," he said. "What can I do for you?"

Daisy was wearing a dark blue dress, a black shawl, and black half boots. The same gold locket she had been wearing before rested in the hollow of her throat.

"Rio, I . . ." Her eyes widened with recognition when she saw Shaye in his bed.

"Shaye, I don't think you two have been introduced."

Shaye sat up. "No, we haven't."

"Shaye, this is Daisy Sullivan. Daisy this is Shaye Montgomery. She's a friend of mine."

"Yes," Daisy said, her voice edged with jealousy. "I can see that." She looked at Alejandro. "I need to talk to you, Rio." She glared at Shaye. "Alone."

"We can talk downstairs," he told her. "Give me a minute to get dressed."

With a last baleful look at Shaye, Daisy stepped into the corridor and closed the door.

Shaye watched Alejandro open a dresser drawer and pull out a clean shirt and a pair of socks. He dressed silently, his expression closed to her. He put on his boots, buckled on his gun belt, grabbed his hat and coat.

He had his hand on the doorknob when he paused. Turning, he crossed the floor to the bed. Bending down, he brushed a kiss across her lips, then left the room.

Shaye stared after him, wondering, as she had before, if it was possible to change the course of history.

Chapter Twelve

He found Daisy in the lobby, pacing back and forth. "Do you want to get something to eat?" he asked.

She shook her head. "I'm not hungry."

Alejandro glanced into the dining room, which was already crowded with hungry miners. "How about a cup of coffee while we talk?"

"No, we can't talk here." She placed her hand on his arm. "Let's go to my place, where we can be alone."

"All right."

They walked down the street in silence. Alejandro nodded to several of the men, smiled automatically at the women, but his mind was on what Shaye had told him. If what she had said was true, and more and more he believed her, what did it mean?

Daisy's house was located at the end of White

Street. It was a nice place, modest in size. New buildings were going up all over Bodie. Town lots were selling for a thousand dollars; lots on Bonanza Street were going for six hundred and more. He'd heard of one man who sold a house and lot adjoining the Miners Union Hall for more than six thousand dollars.

There were about a hundred buildings up on High Peak. The suburbs extended down the ridge to Silver Hill. Most of the houses were occupied by miners who wanted to be closer to their work. There were a couple of boardinghouses and saloons, as well. Some of the mining companies had built boardinghouses near the mines in hopes of keeping the workers away from town and on the job. Captain R. F. Lord, who was the superintendent of the McClinton mine, had built his house at the apex of High Peak so he could look down over the whole town.

Alejandro followed Daisy up the short walkway to the porch and into the house. Cluttered was the only word for the décor. There were fringed pillows and knickknacks everywhere.

"Sit down, Rio," Daisy said. She dropped her shawl over the back of a chair. "Can I get you something to drink?"

"No." He picked up a couple of pillows and tossed them aside, then sat down on the sofa. "What did you want to talk about?"

She perched on the edge of a dainty chair like a bird about to take flight. "It's Dade. I think he's stealing from me."

"What makes you think that?"

"I'm not stupid. Our profits have been down for the last couple of months. He says business is dropping off, but I know that ain't true. I think he's been stealing whiskey, too."

"Why don't you sell him your half and go back home? You always said you'd like to go back, if you had the money."

She shook her head. "Not anymore. I like it here now. Besides . . ." She glanced away. "I don't think I could go home and look my mama in the eye; not now."

"She doesn't have to know."

"No." Daisy met his gaze, reminding him of a defiant child. "This is my home now."

Alejandro ran his hand over his jaw. Would she believe him if he told her what Shaye had said? Hell, he wasn't sure if he believed it.

He was trying to figure out how to tell her when suddenly Daisy was kneeling in front of him.

"I'm afraid of Dade," Daisy said urgently. "Please come back to the Belle. I need you."

"Daisy—"

"Please, Rio. I'll give you my half. I'll give you any—"

He shook his head. "If I'd wanted the saloon, I would have kept it."

He reached down, intending to lift her to her feet, but she rose up on her knees and wrapped her arms around his waist.

She looked up at him, her eyes filled with devotion. "I love you, Rio. I've always loved you! I never

189

stopped. Please stay with me. I'll do anything you want, be anything—"

Unlocking her arms from his waist, he stood up, drawing her with him. "Daisy, listen to me, you've got to get out of town. You're in danger here—"

"It's her, isn't it? That woman in your bed. I saw the way she looked at you. The way *you* looked at her."

"Daisy—"

"It could be good between us, Rio. I could make you happy, I know I could, if you'd just—"

"Daisy, darlin' . . ." He took her in his arms as she began to cry, held her until her sobs subsided.

"I'm sorry." She pushed away from him and turned her back. His heart went out to her as he watched her straighten her shoulders, heard her sniffling softly.

"Daisy, listen to me—"

He put his hand on her shoulder, but she shook it off. "Just go away."

"Dammit, Daisy, you've got to listen to me!"

"Get out!" she shrieked. She whirled around, her finger stabbing toward the door. "Go on! Get out!"

"I'll talk to McCrory." He pulled his hideout gun from his inside coat pocket and laid the derringer on the table beside the sofa. "If he gives you any more trouble, let me know. In the meantime, keep this handy."

Daisy stared at him, her eyes dull and red, her lower lip quivering.

Feeling like a heel, Alejandro left the house.

Women! If he lived to be a hundred, he'd never understand any of them.

While he walked back to the hotel, he thought about what Shaye had told him. It was beyond belief. And yet, she had known things she had no way of knowing. And though he didn't believe in time travel, he did believe that some people were able to see the future. His great-grandfather Red Bow had been a shaman gifted with many mystical powers, among them the ability not only to look into the past, but to see into the future as well.

Shaye wasn't in their room when he returned to the hotel. Going back downstairs, he looked in the dining room. She was sitting at a back table.

"Everything okay?" she asked as he took a seat across from her.

"She thinks her partner's skimming the profits."

"Yes, I know."

He looked at her, a question in his eyes.

"The diary. It's all in there. Did she throw herself into your arms?"

He grunted softly.

"So many women, so little time," she muttered dryly.

"What the deuce does that mean?"

"Nothing. Did you tell her about me?"

"I tried. She wouldn't listen. I'll give her a few days to calm down—"

"Calm down? What did you say to her?"

He muttered an oath. "I didn't say anything. She . . . hell, you said you read her diary. You know what happened." He blew out a breath. "So tell me more about the future."

"I don't know where to start. People travel in automobiles instead of carriages. We have electric lights instead of kerosene lamps. Our houses have air-conditioning to keep them cool in the summer, and furnaces to keep them warm in the winter. We have airplanes—"

"Airplanes?"

She nodded. "It's a way to travel through the air."

"You mean, like flying?"

"Yes. And men have walked on the moon and—"

He laughed out loud at that. "Why would anyone want to walk on the moon?"

It was a good question. She had often wondered that herself. "I don't know. To prove it could be done, I guess."

He shook his head. "You've got a hell of an imagination, I'll give you that."

"I'm not making it up! It's all true. There will be amazing inventions in the next hundred years. Telephones will replace the telegraph. Computers will replace typewriters. Refrigerators will replace iceboxes."

She bit down on her lip, trying to figure out how to explain the miracle of computers and television, stereos and microwaves, washing machines and indoor plumbing, blow dryers and toothbrushes and toilet paper, and all the other things that she had taken for granted and dearly missed.

Alejandro stared at Shaye in bemused bewilderment. It was obvious she believed what she was saying. And he was beginning to. Was she crazy, he wondered, or was he?

Addy Mae sashayed up to their table. "Good morning, Rio. What'll you have?"

"Same as usual, darlin'."

Addy Mae smiled at him, then looked at Shaye. "And you?"

"Just coffee. And a muffin."

Addy Mae laid a hand on Alejandro's shoulder. "I heard about the accident at the mine. I'm sorry about Moose. I know he was a friend of yours."

"Yeah. Thanks."

Addy Mae squeezed his shoulder. "I'll bring your coffee."

Alejandro leaned back in his chair. "The funeral's tomorrow morning."

Shaye nodded, wondering where they would hold the service since there was as yet no church in town. There were over sixty saloons in Bodie, and fifteen dens of iniquity, but not one house of worship. Would they use one of the saloons? Or maybe someone's home. No churches, she mused, but five cemeteries: the people's cemetery for citizens, the Miners Union plot, and the Free Masons' cemetery; the Chinese had their own cemetery, too; and then there was Boot Hill, reserved for the less respectable citizens of the town. Moose would most likely be laid to rest in the Miners Union Cemetery.

"Where will they hold the service?" she asked.

"Over at the Miners Union Hall. Reverend Warrington holds church services there, or sometimes at the Odd Fellows Hall. The Miners Hall is a popular place for dances and recitals and the like. The firemen hold a ball there once a year, and the union has benefits now and then to raise money for the families of men who are killed or injured in the mines."

"Amazing," Shaye remarked. "Thousands of people and two preachers, and no church."

"Hey," he said, "we'll have a church soon. The reverend is soliciting subscriptions now."

Shaye frowned. "If I remember right, you'll have two."

"Two?" Alejandro grinned. "Lord have mercy!"

"As I recall, they'll both be finished in September of next year. The Catholic one will be lost in a fire. But the Methodist one on Green Street is still standing."

Alejandro shook his head. Either she was telling the truth or she was far and away the best storyteller he'd ever heard.

Addy Mae brought their order. Shaye sipped her coffee, wondering if the coffee was getting better or if she was just getting used to it.

"So," Alejandro said, "what are you going to do today?"

"I don't know. Look for a job, I guess."

"What kind of job?"

"I thought I'd ask Philo Richardson if he could use me at the newspaper office."

"You could always get a job dealing cards at the Queen."

"Me? You're kidding, right?"

"Why not you?"

"But I hardly know anything about the game."

"You did all right the other night."

She felt a flurry of excitement at the thought. She'd had fun the other night. "Will you help me?"

"Sure. You can deal at my table until you feel comfortable. You can start next week."

"Will Rojas let me?"

Alejandro grinned at her. "Darlin', he'll love having you there. And so will I."

Chapter Thirteen

Daisy wandered through the house, her heart heavy and aching. She had made a fool of herself with Alejandro, she thought bitterly, but she loved him so much. Why couldn't he love her in return?

She thought about the woman she had seen in his bed, and felt a sharp pang of jealousy. She had offered herself to Rio when she worked at the Rose, and again when they were partners. She had practically begged him to make love to her, and he had refused. And now there was another woman in his life, in his bed.

She picked up the derringer he had left on the table, traced the initials AV carved in the butt with her fingertip. Why couldn't he love her?

Tears stung her eyes and dripped down her cheeks. Maybe she should take Fred Syler up on his last offer, sell him her half of the Belle, and go back home. That had always been her dream, to earn enough money to go home in style. But somewhere along the way, her dream had died, and going home no longer held the appeal it once had. How could she face her mother, look her father in the eye? Her parents were decent, churchgoing people. They would never be able to understand, never be able to forgive her. She put the derringer back down on the table and went into the bedroom.

Sinking down on the bed, she picked up a flaming red pillow one of the miners had brought her from San Francisco. Clutching it to her breast, she let the tears fall, silently praying that somehow, someday, Rio would love her as much as she loved him. She thought of him constantly, relived every moment they had spent together, every word he had spoken to her, every smile, every touch. She rocked back and forth. She hurt deep down inside, hurt with an ache that would never heal.

He was the real reason she didn't want to leave town. Even though he didn't love her, might never love her, he was here. If she went home, she would never see him again.

She wondered what kind of danger he thought she was in, but it didn't matter. She couldn't leave town, not as long as he was here, not as long as there was a chance, however small, that one day he might love her.

Chapter Fourteen

Shaye sat on a hard wooden chair beside Alejandro, her gloved hands folded in her lap, listening as the Reverend Warrington offered comfort to the family and friends of Jacob "Moose" Kenyon.

The coffin, made of pine, rested on a pair of wooden chairs at the front of the hall.

". . . was a fine and honorable man," the reverend was saying. "A good husband and father, a friend to many in this town. He will be sorely missed . . ."

Shaye glanced surreptitiously at the family. Mrs. Kenyon was clad in black from head to foot. Two dark-haired boys huddled against her, their faces pale. She held a third child, a little fair-haired girl who was about a year old, on her lap. What would they do now? Shaye wondered. Would they stay in Bodie?

198

She leaned toward Alejandro. "What will happen to his family?"

"They'll be taken care of," he replied quietly. "The Miners Union will pay for the coffin and the funeral, and he'll be buried in their plot."

She turned her attention to the reverend once more.

"Moose's favorite scripture was the Twenty-Third Psalm. Will you say it with me now? The Lord is my shepherd, I shall not want. He maketh me to lie down in green pastures, he leadeth me beside the still waters. Yea, though I walk through the valley of the shadow of death, I will fear no evil, for Thou art with me. Thy rod and Thy staff, they comfort me. Thou preparest a table before me in the presence of mine enemies, my cup runneth over. Surely goodness and mercy shall follow me all the days of my life, and I shall dwell in the house of the Lord forever. . . . Amen.

"Yes, our brother Moose walked through the valley of the shadow of death, and this day resides with our God in paradise. Let us pray."

Shaye stood beside Alejandro while he offered his condolences to the widow. She felt a surge of tenderness when she saw him slip several greenbacks into the woman's hand, saw the tears of gratitude in the woman's eyes.

"Let me know if you need anything," Alejandro said. "Anything at all." He smiled down at the boys. Shaye was certain the oldest couldn't be more than six or seven. "You two take good care of your ma now, you hear? And your little sister, too."

The boys both nodded solemnly. They looked older already, Shaye thought, as if the weight of responsibility was already settling on their shoulders.

"It's so sad," Shaye remarked as she watched six men load the casket into the back of a black, glass-sided hearse drawn by a pair of black horses. She wondered, fleetingly, if it could be the same conveyance she had seen in the Bodie museum. "What will she do now?"

Alejandro took her hand as they walked toward the hotel. "She has family back in Philadelphia. They'll take her in."

Shaye nodded. Even with family to take care of her, it wouldn't be easy for Moose's widow, not with three small children to support.

Shaye lifted the hems of her skirts as she crossed the dusty street. For a woman who had worn a dress only when absolutely necessary, she was surprised at how readily she had grown accustomed to wearing the frocks of the period. She was even more surprised to find that she rather liked the long skirts and petticoats, though the corset was something she would never get used to.

Lost in thought, she was startled when Alejandro grabbed her arm and jerked her backward. A moment later, a wagon pulled by a pair of wild-eyed horses thundered past.

She heard someone scream, heard a voice yell, "Runaway!"

She was still recovering from almost being trampled by a pair of wild-eyed horses when Alejandro untied a horse from a nearby hitching rack and vaulted onto its back. With a shout, he wheeled the bay around and lit out after the wagon.

He caught up with the runaway carriage before it reached the end of the street. Open-mouthed, she watched him leap from the back of the horse onto the seat of the wagon, grab the reins, and bring the buckboard to a halt.

"What the hell happened?"

She glanced over her shoulder to see Philo Richardson. "I don't know," she replied.

Philo grunted as he shifted his cigar from one corner of his mouth to the other. "Might be a good story there," he mused.

"If there isn't, there will be, if I'm any judge of reporters," Shaye said dryly.

Philo laughed good-naturedly. "Spoken like a woman who knows the breed."

Shaye grinned at him. "You could say that."

She followed him down the street to where a crowd had gathered around the wagon. "What happened?"

That seemed to be the question on everyone's mind as Alejandro jumped to the ground, then turned and lifted his arms. "Come on, Bobby Joe."

Slowly, a curly brown head rose into view. "I . . . I didn't mean nothing."

Alejandro nodded as he lifted the boy to the ground. "You're damn lucky you didn't kill anybody. What are you doing driving this wagon, anyway?"

"I was . . . I was just trying to—"

"Bobby Joe!" A shrill voice cut through the murmurs of the crowd.

A moment later a woman swooped down on Bobby Joe, hugging him tightly. Shaye recognized the woman as the one who had given her a sandwich the night of the cave-in at the mine.

"Are you all right?" the woman asked anxiously.

"I'm fine, Ma," he said, his cheeks flushing with embarrassment.

"Are you sure?" She hugged him close, then ran her hands over his arms and legs, clucking softly.

"I'm sure, Ma," Bobby Joe said, wriggling away. "Rio saved me."

"Well, he won't be able to save you when I get you home, young man!" the woman said, her worry swiftly turning to anger when she realized her son was out of danger. "Just you wait until your father hears about this." She looked at Alejandro. "Thank you, Rio."

"Hell, Jilly, it could be worse," Alejandro said, grinning. "He could be twins."

"Sometimes I think he is," Jilly declared. "That boy is gonna be the death of me yet. Do you know what he did last week? He set off a firecracker in the chicken coop. The hens still aren't laying. And the week before that, he near burned down the outhouse. Right after he decided to swing from the clothesline. One whole load of my clean wash landed in the dirt." She shook her head. "I don't know what I'm going to do with him."

Alejandro ruffled the boy's hair, then pulled a silver dollar out of his pocket and held it before the boy's eyes. "You see this, Bobby Joe? If you behave yourself for one whole month, this is yours."

"A whole dollar? For me?"

Alejandro nodded. "Is it a deal?"

"Yessir!"

Jilly fixed Alejandro with a stern look. "I don't hold with blackmail, Rio."

"It's not blackmail," he replied with a grin. "More like a bribe. Remember now, Bobby Joe," he said, lifting the boy onto the wagon seat. "One whole month."

Bobby Joe nodded vigorously as he scooted over to make room for his mother.

"Remember now, don't be too hard on him, Miss Jilly," Alejandro said. Offering her his hand, he helped her into the wagon. "I got into a pile of mischief when I was a boy, and look how well I turned out."

Jilly looked down at him, her lips curled in a wry grin; then, with a shake of her head, she took up the reins and clucked to the team.

Shaye moved up beside Alejandro. "My hero," she murmured.

He pulled her up against him, his expression intense. "And don't you forget it."

He looked thoughtful as they walked back to the hotel.

"What's wrong?" she asked.

"I was just thinking about what you said earlier."

"About you being my hero?"

"No, about you coming here from the future." He shook his head. "I've given it a lot of thought. Hell, it's hard to believe."

"Tell me about it!" she exclaimed. "But it's true, whether you believe it or not."

He spent the rest of the day teaching her the finer points of playing poker, and when she had the rules down pat, he taught her what to look for if she thought someone was cheating. There were all manner of tricks and gadgets dishonest gamblers used, and Alejandro seemed to know them all. She was aware of some of them, like marking a deck, or dealing off the bottom, or having a shill at the table. He told her that one type of card sharp fastened a bag under the table; it was used for drawing or hiding cards. There were also several kinds of mirrors that enabled a player to see the cards held by the other players. A handy little gadget called a ring holdout made it possible to palm a card. A ring shiner was a ring with a highly polished surface that allowed a dealer to see each card as he dealt it. A sleeve holdout was worn inside a coat sleeve and held one or more cards; when the player brought his arm close to his body, it triggered a mechanism that shot forward, allowing him to palm the cards. A similar item, called a vest holdout, could hold an entire deck.

"There are a lot of gambling games," Alejandro told her. "Faro, roulette, casino, red dog, craps, fantan, three-card monte, blackjack, but there's nothing like a good, honest game of draw poker."

"Are there a lot of cheats?"

He shrugged. "I reckon, though I haven't run across many at the Queen. It's known as an honest house, with honest dealers. You have to watch out for some of the other saloons. The Number Nine is the worst. They're notorious for using advantage cards."

"What are they?"

"Marked cards. You can buy them from Cross and Company in New Orleans, or from E. M. Grandine in New York. You see them advertised in the papers. A dollar a pack, or a dozen for ten bucks. They have complicated patterns on the backs, like stars or calico or vines, so the markings on them are hard to detect, especially if you aren't looking for them. Of course, you can always use an honest deck and mark the cards yourself, or notch a corner."

Shaye shook her head, amazed at the ingenuity of the gadgets he had described, at the lengths men would go to to cheat at a game of cards.

"A lot of men think faro is the only honest game," Alejandro remarked, "but even faro can be rigged." He looked at her and grinned. "I think that's enough for today. It's getting late. What say we go out and get a bite to eat?"

Shaye looked outside, surprised to see that the sun was setting. "Sounds good to me."

He took her to the Excelsior Restaurant on Main Street. He was known to the waitresses here, as well, Shaye noted. They all smiled at him, and of course, he smiled back. He held her chair for her, then took the opposite seat. She couldn't blame the women for vying for his attention, for noticing his presence. He was all man; surely no woman past puberty could resist him.

One good thing about being with Alejandro, Shaye mused, they always got quick service, hot food, and plenty of it. A waitress appeared at their table almost before they were seated.

"Evening, Rio," she said, flashing a warm smile. "Steak tonight?"

He nodded. "What'll you have, Shaye?"

"Steak. Medium-rare, please."

"So," Alejandro said after the waitress moved away. "Do you want to come to the Queen with me tonight?"

"So soon?"

"Why not? You've got to start sometime."

"I guess so. I hope I can . . . what's wrong?"

He jerked his chin toward the entrance. "McCrory's here."

Shaye looked over her shoulder. A man and a woman stood near the door. The man was of medium height, with sandy brown hair, a cavalry-style moustache, and ice blue eyes. His gaze moved over the room, and then he was striding toward them.

"Did you ever talk to him?" she asked. "About Daisy's suspicions?"

"No. I was going to take care of that tonight."

"Valverde, I've been looking for you."

Alejandro pushed his chair back from the table, let

his right hand drop to his lap. "What can I do for you, Mr. McCrory?"

"I had me a little talk with Daisy last night."

"Is that so?"

McCrory nodded. "I don't know what she told you, but mind your own business."

"Daisy is my business."

McCrory planted his fists on the table and glared at Alejandro. "Not anymore."

Shaye glanced around the room. Except for the diners at the nearby tables, no one was paying them any attention.

"I think we'd better take this outside." Alejandro stood up. "I'll be back in a few minutes. Tell Monica to keep my steak warm."

The girl with McCrory placed her hand on his arm. "Dade."

McCrory shook her hand off. "Let's go, Valverde."

"Alejandro—"

"It's all right, Shaye." He ran his knuckles over her cheek. "This has been a long time coming."

She watched the two men leave the restaurant, her heart pounding with trepidation. It hadn't happened this way before, she thought frantically. What if Alejandro were killed? It would be all her fault. If not for her, he wouldn't be dining in the Excelsior tonight. As far-fetched as it sounded, she had wondered, in a distant part of her mind, if Alejandro had died prematurely and she had been sent to the past to save his life.

She frowned, hardly aware that she was walking

toward the door. What if it was Daisy who had died before her time? She felt certain that McCrory had killed Daisy. If that was true, and Alejandro killed McCrory, Daisy's life would be spared. And perhaps Alejandro's, too.

She stepped out onto the street, glanced up and down. Where had they gone?

A commotion drew her attention. Lifting her skirts, she hurried down the street to where a group of men were clustered in the alley that ran between two of the saloons. Standing on tiptoe, she saw McCrory and Alejandro.

McCrory stood with his hands on his hips, his expression arrogant. "Knives or fists, Valverde? It's all the same to me."

Alejandro shrugged out of his coat. "You're a real four-flusher, McCrory. I never should have sold you my half of the saloon, but I didn't think even you were low enough to steal from your own partner."

McCrory snorted as he flung his coat aside. "You don't know a damn thing, you dirty half-breed!"

"I know I'm gonna beat the hell out of you."

"Hah! You're the biggest crook in the whole damn town."

Alejandro shook his head. "Enough sweet talk," he muttered, and drove his fist into McCrory's smirking face.

Chapter Fifteen

Shaye hadn't seen a fistfight since high school when her boyfriend punched Ryan Halestone in the nose for kissing her in the hallway. But that fight had been a tea party compared to this one.

Alejandro fought with a single-minded intensity the likes of which she had never seen, seemingly impervious to the blows he received. Blood oozed from a cut on his lower lip, and another on his right cheek. McCrory looked far worse. He was bleeding from his nose and mouth, his right eye was turning black.

Cheers and catcalls rose from the crowd as the two men exchanged blows. Beside her, men were taking bets on the outcome of the fight. The odds were five to two on Alejandro. She would have bet on him herself, had she been so inclined. Even to her untrained eye, it was easy to see that Dade McCrory was no match for Alejandro. McCrory was tiring rapidly, his punches were badly timed and falling short. Alejandro hit him again, and McCrory went down on his hands and knees. When he came up, there was a knife in his hand.

Alejandro stared at him a moment, and then there was a knife in his hand, too, pulled from the inside of his right boot.

For a moment, the two men glared at each other. There was a subtle shift in the atmosphere, and the crowd fell silent as what had been an ordinary fist fight suddenly turned deadly.

Dade McCrory knew how to handle a knife, and the fight, which had been pretty much one-sided until now, took on a whole new dimension.

Shaye bit down on her lower lip, hardly daring to breathe, as the two men circled each other, bodies slightly crouched, knife hands outstretched. It was a silent and deadly dance, oddly compelling.

Without warning, McCrory lunged forward, and when he pulled away, there was blood dripping from a long gash in Alejandro's left arm.

A buzz ran through the crowd as Alejandro fell back. McCrory pressed forward, his lips pulled back in a snarl, his knife driving for Alejandro's heart.

Shaye gasped, felt her own heart skip a beat, and then, in a swift, catlike move, Alejandro ducked under McCrory's blade. Shaye blew out a deep breath, her fingernails digging into her palms as the two men circled each other again.

They came together in a rush, the sounds of their

labored breathing punctuated by the ring of steel striking steel.

McCrory's blade slid over Alejandro's ribs as Alejandro's blade came down toward his opponent's chest. McCrory's upraised arm deflected the blade, and it sank to the hilt in his shoulder instead of his chest. Alejandro jerked the blade out with a quick twist. McCrory let out a howl, then turned and staggered down the alley.

Several, men followed him. The rest clustered around Alejandro.

Shaye elbowed her way through the crowd. "Are you all right?" she asked.

"I've been better." He cleaned the blood off his knife by wiping it across his pant leg, then slid it back inside his boot. "Damn coward."

"Come on, you need a doctor."

"I'm all right."

"Sure you are." She slid her arm around his waist. "Which way?"

One of the men handed her Alejandro's jacket. Another stepped forward and wrapped a red bandana, which looked none too clean, around the bloody gash in Alejandro's arm. Several men slapped Alejandro on the back as they threaded their way through the crowd.

"Way to go, Rio!"

"McCrory's had it coming for a long time, the damned one-eyed man!"

"You should have put that knife between his ribs."

"One-eyed man?" Shaye asked as they walked toward the mouth of the alley. "What on earth does that mean?"

"Means he's a no-good, yellow four-flusher."

Shaye rolled her eyes. "Speak English."

"He's a cheat," Alejandro said curtly. "I never should have sold him my share in the Belle, but I wanted out. I didn't know what a low-down bastard he was until it was too late."

Shaye glanced right and left when they reached the street. "Which way?"

He grinned at her. "Stop worrying. I'm fine."

"I want you to see a doctor." She looked at the kerchief wrapped around his arm. It was soaked with blood. Blood darkened the front of his shirt, too.

"Shoot, there isn't a doctor in this town that I'd trust. Doctors are responsible for more deaths than mine cave-ins and pneumonia."

Shaye frowned, wondering if he was serious. There was a hospital on Mills Street south of Green if she remembered correctly. "Be that as it may, your arm needs to be stitched up, and I can't do it."

"I can."

She looked up at him. "You?"

He shrugged. "I've done it before."

"Well, you're not going to do it now. Come on."

The hospital was a large two-story frame house. A sign out front said, "Doctor Rogers, M.D."

The waiting room was crammed with people, mostly miners with a variety of injuries that seemed to range from sprains and breaks to pneumonia. There was no place to sit down.

The doctor emerged from his office a moment later. He surveyed the patients, then summoned Alejandro.

"Hey," one man complained. "We was here first."

"Yes, indeed, you were," the doctor replied. "But all you've got is a sprained ankle. This man's bleeding."

"Dammit, doc—"

"I've put in twelve hours today," the doctor said brusquely. "I haven't had lunch and I've missed my supper. You can wait your turn, or you can leave. You," he said, pointing at Alejandro. "Come with me."

Shaye hung Alejandro's coat on a hook beside the door, then glanced around the room. Like every doctor's office she had ever been in, there was a pile of old magazines on a table: *Scribner's Monthly, Ladies Home Journal, Carriage Monthly, The Illustrated Police News.*

She skipped the magazines and picked up an old newspaper. Thumbing through the pages, she perused the ads. Joseph Wasson was running for State Assembly for Mono and Inyo Counties, the Patterson Brothers were advertising their photography shop, Silas B. Smith was having a going-out-of-business sale. The ad for Boone & Wright, located at the corner of Green and Main Streets, stated they were dealers in General Merchandize, including groceries, crockery and glassware, pure whiskeys and brandies, wines and cigars. They were also agents for Weiner's Milwaukee Beer, Ale, and Porter. They also had stabling facilities for two hundred horses. An interesting combination, Shaye mused.

A small article on the back page listed the businesses operating in Bodie. One opera house, five newspapers, six stage lines, four shoemakers, a dozen cigar stores, fifteen restaurants, forty Chinese wash houses, ten barbershops, two banks, sixteen law offices, four drug stores, two assay offices, one harness maker, twenty-one lodging houses, as well as a number of bakeries, stables, and clothing stores.

She folded the paper and put it back on the table, glanced at the closed door of the doctor's office, tapped her foot impatiently. Finally, unable to stand it any longer, she crossed the floor and entered the office.

Beyond the office, which was sparsely furnished with a small desk and a large file cabinet, was a curtained-off area. She hesitated a moment, then drew back the curtain. Alejandro was stretched out on a narrow table, his eyes closed. A wide bandage was wrapped around his middle. It looked very white against the dark bronze of his skin. His shirt had been carelessly tossed on a wooden stool in the corner.

The doctor was frowning in concentration as he stitched the long, narrow gash in Alejandro's forearm. The cloth under Rio's arm was stained with blood. Shaye felt her stomach turn over at the sight.

The doctor looked up. "Is something wrong?"

"No. No, I was just—"

"I'd advise you to sit down," the doctor said, gesturing to a chair, "and put your head between your legs."

"I'm fine," she said weakly.

"You're about to faint," the doctor said curtly. "Sit down."

"If anyone's going to faint, I think it should be me," Alejandro remarked dryly.

Shaye sat down, lowered her head, and closed her eyes. The sight of blood had always made her sick to her stomach.

Some time later she felt a hand on her shoulder. Looking up, she saw Alejandro grinning at her. It was a rather lopsided grin, since his lower lip was swollen on one side. He had put on his shirt. It was, she noted, past saving. His right arm had been bandaged from his elbow down to his wrist.

"You think you can make it back to the hotel?" he asked.

"Oh, shut up."

He paid the doctor, Shaye retrieved his coat, and they left the hospital.

"I'll say one thing about living in the past," Shaye muttered as they walked back to the hotel. "It's never dull."

Chapter Sixteen

Shaye glanced around Alejandro's new room, which was very much like his old one: a double bed, a four-drawer chest, a single chair, a window that overlooked the street.

"Can I help you with anything?" Folding his coat, she laid it over the back of the chair.

He shook his head. "Thanks. I'll be all right."

"Okay. I guess I'll see you tomorrow, then."

"Were you serious about dealing at the Queen?"

"Yes, if you really think I can do it."

"There's no time like the present to find out."

"What do you mean?"

"I'm due at the Queen in an hour." He lifted his wounded arm. "The doc told me to take it easy for a few days. Said I shouldn't deal. But you can."

"Tonight? You mean tonight? But I haven't had enough practice."

Alejandro's gaze moved over her. "Darlin', the men won't be paying any attention to their cards."

She stared at him a moment, felt her cheeks grow warm as she realized what he meant. "But—"

"Wear something . . . provocative."

"Provocative? Like what, my shorts?"

"What are shorts?"

"You know, the short pants I was wearing when I came here."

"I remember," he said with a grin. "You've got nice legs."

"Thanks," she muttered dryly.

"I need to get cleaned up," he said, glancing down at his ruined shirt. "How soon can you be ready?"

"I don't know. Thirty minutes?"

"All right. I'll come for you in three-quarters of an hour. And don't worry. You'll be fine."

"If you say so."

She hadn't been kidding when she'd said the only provocative thing she owned were her shorts. The outfits from Madame Sophie's were all demure in the extreme with their high necks and long sleeves.

In the end, she picked the white blouse with the ruffled front and the wine red skirt, which had a modest bustle. She wore her hair down, something she rarely did.

She applied her makeup carefully, put on a clean pair of stockings, laced up her boots.

She blew out a sigh when Alejandro knocked on the door. *Ready or not*, she mused, *here I come.*

The Queen of Bodie was in full swing when they arrived. Every table was filled to capacity. Men stood three deep at the bar, drinking and laughing. The saloon girls moved through the room, their gaudy dresses making them look like exotic birds.

Digger, Henry, and Spooner were sitting at Alejandro's table, along with two other men unknown to Shaye.

" 'Bout time you got here, Rio," Digger said. "Hell, man, what happened to your arm?"

"I got into a little disagreement with McCrory. I'll take over now, Murphy."

"Suits me." Murphy swept up his cash and left the table.

Alejandro pulled out a chair for Shaye, then dropped into the one Murphy had vacated.

Spooner made a sound of disgust. "McCrory! That dirty sonofa—" He glanced at Shaye, cleared his throat, and looked back at Alejandro. "What did he do?"

"He's dipping into the till over at the Belle."

"The bastard. Oh, sorry, Shaye."

"It's all right, Spooner," she said with a grin. "I agree with you."

"So I guess you set him straight," Henry said. "Right?"

"We talked," Alejandro said curtly.

Spooner grunted. "Must have been some conversation. Does he look as bad as you do?"

Alejandro laughed. "Worse."

"We playin' poker or gossipin'?"

"Hold your horses, Mercer," Digger admonished. He gestured at Alejandro's injured arm. "You gonna be able to deal?"

"No. Hurts like the devil when I move my hand. Shaye's gonna deal, if you've got no objections."

"Shaye!" Henry exclaimed. "Why, I think that's a hell of . . . I mean, that's a fine idea."

"I don't care who deals," Mercer muttered irritably. "Let's play cards."

Alejandro winked at Shaye as he handed her a fresh deck.

She smiled her thanks, broke the seal, and shuffled the cards, grateful that her hands weren't shaking. She wasn't sure why she was nervous. She had sat in with Spooner, Digger, and Henry before.

The four men each tossed twenty dollars into the pot.

Shaye looked over at Alejandro. "I didn't bring any . . ."

He shook his head as he reached into his pocket and withdrew a roll of greenbacks and a handful of coins. "You're dealing for me," he said as he tossed a double eagle into the pot. "It's only fair that I foot the bill."

Shaye pushed away from the table and stood up, stretching. She couldn't believe how quickly the last four hours had passed. What was even more amazing was the fact that she had come out more than seven hundred dollars ahead.

Alejandro sat back in his chair. "You're a natural, darlin'." He smiled at her, a warm, wonderful smile that made her go weak in the knees. "I thought Mercer was gonna shit his britches when you turned over that fourth jack."

Shaye laughed. She had taken a big chance on the last hand, and it had a paid off. She gathered up her winnings and pushed them toward Alejandro. "Thanks for backing me."

Alejandro counted the greenbacks, gold, and silver. After deducting the amount he had given her up front, he split the rest in half and slid one half across the table.

"What's that for?"

"You worked hard. You earned it."

"But I still owe you—"

"You don't owe me anything, darlin'." He picked up her half and put it in his pocket. "Mine in the left, yours in the right," he said, and stood up. "Ready to go?"

She nodded, felt her whole body tingle when he took her hand in his.

They walked slowly toward the hotel. Caught up in his nearness, she paid little heed to the crowds on the street, hardly heard the ever-present noise of the stamp mill. His hand was large and warm around hers.

The air around them felt charged, thick with tension, like the air before a storm. Her heart was pounding by the time they reached the hotel. He walked her up the stairs, waited while she unlocked the door. Stepping inside, she lit the lamp on the bedside table, her heart racing a little as she wondered if he would stay awhile.

When she turned around, he was standing just inside the door. "Should I go?"

She shook her head, felt a nervous quiver of excitement in the pit of her stomach as he closed and locked the door behind him.

She stood there, feeling as though she were poised on the brink of a precipice, while he closed the distance between them, then slid his good arm around her waist and drew her close.

"Shaye." He looked into her eyes, a wry smile on his lips. "I love the sound of your name."

"I love the way you say it." She swayed toward him, eyelids fluttering down as he bent his head toward her.

His kiss, when it came, was warm and sweet and infinitely tender. Rising on her tiptoes, she wrapped her arms around his waist and kissed him back.

"Rio . . ."

He ran his finger over her lower lip. "I know, darlin'," he murmured.

"Does your arm hurt very much?"

"Yeah," he admitted. "Would you mind if I spent the night?"

She batted her eyelashes at him in her best Southern belle style. "Why, sir, whatever are you suggesting?"

"When I'm suggesting something, darlin', you'll

know it," he said with a wicked grin. "You won't
have to ask."

"Of course you can stay." She unbuttoned his shirt,
taking care not to jar his injured arm as she slipped
his shirt off and tossed it on the chair.

She unbuckled his gun belt, coiled it around the
holster, and laid it on top of his shirt.

When she started to unbuckle his belt, he laid his
hand over hers. "I think I'd better take care of the
rest myself."

She nodded. Turning her back to him, she began
to get undressed.

He whistled under his breath when he saw her
standing there clad in nothing but her bra and panties.
"What the hell are you wearing?"

She glanced at him over her shoulder. "This is what
ladies' underwear is like where I come from."

"Damn," he muttered, "I'm gonna have to go
there."

She made a face at him. When he turned away, she
removed her undergarments, pulled on her nightgown,
then drew back the covers and slid under the sheets.

A few moments later, he crawled into bed beside
her.

"I've been thinking about what you said," Alejandro remarked.

"What I said about what?"

"About your coming here from the future."

"Do you believe me?"

"I don't know." He put his arm around her and
drew her up against his side. "It seems impossible."

"But here I am." She turned her head so she could see his face. "You'll leave town the end of July, won't you?"

"If you'll go with me."

She nodded, knowing she would gladly go anywhere he asked. "What about Daisy?"

"I don't know. I guess we'll just have to take her with us."

"That'll be a lot of fun," Shaye muttered. But she knew he was right. They couldn't leave Daisy behind. And once again, she couldn't help wondering what effect, if any, all this would have on the future.

She settled her head on his shoulder, thinking how right it felt to be lying there with him. Only a few days ago, she had been afraid she would never find her way back home; now she wanted to spend the rest of her life here, with him.

Chapter Seventeen

The days that followed passed quickly. She took Alejandro's place at the poker table each night, sometimes dealing for herself, sometimes for the house. There were always men eager to sit in, certain they couldn't be beat by a lady gambler. It never ceased to amaze her that she won more than she lost. Alejandro said she was a natural-born gambler, that she had a "feel" for the cards, an inborn sense of when to hold 'em and when to fold 'em. It was something that couldn't be taught, he said. You either had it or you didn't.

He was proud of her ability. She could see it in his eyes each time she won a hand. She had a feeling that his arm had healed enough so he could take over, but when she asked him about it, he just shook his head and told her she was doing fine.

"Maybe I should buy back my share of the Belle," he remarked one night as they walked home. "Give you a place of your own."

"Me and Daisy under one roof?" Shaye had replied with a laugh. "I don't think so."

His wounds were healing nicely. He had gone back to the doctor to have the stitches removed, but his arm was still tender. The cut over his ribs hadn't been deep enough to require stitching. She hated to think of how close that knife had been to his heart. Just a few inches deeper and he might have been killed.

They stayed up late and slept late, eating breakfast at their leisure, spending their afternoons shopping or taking long walks, or just finding a relatively quiet spot on the outskirts of town to sit and talk. He asked endless questions about the future, seemed fascinated by the idea of television and cars. He asked if gambling was a way of life in the future, and she told him about the luxurious casinos in Monte Carlo and Las Vegas, horse racing at Santa Anita and Hollywood Park, the Lotto, the card clubs in Gardena, the bingo games on the Indian reservations, the riverboats in the South.

"I can just imagine you on one of those floating gambling houses," Shaye had remarked, "all decked out in a pair of tight black slacks and a fancy white shirt with black cuffs, smiling that killer smile. Surrounded by women."

"I knew it!" he had replied. "I was born in the wrong time!" And then he'd looked at her, one black brow arched. "Killer smile?" he had asked innocently.

She'd had to laugh at that.

She grew to love him more with every passing day. It grew harder and harder to tell him good night at her door, to settle for a few lingering kisses and sweet caresses when she wanted so much more. He hadn't asked to stay the night again, and though she was sorely tempted to ask him, she never did, all too aware that she could be zapped back to the future at any minute. Every time she walked into the Queen of Bodie, she held her breath, wondering if she would suddenly find herself back in her own time, walking down Bodie's deserted main street. It would be painful enough to leave him now; if they made love, she knew the separation would break her heart beyond repair. She had known him only a short time. How had she fallen so hard, so fast?

The morning of the Fourth of July bloomed bright and clear. Alejandro had told her Bodie celebrated the event in grand style, and he hadn't been exaggerating.

A thirteen-gun salute roused the town.

A short time later, Alejandro was knocking at her door. He swept his hat off when she opened the door. "Good morning, fair lady," he said.

"Good morning, sir," she replied, smiling. He was like the sunshine, she thought. Just seeing him warmed her clear through. He was so handsome. He wore a white shirt, a burgundy cravat, a black broadcloth coat with a velvet collar, black trousers. And a black vest embroidered with gold fleurs-de-lis.

She looked up at him, a sinking feeling in the pit of her stomach.

"Shaye, are you all right? You look like you've seen a ghost . . ."

"That vest . . ."

He glanced down, only then recalling that she had described the vest once before, that she claimed to have seen his ghost wearing it in the jail, over a hundred years in the future.

He settled his hat on his head, wondering if his face looked as pale as hers.

"Rio, I'm scared."

He drew her into his arms and held her close, aware of a tightness in his chest, a tingling in his skin. The air around them seemed heavy somehow. He could hear the beat of his heart, imagined he could hear hers, too, pounding as loudly, as wildly, as his own.

She looked up at him, her eyes wide and scared. "Rio. . . ."

"Yeah, I feel it, too. I think maybe you're right. Maybe we should leave town."

"Today?"

"There won't be any stages leaving today. The town is celebrating." He smiled down at her. "We might as well enjoy it."

Shaye nodded. He hadn't been arrested until August ninth. They had plenty of time.

They ate a quick breakfast, then went outside to join the crowd. Shaye put her fears behind her, determined to do as Alejandro had suggested and enjoy the day. There was nothing to worry about. They would leave town tomorrow. Even if she was sent back to her own time, at least Alejandro would be all right.

About ten-thirty, the celebration officially began with a parade composed of several hundred townspeople. Both sides of the street were lined with thousands of men, women, and children all dressed in their Sunday best. Kids holding flags ran up and down the sidelines. More people stood on the balconies of the hotels, waving and cheering.

Shaye stood beside Alejandro, caught up in the excitement as the parade began. The Bodie Band marched at the head of the parade, the music punctuated by the pop of firecrackers and an occasional gunshot. The Grand Marshal and his aides rode in a carriage behind the band, followed by members of the Veterans of the Mexican War, Officers of the Day, President, Orator, Reader, and Poet of the Day.

Shaye nudged Alejandro. "Poet of the Day?"

Alejandro grinned at her. "Yep. Never let it be said that Bodie lacks class."

Happiness bubbled up inside her as she grinned back at him.

There were representatives from the Miners Union, the Odd Fellows, the Masons, and Mexican Patriots, Veterans of the Civil War. There was even, to her surprise, a baseball team.

Shaye pulled her camera from her reticule and took several pictures of the men attired in the faded gray uniforms of the Confederacy as they passed by. Strange to think that, in this time and place, the Civil War had ended just fifteen years ago.

"Are you going to take pictures of everything?" Alejandro asked.

"Darn right," she said, and snapped a picture of a wagon carrying thirty-eight little girls, each holding a flag representing a state of the union.

Alejandro squeezed Shaye's hand. "Did I tell you how pretty you look today?"

"Why, no, sir, you did not," she replied in her best Southern drawl.

He swept his hat off his head and held it over his heart. "Forgive me, fair lady," he said, his fake drawl as thick as molasses in winter.

Shaye grinned at him. "I forgive you, sir."

"Ah, you are too kind, ma'am." He settled his hat back on his head; then, taking her hand, he kissed her fingertips. "The parade seems to be about over, Miss Montgomery. Perhaps you will allow me to buy you a piece of Miss Maybelle's cherry cobbler and a glass of lemonade."

"Why, thank you, Mr. Valverde." She tucked the camera into her reticule, then placed her hand on his arm. "That would be most kind."

Side by side, they strolled down Main Street toward the Miners Union Hall. Shaye nodded and smiled at everyone they passed. Alejandro tipped his hat to the ladies, greeted the men he knew. All the saloons were open and doing a brisk business. She supposed most of the town's male inhabitants would be drunk well before nightfall, and that the girls who occupied the little cabins along Maiden Lane would have more business than they could handle.

229

As they passed one of the saloons, a girl with dyed red hair called Alejandro's name. He turned and waved at her.

Shaye slid a sidelong glance at Alejandro, wondering if, or how often, he visited Maiden Lane.

He met her gaze and lifted one brow. "What's that look for?" he asked.

"Oh, nothing. I was just wondering. . . . never mind."

Alejandro frowned. "Is something wrong?"

"No." It was none of her business if he spent every night in one of those horrid cribs.

"Dammit, Shaye, what's wrong?"

"Have you ever . . . do you . . . never mind."

He shook his head, his dark eyes alight with amusement. "Still jealous, I see."

"Should I be?"

"No, darlin'."

"So you've never visited any of the doves in their . . . um . . . never bought their services?"

He looked offended. "Darlin', I've never had to buy it."

"Bragging, are you?"

He shrugged. "Why, no, Miss Montgomery, just stating a fact."

She punched him on the arm, careful to make sure it wasn't his injured one.

"Feel better?" he asked.

"No. You probably have to beat the women off with a stick."

"Well, not quite," he said, laughing.

"I'll bet."

"Well, darlin', just in case you were wondering, I'd never beat you off with a stick."

"Thanks a lot."

He came to an abrupt halt, drew her into his arms, and kissed her full on the lips, right there in the middle of Main Street. Heat suffused her, flooding her cheeks with warmth, flowing like sun-warmed honey through her veins, until she thought she might melt beneath the onslaught of his kiss. She moaned softly, aware of nothing at that moment but his mouth on hers.

When he let her go, she stared up at him, only dimly aware of the whistles and catcalls from the men around them. "Kiss her again, Rio!" someone shouted.

"My pleasure," he murmured, and claimed her lips a second time.

And everything else faded away . . . the crowd, the noise, the dust, the heat. It didn't matter that she didn't belong here, that she might wake up and find herself back in her own time. Nothing mattered but his lips on hers, the feel of his arms holding her close, the heat and hardness of his body pressed intimately against her own. Alejandro . . .

He drew back, his gaze hot, his dark eyes smoky with desire. A thrill of anticipation ran through her as he brushed a kiss over her cheek, then slid his tongue over her earlobe.

"You're the only woman I want, darlin'," he said, his voice low and husky, "and I mean to have you."

He grinned at the crowd gathered around them. "But not here."

As Alejandro took her hand in his, a flash of movement caught Shaye's eye. Glancing over her shoulder, she saw Daisy Sullivan turn and run down the street, but not before she saw the tears glistening in Daisy's eyes.

The Miners Union Hall was a long, narrow building with windows on either side of the door, and more windows along the walls. There were at least two dozen tables set up inside, each one laden with iced cakes and cupcakes, a variety of cobblers and pies, cookies and gingerbread men, cinnamon rolls and flaky biscuits, as well as jugs of apple cider and bowls of punch and lemonade. Red, white, and blue bunting was draped on the walls. Streamers and balloons hung from the ceiling.

The food and drinks had been donated by the ladies of the town; the proceeds would go into the Miners Fund for Widows and Orphans.

Alejandro bought two plates of cherry cobbler, a cup of lemonade for Shaye, a cup of cider for himself. There was no room to sit down inside, so they went outside and found a place in the shade behind the building.

The cobbler was delicious and gone too soon.

"That Maybelle Carpenter is a mighty fine cook," Alejandro remarked.

"Yes, indeed," Shaye replied.

He leaned forward and licked a bit of cherry filling

from the corner of Shaye's mouth. "But I've never tasted anything as sweet as you."

She felt herself blushing, she who rarely blushed. What was it about this man that caused her to react as if she were a naive young girl instead of a woman who had been married and divorced?

Several shouts rose above the noise and confusion around them.

"What's that?" Shaye asked.

"Some of the Mexicans are showing off their riding skills," Alejandro said.

"Can we watch?"

"Sure."

They put their dishes in one of the big washtubs set out for that purpose, then walked down the street. The cheering grew louder as they approached.

Shaye's eyes widened at what she saw. A live rooster had been buried in the ground so that only its neck and head showed. About twenty riders were lined up some fifty yards away.

Shaye gasped as one of the riders spurred his horse forward. He leaned far over the side of his mount, his fingers skimming the ground as he made a grab for the rooster's head, but the frightened rooster dodged out of his way, and the man came up with a handful of dirt and a few feathers.

She took several pictures, dismayed when she reached the end of the roll.

Betting was hot and heavy, the odds rising higher and higher as one rider after another tried to pull the rooster from the ground, and failed.

Shaye seemed to be the only one present who felt sorry for the rooster.

Feeling as though she were being watched, she glanced across the way, and met Daisy Sullivan's gaze. There was no mistaking the jealousy in the girl's eyes, or the unabashed yearning when Daisy looked at Alejandro.

Feeling a wave of sympathy for the girl, Shaye tugged on Alejandro's arm.

He looked down at her and smiled. "Are you ready to go?"

"No." She inclined her head in Daisy's direction. "Maybe you should go say hello to her."

Alejandro grunted softly when he saw Daisy. "I don't think so."

Daisy looked at Alejandro, naked longing in her eyes, before she turned and walked away.

"We'll make her leave town with us, won't we?" Shaye asked.

"Sure, darlin', even if we have to hogtie her."

Shaye squeezed his hand, her attention drawn back to the contest as, with a triumphant shout, a young Mexican riding a wild-eyed bay pulled the rooster from the ground.

"Well," Shaye exclaimed, "I've never seen anything like that."

Alejandro grinned at her. "Guess they don't do that in the year two thousand."

"Not that I know of."

"Come on, let's go get a beer. All this dust has given me a powerful thirst."

Members of the Miners Union were dispensing beer from a keg in front of the firehouse. Alejandro got two glasses. Shaye sipped hers slowly, amazed, once again, to find herself in this time and place. Women in long dresses and their Sunday-best bonnets stood in small groups, talking about babies, exchanging recipes, complaining about the dirt and the dust. A bunch of men were playing horseshoes across the street. Someone was playing "Oh, Dem Golden Slippers" on the piano at the Sawdust Saloon down the street. And over all hung a haze of dust, and the ever-present sound of the Standard Stamp Mill.

There were games and contests throughout the day—a pie-eating contest, a shooting contest, a washtub where kids bobbed for apples, a cakewalk. The Poet of the Day recited a dozen poems. A barbershop quartet sang "My Old Kentucky Home" and "Silver Threads Among the Gold" and "Jeannie With the Light Brown Hair." There was a baseball game between the Odd Fellows and the Masons.

And that night, there was to be a dance.

"Don't we have to go to the Queen tonight?" Shaye remarked as they went back to the hotel to change.

Alejandro shrugged. "And miss a chance to dance with the prettiest girl in town?"

"So we're just not going to show up?"

"I told Rojas last night that we wouldn't be there."

"Had it all planned out, eh?" she teased, and felt her heart swell with happiness because he wanted to spend time with her; because when she looked into

235

his eyes, she saw the answer to her every unspoken hope, every longed-for dream.

When they reached the door of her room, he drew her into his arms. His kiss, when it came, was long and deep and filled with promise.

"Pick you up in an hour?" he asked, his voice husky.

"I'll be ready."

It was, she mused, going to be a night to remember.

Chapter Eighteen

Shaye looked around the hall, amazed and delighted
with what she saw. The lamps, turned low, filled the
room with a soft amber light. At least a dozen tables
were crowded together at one end of the hall. The
women of the town must have been baking for days,
she thought. She could almost hear the tables groan-
ing beneath the weight of all the desserts heaped upon
them: layer cakes, apple pies, sugar cookies, and cobblers.

The dance floor was crowded with couples, the
women looking like colorful butterflies as their partners twirled them around the room.

Alejandro swept her into his arms and soon they
were caught up in the crush.

"Did I tell you how beautiful you look in that
dress?" he remarked.

She smiled up at him. "Yes, but tell me again."

"You're the prettiest girl here," he said. "The color makes your eyes glow like emeralds."

Shaye laughed softly. "You sweet-talker, you."

His gaze moved over her face, lingering on her lips. "I mean every word."

How could she doubt him when he was looking at her like that? She was acutely aware of his arm around her waist, of the warmth of his hand holding hers, of the way their bodies swayed together, as if they had been dancing together for years. He drew her closer, so that, with each movement, his body brushed against hers, teasing, tantalizing.

How handsome he was. His black coat was the perfect foil for his long black hair and deep brown eyes. Her gaze moved over his mouth, and when he smiled, she knew he was aware of her thoughts, knew that she was wishing they were alone.

Leaning forward, he whispered, "Later," in her ear.

When the music ended, Lottie Johl sashayed toward them. "Rio Valverde," she exclaimed, jabbing the end of her closed fan against his chest, "didn't you tell me you had to work tonight?"

Alejandro's arm curled around Shaye's shoulders. "There was a change of plans, Miss Lottie."

Lottie looked at Shaye and winked. "Yes, I can see that. And a mighty pretty change she is, too."

Alejandro laughed. It was a deep rich, wonderful masculine sound, and it wrapped around Shaye's heart like a warm blanket on a cold day.

"You saved me a dance just in case, didn't you?" Alejandro asked.

Lottie opened her fan with a snap. "What do you think?"

"I think your dance card is full," he said, a woeful expression on his face.

Lottie batted her eyelashes at him. "Of course it is," she replied with a saucy grin, "and one of the dances is yours."

"Let me know which one," he said, "and I'll be there." He glanced down at Shaye. "As long as my lady has no objections."

Shaye pretended to think about it for a moment, then sighed dramatically. "I suppose I can spare you for one dance," she said, faking a much put upon expression.

"I will see you later, then," Lottie said. She smiled at the man walking toward her. "George," she said, pouting prettily as she placed her hand on his arm, "I thought you had forgotten all about me."

Shaye shook her head as the man swept Lottie onto the dance floor. "Oh, look," she said, "there's Madame Sophie."

The dressmaker looked elegant in a gown of black and white striped taffeta. She nodded at Shaye, smiled at Alejandro as she swept past on her husband's arm.

"Shall we?" Alejandro asked, gesturing at the dance floor.

"Yes," Shaye answered, and felt a thrill run through her as he drew her in his arms again.

She stared at one of the couples waltzing by, recognizing James and Martha Cain from the photograph in the guidebook.

As the evening went on, she heard other names that were familiar: Henry Metzger, S. B. Burkham, Frank McDonnell, Tom Miller, Lester Bell. It was unreal, she thought. She was actually here, in the past, mingling with people she had read about in the guidebook.

It was a wonderful night, filled with magic. The band played waltzes and polkas, and a quadrille, which she discovered was very much like square dancing back home. As usual, the men far outnumbered the women, and while Alejandro danced with Lottie and Sophie, Shaye danced with Henry and Spooner, both of whom paid her outrageous compliments.

She was shocked when Dade McCrory asked her to dance. Taken by surprise, she let him lead her onto the dance floor. She glanced around the room, looking for Alejandro, saw him dancing with Addy Mae.

"So," McCrory said, "it's all over town about you and Valverde."

"What's all over town?" Shaye asked.

"You know, how the two of you are sharing a room."

"I don't see as how what I do is any of your business," Shaye retorted.

His arm tightened around her waist. "I'd like to make you my business."

"No way!" She jerked her head back when he tried to kiss her. "What do you think you're doing?"

"Come on, honey, I'll bet that damned 'breed can't please you near as good as I can."

"That's enough, McCrory!"

"Go to hell, Valverde, we're dancin' here."

"Not anymore. Take your hands off her!"

"Sure, sure," Dade said. He backed away from Shaye, nodding and smiling, and then, with no warning, he drove his fist into Alejandro's face.

Alejandro staggered backward. Slowly, he lifted the back of his hand to his mouth.

The dancers nearest Alejandro and McCrory stopped dancing. Like ripples in a pond, silence spread around the three of them until even the band fell silent.

Shaye stared at the blood dripping from Alejandro's mouth, clenched her fists as he lunged at McCrory. The two men reeled backward, crashing into one of the tables. Punch slopped over the sides of the bowl to stain the white lace cloth.

A sense of helpless frustration rose up in Shaye. How could he fight? He hadn't healed up from his last encounter with that vile man.

Several women screamed as Alejandro and Dade began to trade blows. The men cheered them on. Shaye felt a sense of déjà vu as she overheard several of them making bets on the outcome. Most favored Alejandro to win.

"Men! They are such . . . such animals!"

Shaye turned her head and saw Madame Sophie standing beside her.

241

Madame Sophie clucked softly. "Every year it is the same! Always the fight."

Shaye nodded, only half listening as the dressmaker went on and on about men and how they spoiled every get-together with their childish behavior.

Shaye took a step forward, craning her neck to see what was happening. Alejandro was pummeling McCrory, his fists making a dull thudding sound as he struck McCrory again and again.

"All right, that's enough." The crowd parted as the sheriff pushed his way through. "What the devil's going on here?"

Philo Richardson caught the sheriff's arm. "Nothing for you to be concerned about, Sheriff. Just a little spat over a pretty woman."

Alejandro stood up and moved to Shaye's side.

Two men helped McCrory to his feet.

"Who started the ruckus?" the sheriff asked, his gaze moving from Alejandro to McCrory and back again.

Neither man said anything.

The sheriff grunted. "So that's the way it's gonna be."

"Now, Sheriff, why make a fuss?" Philo asked good-naturedly. "It's not the first time two men have squabbled over a woman, and it sure as hell won't be the last."

"I reckon you're right about that," the sheriff said.

"Sure." Philo slapped the sheriff on the arm. "Let's go over to the Sawdust. I'll buy you a drink."

The sheriff fixed Alejandro and McCrory with a

warning glance. "No more fightin'," he said gruffly, "or I'll lock ya both up."

Alejandro nodded, his gaze on McCrory, who was walking away, one arm wrapped protectively around his rib cage.

"Remember what I said," the sheriff warned, then followed Philo Richardson out the door.

Shaye looked up at Alejandro. "Are you all right?"

"Yeah, I'm fine." Pulling a handkerchief from his pocket, he wiped the blood from his mouth, ran his hand through his hair. "Come on, let's dance."

She was conscious of the stares they received as Alejandro waltzed her around the floor, but she refused to let it bother her, refused to let anything spoil this night. She was all too aware of time passing, of the fact that she could be whisked back to her own time at any moment, that every second she spent with Alejandro might be her last.

Thirty minutes later, the band took a break.

"Let's go outside," Alejandro suggested.

"All right."

Shaye picked up two cups of apple cider and a napkin and they left the building. They found a relatively quiet place behind the hall. Using the napkin, Shaye wiped a spot of blood from the corner of Alejandro's mouth, then handed him a cup of cider. She sipped hers slowly.

It was a beautiful night. The sky was like rich dark velvet, a vast indigo vault peppered with millions and millions of twinkling silver stars accented by a bright butter yellow moon.

On this night she was only dimly aware of the noise and the dust and the people. On this night she was mainly aware of the man standing beside her, of the way her skin tingled whenever he touched her, the way her pulse raced and her heart beat fast in anticipation of the time when they would be alone in her room, just the two of them.

Putting her empty cup on an overturned crate, she moved closer to Alejandro, placed her hand on his chest. "Are you all right? Your arm—"

"I'm fine, darlin', stop worrying." He gazed deep into her eyes. Put his cup down next to hers. Wrapped her in his embrace. "Shaye . . ."

His kiss was warm and sweet, filled with promise and an unspoken question.

Her heart was pounding with anticipation when he took his lips from hers. "Let's go back to the hotel."

Every saloon they passed was overflowing with miners and townspeople. There were gatherings at most of the houses, as well, and another dance at the Odd Fellows Hall. They passed a group of older boys who were lighting firecrackers and blowing up bottles and tin cans.

Shaye paid little attention to the noise and the music and the people. Every sense was attuned to the man walking beside her, to the feel of her hand in his. Soon, she thought, soon she would be in his arms. The thought was exhilarating, and frightening. She hadn't been sexually intimate with a man since her divorce. She'd had offers, of course, but sex without love, without any meaning other than the gratification of the moment, held no appeal. She recalled a line from a movie, something about women needing a reason and men just needing a place. The thought made her smile, and then gave her pause. Was that all she was to Alejandro? He'd never said he loved her, never mentioned love at all. Of course, neither had she. When had she fallen in love with him? Did anyone really know the exact moment when the magic happened, or why?

Alejandro squeezed her hand and she looked up, felt the warmth of his gaze seep into her very soul.

The hotel lobby was practically empty. The clerk glanced up from the paper he was reading when they stepped inside. Shaye paid him hardly any attention, too caught up in Alejandro's nearness, and what was about to happen between them, to spare a thought for anything or anyone else. Until a woman in a bright red dress emerged from a shadowy corner.

Alejandro swore softly as Daisy staggered toward them.

Shaye felt a wave of pity sweep through her as Daisy threw her arms around Alejandro's neck.

"Rio!"

"Daisy, what are you doing here?" He tried to disengage her arms from around his neck, but she clung to him like a burr to a saddle blanket.

"You don't need her!" Daisy said, sobbing. "You don't need anyone but me. I'll make you happy, Rio, I'll—"

"Daisy, that's enough."

"Get her out of here," the clerk called. "This is a

decent establishment. We don't want her kind in here."

Alejandro quelled the desk clerk's outburst with a single withering glance; then he looked at Shaye over the top of Daisy's head. "She's drunk. I'd better take her home."

Shaye nodded.

"I'll be back in a few minutes," Alejandro said, and there was a wealth of promise in his voice.

Daisy leaned heavily against him as he guided her out of the hotel. Outside, the streets seemed uncharacteristically empty. She stumbled once, and he slipped his arm around her waist to steady her.

Alejandro nodded at several men as they neared White Street.

"She ain't gonna be any use to ya tonight," one of the miners called out good-naturedly.

"That's right, Rio," came a honeyed voice. "Why don't you come see me instead?"

Alejandro winked at the scantily clad woman leaning over the railing in front of the saloon on the corner. "Some other time, Katie, darlin'."

Alejandro was practically carrying Daisy by the time they reached her house. Deciding that would be easier, he swung her into his arms, opened the front door, and carried her through the dark house to her bedroom.

She clung to him when he put her down on the bed. "Don't leave me."

"I'm here." He disengaged her hands from his neck, kissed her cheek. "Just lie still."

Alejandro reached for the matches on the bedside table, his fingers brushing against the derringer he had given her. He lit the lamp and turned the wick down when she groaned and turned away from the light.

He removed her boots and stockings, slipped off her petticoats, drew her dress over her head. He found her nightgown and helped her into it, then tucked her beneath the covers.

"I'm sorry." She reached for him again, capturing his hand in hers. "Don't be angry."

"I'm not angry with you."

"I love you, Rio. I'll never love—" She hiccoughed. "Never love anyone else. Just you." She squeezed his hand. "Just you. We could be happy, Rio." She looked up at him through wide, hopeful eyes. "I know we could, if you'd just . . . just give us a chance."

She was young, he thought, so damn young. He didn't want to hurt her, but it would be no kindness to let her go on hoping.

"Daisy—"

"Why? Why can't you love me?" She flung his hand aside, her expression suddenly cold and bitter. "It's her, isn't it? That woman you were with to-night."

Alejandro shook his head. "No, Daisy, it's me. I've never had a steady woman in my life. I'm a drifter, and I always will be. That's no life for a woman. Any woman."

He extinguished the lamp, then leaned down and brushed a kiss across her forehead. "Get some sleep, darlin'. You'll feel better in the morning, and you'll see that I'm right."

She looked up at him, her eyes suddenly clear. "I'm tired." She turned over on her side, putting her back to him.

Something in her voice sent a chill down his spine. "Daisy . . ."

"Good-bye, Rio."

Laying his hand on her shoulder, he gave it a squeeze. "Good night, Daisy."

Shaye stared out the window, wondering what was taking Rio so long. She had removed her shoes and stockings, turned down the bed, brushed out her hair. Every time she heard a footstep in the hallway, she felt a thrill of anticipation, followed by a keen sense of disappointment.

What was taking him so long? Daisy's house wasn't that far away. She drummed her fingers on the windowsill. Had Daisy convinced him to stay awhile? To stay the night?

She banished the thought as soon as it formed and forced herself to think of something else, of what she would do if she was stuck in the past. She realized that she wouldn't mind, so long as Alejandro was here with her. It would be hard on her parents, of course, never knowing what had happened to their only daughter, and she had a few close friends who would miss her for a while, but life went on and they would no doubt forget about her soon enough. She could be replaced at work. She shook her head. It was kind of sad, actually, that there were so few people who would be worried by her disappearance.

She blew out a sigh. Where was he?

Just when she was beginning to think he wasn't coming back, she heard the door open. She felt a rush of anticipation as he came up behind her, his arms sliding around her waist.

"Miss me?" he asked.

"What do you think?"

He nuzzled the back of her neck, his breath warm against her skin. "I want to hear you say it."

"I missed you." She leaned back against him. "I was beginning to wonder if you'd changed your mind."

"No, darlin', not for a minute."

She had thought she would feel apprehensive, shy, embarrassed, but all she felt was contentment as he turned her in his arms, lowered his head, and kissed her. It was the Fourth of July, she thought. Independence Day. And Alejandro was setting her free.

His hands moved up and down her back, slowly, sensually, the heat of his hands penetrating her clothing, warming the skin beneath. His tongue skimmed over her lower lip, a living flame. Her breasts were flattened against his chest as he drew her closer, closer. He deepened the kiss, and she moaned softly, her arms sliding around his waist, her hands delving under his shirt to caress the firm, warm skin of his back.

"Shaye . . ." He rained kisses on her nose and eyelids, on her cheeks, down her neck, his hands deftly disposing of her clothing until she wore only her chemise and pantalets. No small feat, she mused, considering the layers she wore.

Her hands had been equally busy, stripping away his tie, his coat, his vest, his shirt, until he wore only his trousers.

Their gazes met then, hers supplying the assurance that his sought.

"I think I've been looking for you my whole life," he murmured, and sweeping her into his arms, he carried her to bed.

His bed. Every night since he had moved out of this room, she had imagined lying here in his arms, running her hands over his skin, through his hair, feeling his hands moving over her body. Reality, she mused, was ever so much better.

The sheets were cool in vivid contrast to the heat of Alejandro's body as he pressed her down onto the mattress, his body a welcome weight. She ran her hands over his back and shoulders, over his buttocks and thighs, wanting to touch all of him at once.

"Rio . . ." She gasped as the need within her grew stronger, more urgent.

"I know, darlin', I know." His voice was husky with desire as he claimed her lips yet again, his hands caressing her until she writhed beneath him, wanting, wanting.

A sharp knock at the door filtered through the haze of passion. She stared up at Alejandro, breathless. "Who can that be?"

He shook his head.

The knock came again, louder and more insistent. "Open the door, Miz Montgomery, we know you're in there."

Alejandro swore under his breath. "It's the sheriff."

"The sheriff! What does he want with me?"

"Beats the hell out of me. I guess you'd better let him in."

"I guess so." She was about to get out of bed when the door opened and the sheriff stepped inside, followed by four armed deputies. She could see the desk clerk standing in the hall, a smirk on his face, a key in his hand.

Shaye grabbed the sheet and drew it up to her chin. "What's the meaning of this?" she exclaimed as the sheriff drew his gun and leveled it at Alejandro.

"Put your pants on, Valverde, you're under arrest."

Alejandro swung his legs over the edge of the bed and stood up. "I didn't know it was against the law to spend the night with a lady," he drawled.

The sheriff grimaced. "Get dressed."

Alejandro reached for his pants and pulled them on. "You mind telling me why you're arresting me?"

"For the murder of Daisy Sullivan."

"He didn't do it!" Shaye said. "He couldn't have."

Alejandro glanced over his shoulder. "Shaye, keep out of this."

"Something you want to tell me, Miz Montgomery?" the sheriff asked.

She shook her head. "He didn't do it. I know he didn't. He's been with me all day. And all . . . all night." The lie tasted sour in her mouth.

The sheriff jerked a thumb in the desk clerk's direction. "Cliff here says different," the sheriff replied. Pulling a pair of handcuffs from his back pocket, he handcuffed Alejandro's hands behind his back. "All I know is, the woman is dead and Valverde's gun killed her."

"But—"

The sheriff lifted his hand, cutting her off. "Save it for the judge. He might believe you. Let's go, Valverde."

"Rio—"

"Take care of yourself, darlin'."

She wanted to go to him, to throw her arms around him and hold him tight. Tears stung her eyes and clogged her throat as she watched the sheriff handcuff Alejandro. Several people stood in the hallway, eyes widening as they watched the sheriff and his men take Alejandro away.

The last deputy out the door tipped his hat to Shaye. "Sorry for the intrusion, ma'am," he said, and closed the door behind him.

Shaye sank down on the bed, stunned by the unexpected turn of events. It wasn't supposed to happen this way! He wasn't supposed to be arrested until August ninth. What had changed? Yet, even as she asked herself that question, she knew the answer, knew that her presence in Bodie had altered the past, and perhaps the future.

She had a sudden image of the tears shining in Daisy's eyes earlier in the day. Shaye had been certain that Dade McCrory had killed Daisy, but now . . .

she bit down on her lower lip as a horrible thought occurred to her. What if seeing Shaye and Alejandro kissing on the street had been more than Daisy could bear?

Oh, Lord, what if Daisy Sullivan had taken her own life? Shaye groaned softly. What if it was her fault?

Chapter Nineteen

Alejandro paced the floor of his cell, his hands thrust deep into his pockets, his jaw clenched. Any doubts he'd had about Shaye's claim of being from the future had been swept away the minute he heard the cell door close behind him. Why the hell hadn't he listened to her? He lifted one hand to his neck. He had seen men hanged before. It was not a pretty sight, especially if the drop didn't break the victim's neck and he was left to hang there while he slowly strangled to death. It happened more times than he cared to think about.

Going to the window, he stared out into the darkness. The town was still celebrating. The sounds of music and laughter, gunshots and firecrackers, drifted to him on the breeze. The drunk in the next cell was snoring loudly. He heard the whinny of a horse from the barn next door.

Damn it all to hell! Why hadn't he grabbed Shaye and left town the minute she told him about his fate? Even now, even knowing she was telling the truth, it still seemed incredible.

His hands curled around the bars as he thought about Daisy. It was his fault she was dead. He should have made her leave town, should have put her on a stage himself, gone with her, if necessary. Guilt burned through him. Dammit, he might as well have shot her himself.

Too restless to stand still, he began to pace the floor again. He had to get out of here, had to find out who killed Daisy. Dade McCrory was the obvious answer. But why?

Alejandro frowned as he reached the far side of the room. Muttering an oath, he slammed his fist against the wall. The answer was obvious. Daisy had come to him for help, and he'd failed her, so she had threatened to go to the sheriff, and McCrory had killed her to shut her up. With Daisy out of the way, McCrory would be sole owner of the Queen. Using the gun Rio had left for Daisy had been a nice touch on McCrory's part, he mused bitterly. And leaving it next to the body had been the ace in the hole.

Dammit, he had to get out of here!

Wrapped in a blanket pulled from the bed, Shaye stood at the window, her fingertips drumming restlessly on the sill as she gazed down into the street, unable to believe what had happened. Alejandro wasn't supposed to be arrested until August, yet something had caused a shift in the timeline of the past, and she knew that she was that something. She thought over the events of the past few days, wondering what she had done that had altered his destiny, wondering if whatever shift had occurred would also change the date of his hanging.

She sighed, distraught at the idea that she was somehow responsible. And then a new idea bloomed in her mind. What if she had been sent to the past because she was supposed to change it? What if Alejandro wasn't supposed to die at all?

The thought gave her pause. What if she had been destined to come here to save him? What if she was the only one who could? Others had felt his presence, but she was the only one able to see him. Maybe they were destined to be together. . . .

She shook her head. That was too far-fetched to be believable. She was a reporter. She dealt in facts, not fiction. And yet, what if it was true? Why else would she be here? If she was here . . . Maybe it was all just an elaborate dream. Maybe she was crazy, locked up in an asylum somewhere, and all this was just a drug-induced hallucination.

Turning away from the window, she pulled on her dark green calico dress, slipped on her Nikes, and left the hotel.

The celebration was over, and for once the streets were almost quiet, with only the last of the revelers staggering down the street, and only the saloons showing any signs of life.

She moved through the dark streets, her heart pounding with a vague sense of déjà vu as she walked down Main Street, past the carpenter shop and the barbershop and the assay office, remembering how they had looked when she'd first seen them. She turned left on King Street, passing the Kirkwood Stable, and then she was at the jail. The door to the sheriff's office was closed. She tiptoed past, her heart beating faster as she approached the jailhouse window and peered inside.

And Alejandro was there, just as she had seen him before. Clad in black pants, a white shirt, and a vest embroidered with tiny gold fleurs-de-lis, he was stretched out on a narrow cot, one arm folded behind his head. A thin plume of smoke rose from the cigarette he held in his left hand. The cell looked exactly as she remembered it. His coat was folded over the back of one of the chairs. She heard the sound of snoring coming from the sheriff's office adjacent to the jail.

Alejandro took a deep drag on the cigarette. Sitting up, he dropped the butt on the floor, ground it out with his boot heel. He sat there a moment, and then he stood up and began to pace the floor, his long legs carrying him quickly from one side of the room to the other. Her breath caught in her throat as she watched him turn and walk toward the window.

"Shaye!" he exclaimed softly. "What are you doing here?"

She expelled her breath in a long sigh, feeling as though she were waking from a dream. "It's exactly as I remember."

He frowned at her. "What are you talking about?" he said, and then he knew. Knew why he'd always felt as if he had seen her before. "You were wearing a black shirt..." He dragged his hand across his chest. "It had writing on it. Here."

"Jekyll and Hyde. It's a stage play."

Disbelief and astonishment chased themselves across his face, and then he swore a short, pithy oath. "It's true, isn't it?" he said, his voice little more than a whisper.

Shaye nodded. "You did see me that night, didn't you?"

Alejandro nodded. He had known from the first that he had seen her somewhere before, but to have seen her when he was dead... Damn, maybe his grandfather had been right. Maybe spirits did walk the earth. And he had been one of them, a ghost trapped in this jail.

"I knew you had seen me," Shaye said. "I felt it. I felt you." She leaned closer. "I felt what you were feeling." She smiled faintly. "What you're feeling now. But it isn't hopeless."

He reached through the bars to cup her face in his hand. "I thought I'd imagined you."

"I couldn't stop thinking about you." She reached up to cover his hand with her own, suddenly certain that she had, indeed, been sent back in time to meet this man. "Or dreaming about you."

"Shaye . . ."

"Do you believe me now?"

"Oh, yeah," he said with a wry grin. "I believe you."

"I'm going to get you out of here," she said fervently.

"And how do you plan to do that?"

She rubbed her cheek against his hand. "I'm not sure, but I will. You'll see." She turned her head and kissed his palm. "Just be ready."

"I'll be ready," he said. "The sooner, the better."

"Good. Do you think I should . . ." She went still as the sound of voices drifted on the wind. Leaning forward, she kissed him quickly, then disappeared into the shadows.

Alejandro stared after her, wondering what manner of escape she had in mind. Not that it mattered. Whatever she came up with would be fine with him as long as it got him out of here.

Hanging. Damn. What a horrible way to die. He grinned into the darkness as he remembered telling Shaye that there weren't many good ways that he knew of.

He stared into the darkness, his smile fading as his hands wrapped around the bars. What if it didn't matter what she did? She said he had died on August twelfth. He had a horrible feeling in his gut that no matter what happened between now and then, he'd be standing on the gallows on that day, a rope around his neck.

"Shaye." He whispered her name. For the first time in his life, he had something to live for, someone he cared for. It wasn't fair that he should lose her when he had just found her.

Chapter Twenty

When she reached her room, Shaye locked the door, put on her nightgown, washed her hands and face, and crawled into bed. But sleep wouldn't come. There were too many thoughts and fears running through her mind. How would she get Alejandro out of jail? Where would they go? What if he was killed during the escape? What if she was?

She turned over on her stomach, punched her fist into the pillow, and closed her eyes. And thought about Daisy. It was sad that she should have died so young, so violently. Why had McCrory killed her? What if it hadn't been McCrory at all, but someone else? Or Daisy herself?

She rolled onto her side, beset by a new fear. She had been so certain she had been sent her to solve the mystery of Daisy's death and save Alejandro from hanging. What if she failed? What if she solved the riddle of who killed Daisy, and Alejandro was hanged anyway, and she was left here without him? She liked the excitement of the town, she liked the people, especially Digger and Spooner and Henry. And Sophie. But as much as she liked Bodie and its inhabitants, she didn't want to stay here without Alejandro . . .

She woke to the sound of gunshots, sighed, and rolled over. Another man for breakfast, she mused, shocked by how readily she accepted that fact of life in Bodie. Maybe it was because she'd lived in Los Angeles. The City of Angels usually had a man for breakfast, too, she mused ruefully, and more often than not, more than one.

She closed her eyes, wishing she could get back to sleep. It had taken hours to fall asleep last night, and then she had tossed and turned restlessly, her dreams dark and ominous, filled with grisly images of Alejandro being led to the gallows, of a rope being dropped over his head, the thick knot just behind his ear. She heard her own screams as he dropped through the trapdoor. She had awakened then, drenched with sweat.

But it had only been a dream. Hadn't it?

Somewhere in the distance, she heard a clock chime the hour. Ten, eleven, twelve. Good heavens, it was noon. She never slept that late.

Throwing back the covers, she got out of bed, dressed hurriedly, and left the hotel.

As usual, the streets were crowded with miners and gamblers. Chinamen peddled firewood and vegetables, a couple of shady ladies stood in the doorway of the Strike It Rich saloon, drumming up business. Men were unloading a huge wagon filled with merchandise in front of the general store, but she paid little heed to her surroundings as she pushed through the throng on her way to the jail. She had to see him, had to know he was still there.

She was breathless when she reached the jail. Relief swept through her in a long, heartfelt sigh when she saw he was there, sitting at the table, drinking a cup of coffee. A plate with the remains of a ham and egg breakfast was pushed to the side. She recognized the dish as one from the hotel dining room and wondered if Addy Mae had brought it personally.

"Alejandro." His name whispered past her lips.

He glanced over his shoulder, smiled when he saw her. Putting the cup on the small, scarred table, he stood up and walked toward her.

"I had a nightmare." She reached through the bars, needing to touch him.

He took her hand, his fingers curling around her palm. "Yeah," he said with a wry grin. "So did I."

"Have you heard anything? When's the trial going to be? Do they have any evidence besides your gun?"

"The only thing I've heard is that Daisy's funeral is this afternoon at three over at the Odd Fellows Hall." He swore under his breath. "I should have made her leave town. Dammit, this is all my fault." He swore again. "I should have believed you sooner."

"That doesn't matter now. Nothing matters now except getting you out of here."

"I don't know how you're going to do that."

"Me, either. But I will. You'll see."

"Hey, what are you doing here?"

Shaye whirled around, startled to find the sheriff standing at her elbow. Oh, Lord, she thought, how much had he heard? "I'm not doing anything," she said, and immediately wished she could take the words back. They made her sound just like a kid caught with a hand in the cookie jar. She composed herself and smiled. "I just came by to see Rio."

"Yeah, you and every other woman in town," the sheriff replied gruffly. "Been a regular parade all morning." He made a shooing motion with his hand. "Go on, get the hell out of here."

Shaye looked over her shoulder at Alejandro. "A regular parade, eh?"

He shrugged, then grinned at her as if to say, What can I do?

Shaye scowled at him. No doubt Addy Mae and Lily and all the doves at the Queen and the Bodie Belle had been by. And Sophie and Lottie, too, and who knew how many other women. They had probably all stopped by while she was at the hotel worrying herself sick. She chided herself for being jealous at such a time, but she couldn't help it. Right or wrong, she wanted to be the only woman in his life, in his heart.

"Come here," he said, and leaning forward, he kissed her through the bars.

At the touch of his lips, she forgot the sheriff was watching, forgot everything but the never-ending wonder of his touch and the fact that she loved him beyond words.

"Okay, you two," the sheriff muttered, "that's enough. You're breaking my heart."

She squeezed Alejandro's hand. "I'll see you soon."

Alejandro smiled down at her and winked. "I'll be here."

Back at the hotel, she went into the dining room. She glanced at the menu, suddenly homesick for a pepperoni pizza and an ice-cold Seven-Up.

A few minutes later, Addy Mae came by to take her order. "I guess you heard about Rio," she said.

"Yes," Shaye replied, then couldn't help adding, "I was with him when they arrested him."

Addy Mae nodded. "It's all over town, 'bout you and him," she said, her voice edged with jealousy and resentment.

"What's all over town?"

Addy Mae shrugged. "You know, how you're sleeping in his old room, and not alone."

A wave of color swept up Shaye's neck, heating her cheeks. Blast that hotel clerk and his big mouth. "We're not sleeping together," she retorted. It was the truth and a lie, she thought. They had slept together but they hadn't *slept* together, not that way. Not yet.

"Are you in love with him?" Addy Mae asked.

"Yes," Shaye replied quietly. *Just like every other woman in town.*

"Well, get in line," the waitress said. "What can I bring you?"

Shaye ordered chicken and dumplings and a cup of coffee. Sitting back in her chair, she listened to the conversations around her while she waited for her lunch to arrive. As expected, most of the talk concerned Alejandro, and whether he was guilty or not. From what she overheard, most of the men were of the opinion that, while he might be capable of killing in self-defense, he wasn't capable of murder. No one seemed to believe he was capable of killing a woman.

"Ah, Miss Montgomery."

Shaye looked up to see Philo Richardson striding toward her. He cut a dapper figure in a dark blue pinstripe suit, his black bowler hat cocked at a jaunty angle.

"Hello, Mr. Richardson. Would you care to join me?"

"Thank you, my dear." Removing his hat, he hung it on a peg, then sat down across from her. "How are you holding up?"

"All right, I guess. I'm worried about Rio."

"Ah, yes, Rio," Richardson remarked with a shake of his head. "His arrest made the front page this morning. I can't believe he did it."

"He didn't do it! I know he didn't."

Richardson nodded. "I'm quite sure he's innocent, my dear, and that the judge will find him so."

Suddenly on the brink of tears, Shaye shook her head. "He's going to hang."

"Now, now." Philo covered her hand with his. "We

have to hope for the best. Judge Krinard is a fair man."

"You don't understand!" Shaye exclaimed.

Richardson observed her for a moment. His instincts, honed over thirty years as a newspaper man, told him she knew more than she was telling. He moved his chair closer to hers, then glanced right and left to make sure no one was listening. "What is it?" he asked quietly. "What aren't you telling me?"

He drew back as Addy Mae approached the table with Shaye's order. "Hi, Philo, honey," she crooned. "Can I get you anything? I saved a slice of apple pie for you. Modean just made it this morning."

"That'll be fine, Addy Mae. And a cup of coffee."

"Black, with two teaspoons of sugar," Addy Mae said. "Just the way you like it."

The girl was a natural-born flirt, Shaye mused as she watched her walk away.

Addy Mae returned a few minutes later with Philo's pie and coffee. "Anything else I can get for you, honey?" she asked.

"Not just now," Philo said.

She gave his shoulder a playful squeeze, then hurried off to clear one of the other tables.

Shaye stared at her plate, her appetite gone. How could she even think of food when Alejandro was in jail?

"You've got to eat," Richardson said.

"I can't."

Philo looked around the room, which was getting more crowded by the minute. "We can't talk here."

He took a bite of his pie and smiled with pleasure. "That Modean's one helluva good cook. If she wasn't already married, I'd marry her myself. Why don't you come by my office later this afternoon? Say about five?"

"I don't know."

"Well, I'll be there if you decide to tell me what you know, or think you know." He finished his pie, drained his coffee cup, and stood up. "Try not to worry," he said, reaching for his hat. "There's only been one hanging in Bodie since I've been here, and he deserved it."

Shaye smiled weakly. Delving into her bag, she withdrew a dollar and dropped it on the table, then left the dining room.

At a loss for something to do, she went for a walk. To occupy her mind, she studied the houses she passed, wondering if she would recognize the house Clark McDonald was staying in if she saw it.

For the first time, she wondered what was happening in her world. Her parents would have worried when she didn't show up and didn't answer her phone. And what about her editor? She was due back at work in three days, assuming twenty-four hours in the past was the same as twenty-four hours in the future. What would Frank think when she didn't show up, didn't call? She had tickets to a play at the end of the month. Her rent was due the first of August.

She frowned as a new thought occurred to her. What if time in the past didn't unwind at the same speed as time in her world? She might have been gone for months, or only a few moments. If she made it back home, no one would ever believe her, she thought, and then smiled in spite of herself. If she ever made it back to her own time, the first person she wanted to see was Clark McDonald. He would believe her.

By accident or design, she wound up at the Odd Fellows Hall at three o'clock. Going inside, she took a seat in the back. A rough-hewn pine coffin rested on the floor. There was no grieving family at this service, only a handful of working girls wearing their most subdued dresses. She was surprised to see Dade McCrory sitting off to one side, hat in hand.

Reverend Warrington presided here, as well. However, where his words had been filled with comfort and hope for Moose's family, his eulogy for Daisy held little hope for a better world in the afterlife due to the "ill-fated road she chose to follow," and though he never came right out and said her soul was "bound for hellfire and damnation," he implied it with the tone of his voice and his solemn expression. Every word, Shaye thought, was a less than subtle warning for the doves who were sobbing none too quietly.

When the service was over, the same glass-sided black hearse carried the casket to the cemetery. Daisy would, Shaye knew, be buried in Boot Hill with the other prostitutes, many of whom had died by their own hand. She remembered reading that most of the women who pursued that line of work died young. Many became opium addicts. Shaye stared after the hearse, wondering if she was in some way responsible for Daisy's death.

"Well, well, if it isn't Valverde's woman."

She turned to see Dade McCrory smirking at her. He was looking prosperous in a dark blue pinstripe suit that was obviously new, as were his boots and hat. A diamond stickpin sparkled in his cravat.

She wanted to ask him why he had killed Daisy and how he had the nerve to attend her funeral, but some inner voice warned her to say nothing. Turning, she started back toward the hotel.

"Tell Valverde I'll be at the hanging," McCrory hollered. "Right up front, where I can watch him squirm."

Shaye forced the gruesome image from her mind. She had more important things to think about. Like where to get hold of a gun. And what was the best time of night to make a jailbreak.

Chapter Twenty-one

She needed a gun. Buying one shouldn't be much of a problem, she mused, since everyone in town seemed to carry at least one. And, unlike modern-day Los Angeles, Bodie had no waiting period.

Walking down Main Street, she turned left on Green. She passed the Boone Store and went into Westlake's Gunsmith Shop. Ten minutes later, she left the store, a derringer tucked inside her reticule.

Back at the hotel, she tossed her shorts, tee shirt, underwear, Nikes and socks into her backpack, as well as a change of clothes. She packed the shirt Alejandro had left in her room, too. It seemed a shame to leave all her new dresses behind, but there was no way to take them with her.

She glanced around the room, making sure she had packed everything she had brought with her from the future, then went to the window and stared down into the street. She was going to miss Bodie, she thought with some surprise. Even though she had only been here a short time, there was something about the town, both present and future, that appealed to her. She would miss Spooner and Digger and Henry, Philo Richardson, and even Miss Sophie, and that was odd, she thought, because she didn't really know any of them very well. She was going to miss the noise and the crowds and the sense of always being on the brink of discovery.

Changing into one of her cotton everyday dresses, she grabbed her reticule and, after putting the derringer under the mattress, she left the hotel. At the dry goods store, she bought a black skirt and a dark print shirtwaist. All the better for blending in with the night, she mused as she paid the clerk.

From there, she crossed the street and went to the United States Bakery and Chop Stand. She bought two loaves of bread and a dozen assorted rolls. Leaving the chop stand, she went to West and Bryant's grocery store and bought a jar of jelly and some canned goods, a hunk of cheese, a dozen apples, some hard-boiled eggs.

She was on her way back to the hotel when she passed a candy store. Pausing, she looked over the assortment of hard candy displayed in large glass jars, thinking she would give anything for a dark chocolate Milky Way or a Baby Ruth. In the end, she bought a bag of saltwater taffy and a bag of peppermint sticks.

Once again, she felt a twinge of regret at the

thought of leaving Bodie. Everyone was so friendly. Even the miners, as tough a bunch of men as she had ever seen, treated her politely, tipping their hats, holding doors for her, calling her "ma'am."

She bought a satchel to hold her purchases and made her way back to the hotel. In her room, she put her backpack and the satchel near the door, took off her boots, and settled down on the bed with a newspaper to wait.

Alejandro paced the jailhouse floor, his restlessness growing. The sheriff had come in earlier to bring him his dinner and let him know that his trial was set for tomorrow morning. He lifted a hand to his throat. According to Shaye, he had been hanged on August twelfth. He swore under his breath. She'd also said he would be arrested on the ninth, but today was only the fifth of July. If she was wrong about that, she could be wrong about August twelfth, too. Damn!

He went to the window, his hands wrapping around the bars as he stared out into the night. His old man had always predicted he would meet a bad end. Resting his head against the bars, he closed his eyes, his mind going back in time, back to those long summer days when he had spent his summers with his mother's people. He had loved the Lakota way of life, where every day was a new adventure. He had learned to hunt and track with the other boys, how to survive off the land, how to skin game. His grandfather had told him the stories of Coyote the Trickster. His life would have been far different if he had gone to live with his mother's people when he left home, he mused ruefully. He would have become a warrior instead of a gambler. He wouldn't be locked in a cell accused of killing his ex-partner. Daisy. Who had killed her, and why? McCrory was the obvious answer.

He opened his eyes, his hands tightening around the bars. Dammit, maybe he was blaming the wrong man. Maybe he should be blaming himself for Daisy's death. If he hadn't sold his share of the Belle to McCrory, none of this would have happened.

Muttering an oath, he began to pace the floor again. "I don't know what you're planning, Shaye," he murmured, "but you'd best do it right quick."

It was a little before three in the morning when Shaye left the hotel carrying her backpack and satchel. She had changed into the dark shirtwaist and black skirt, tied her hair back in a ponytail, laced up her Nikes. The gun, pulled from under the mattress, felt heavy in her skirt pocket.

The town was as quiet as it ever got as she made her way toward King Street. In the background, like the heartbeat of the city, was the ever-present sound of the Standard Stamp Mill, punctuated by an occasional shout of raucous laughter.

No lights burned in the jail.

Two men speaking rapid Chinese hurried past her on their way to Chinatown.

The pounding of her heart drowned out every other sound as she neared the jailhouse window. What would happen if, instead of freeing Alejandro, she was caught? Would they put her in jail, too?

She thrust her fears to the back of her mind and concentrated on the task at hand. She had to get Alejandro out of here. Now.

But how? That was the question that came to mind as she put her hand to the doorknob, and discovered that it was locked. How could she have been so stupid? Of course, it would be locked! Damn! She supposed she could knock on the door, but what business could she possibly have at the jail at this time of the morning?

What would MacGyver do? Reaching into her backpack, she found her wallet and withdrew her Visa card and slid it, very carefully, between the door jamb and the edge of the door. There was a lot of room, and she wiggled the card up and down until she freed the latch. Success! She smiled as she shoved her credit card back in her pack. She just hoped there wasn't also some sort of bar in place.

Hardly daring to breathe, her heart pounding wildly, she took hold of the handle and gave a careful push, exhaling in relief as the door opened.

Taking a step inside, she glanced around the room. In the faint light filtering through the open door, she saw a pot-bellied stove to her right, the jail cells to her left. There was a large desk directly in front of her, with a chair behind it. Beyond the desk, she could just make out the shape of a man sleeping on a cot. And sleeping soundly, she thought, if his snoring was any indication.

A key, she thought; she needed the key to the cell door. On tiptoe, she crossed the floor toward the desk, grimacing when one of the floorboards creaked beneath her foot. She paused, fearful of being discovered, then moved on. She ran her hand lightly over the desk top, encountering papers, a tin mug, a set of handcuffs. But no key.

"Shaye."

Glancing over her shoulder, she saw Alejandro peering at her through the bars.

"Where's the key?" she whispered.

"I don't know. Try the top desk drawer."

Moving as quietly as she could, she moved the desk chair out of the way. Biting down on her lower lip, she eased the drawer open. She was searching the contents as quietly as she could when she heard the cot squeak. She froze, her heart pounding wildly.

"Who's there?" There was the scent of sulfur as the sheriff struck a match. Light from a stub of a candle filled the room.

"Dammit, woman, what are you doing here in the middle of the night?"

She searched her mind for some plausible explanation.

The sheriff frowned at her as he swung his legs over the side of the cot. "Speak up, what are you doing here? Are you in trouble?"

"Yes. No."

"Well, which is it?" He glanced at the door. "How the hell did you get in here, anyway?"

"Oh, hell," Shaye muttered, and sticking her hand

in her skirt pocket, she withdrew the derringer.

The sheriff looked momentarily astonished, and then he laughed. "You're Rio's gal, ain't ya?" he asked, and laughed again.

"What's so funny?" Shaye demanded.

The sheriff gestured at the gun in her hand. "Hell, gal, you can't hit anything with that popgun."

"Maybe not," Alejandro said, "but I don't think I can miss with this."

The sheriff looked at Alejandro, his face suddenly pale.

Perplexed, Shaye glanced over at Alejandro, surprised to see him holding a revolver. "Where did you get that?"

Alejandro pointed at the chair she had moved away from the desk. The sheriff's holster, now empty, had been draped over the back. "Damn, Shaye, I can't believe you brought a derringer to a jailbreak."

"Well," she retorted, "it's my first one. I'll do better next time."

"Right," Alejandro said dryly. "Next time. Get the key."

Shaye looked at the sheriff. "Where is it?"

"I ain't sayin'."

"And I'm not asking you again," Alejandro warned.

The sheriff snorted. "What're you gonna do, shoot me? Go ahead. Somebody's sure to hear the shot and come a-runnin'."

"It won't matter to you, you'll be dead. Anyway, I don't think anybody will pay any attention. Boys have been setting off left-over firecrackers all night."

Shaye glanced from Alejandro to the sheriff. For all his bold talk, the lawman didn't look very confident. She didn't blame him. There was a hard, cold look in Alejandro's eyes that she had never seen before.

"Open the damn door," Alejandro said.

The sheriff hesitated a moment. Shaye could almost see the wheels turning in his head. Apparently deciding that Alejandro meant what he said, the sheriff reached into his pocket, withdrew a large brass key, and opened the door.

Alejandro motioned the lawman into the cell. "Face the wall. Shaye, bring me the handcuffs on the desk."

Slipping the derringer back into her skirt pocket, she did as he asked.

Taking the cuffs, Alejandro handed her the sheriff's gun. "If he twitches, shoot him."

She held the gun in both hands while Alejandro handcuffed the sheriff's hands behind his back, securing him to one of the iron bars.

"If you run, it's the same as saying you're guilty," the sheriff remarked.

"Shut up."

"Think about what you're doing, Valverde. If you run, they'll hang you for sure when they catch you."

"I didn't run the last time, and they still strung me up," Alejandro muttered. Removing the sheriff's kerchief from his neck, he stuffed it in the lawman's mouth. That done, he grabbed his coat from the back of the chair and exited the cell. Shutting the door, he turned the key in the lock. He buckled on the sheriff's gun belt, took the revolver from Shaye's hand, and slid it into the holster. "Come on," he said, taking her by the arm. "Let's get the hell out of here."

Outside, he dropped the key into the horse trough, shrugged into his coat, and headed for the stable.

Shaye grinned. She remembered overhearing a tourist remark that having the stable next to the jail might be a right handy thing.

She waited just inside the doorway while Alejandro went inside. She heard the sound of a scuffle; a short time later, Alejandro appeared leading two horses, both dark. It occurred to her that she probably should have mentioned that she hadn't been on a horse since she was nine or ten and her mother took her horseback riding in the park. But there was no other alternative for a quick getaway. There were no stages leaving at three in the morning. A wagon would be too slow. She only hoped that riding a horse was like riding a bicycle, something that, once learned, was never forgotten.

Rio secured her carpetbag behind the cantle of the larger horse, strapped her backpack behind the saddle of the second animal, then offered her the reins to the smaller horse.

"You can ride, can't you?" he asked when she hesitated to take the reins from him.

"Well . . ." She shrugged. "I haven't for a long time." One thing that had been drummed into her head was that you didn't ride in tennis shoes. You wore boots with heels to keep your feet from slipping through the stirrups.

He muttered something that sounded like a curse, then picked her up and set her in the saddle. He quickly adjusted the stirrups, then handed her the reins. "Just hang on the best way you can," he said, and swung effortlessly into his saddle.

He reined his horse around and rode north, past Chinatown, past Mastretti's Warehouse, toward Bodie Canyon, which led to Aurora about seventeen miles away. Aurora was another boomtown. She recalled reading in one of the books she had bought at the museum in Bodie that Mark Twain had lived in Aurora sometime in 1862, where he had held a major interest in the Wilde West mine.

Seventeen miles over rough country on horseback. If only they could go to the parking lot and get her Rover. She thought longingly of the six-pack of Seven-Up waiting for her in the ice chest in the backseat along with the dark chocolate Milky Way awaiting her pleasure in a Tupperware container so it wouldn't melt or get wet.

Her mount followed Alejandro's without any urging. She grabbed the saddle horn as the horse moved forward. Telling herself to relax, she tried to remember the riding lessons she had taken so many years ago. Hold the reins lightly. Sit down in the saddle, back straight but not stiff, arms bent, elbows close to her sides.

She had always loved horses even though she was a little afraid of them. Every birthday, every Christmas, she had begged for a pony. Finally, her parents had given her riding lessons, and after that, her mother had taken Shaye riding once a week. Her interest in horses had ended when she discovered boys.

Leaning forward, she gave her horse a pat on the neck. This one seemed docile enough and had a smooth, steady gait.

The sound of the stamp mill followed them for several miles until it gradually faded away. The night closed in around them, dark and quiet.

"Are we going to stay in Aurora?" she asked.

"No. That's the first place a posse will look."

"Where will we go from there?"

"Damned if I know. Hang on," he said, and put his horse into an easy canter.

Shaye grabbed the saddle horn as her horse bounded forward. It took only a few minutes to find the rhythm, and she relaxed once again. She had forgotten how much she'd loved riding, although she wasn't sure she cared for it in the dark.

She took a deep breath in an effort to calm her fears. The horse seemed sure-footed enough, and Rio seemed to know where he was going. No doubt he'd been this way before. Still, she couldn't help being apprehensive. Better riders than she had been injured when their horse went down.

She thought about Daisy instead, and wondered if she had inadvertently been the reason for altering Daisy's date with destiny, wondered if there hadn't been something she might have done to prevent the girl's death. Wondered, in the back of her mind, if this was all a dream that wouldn't end. Maybe she was in a coma somewhere, and none of this was real. . . .

After a time, Alejandro slowed his horse to a walk again, and they rode side by side.

"How long before they come after us?" Shaye asked.

"Depends on whether Conner can work that gag out of his mouth and holler for help. If he can't, we'll get a good head start. O'Brien doesn't come in to relieve him until after nine."

"What time do you think it is now?"

He glanced up at the sky. "Right around five. You all right?"

She smothered a yawn with her hand. "Yes. Just tired."

"We'll rest a few hours in Aurora."

"How long will it take us to get there?"

"We should be there in a couple of hours."

She groaned softly. They had only been riding for about two hours, and she was already feeling it in her back and legs.

"Thanks, darlin', for getting me out of there."

He smiled at her and she smiled back, more certain than ever that he was the reason she was here, that they had been destined to be together long before she was born, and that her journey into the past was Fate's way, however bizarre, of bringing them together.

When they reached Bodie Creek, they paused to rest for a short time. Alejandro helped Shaye dismount, and she leaned into him, grateful for his nearness, his warmth, his strength.

She looked up at him, and he kissed her, the touch of his lips chasing away every other thought. She was in his arms, where she belonged, and nothing else mattered.

His arms went around her, holding her close. With a sigh, she snuggled against him, her hands locked behind his neck.

"Dammit, Shaye," he muttered.

"What?"

"Darlin', you feel so good."

"Hmm, so do you."

He had to have her, he thought, and soon, or he'd go crazy. Even now, knowing there was no time to waste, certain Conner would come after him as soon as he was able, he was tempted to spread his saddle blanket on the ground and make love to her there and then. But she deserved better than a quick roll in the sagebrush. He wanted their first time together to be something she would never forget.

He rested his chin on the top of her head and grinned. On sagebrush or satin sheets, she was never going to forget it. He would see to that.

Chapter Twenty-two

It was a little after seven in the morning when they rode into Aurora. Shaye fell into Alejandro's arms when he lifted her from the back of her horse. Her legs felt like rubber, her back ached, her shoulders ached, and she was tired. So tired she had almost fallen off her horse a time or two.

He put his arm around her shoulders, and she leaned against him while he told the man at the livery stable to take good care of their horses and have them saddled and ready to go by five. Grabbing her valise and pack in one hand, he took her arm and they headed down Main Street.

They stopped at the first hotel they came to. Alejandro paid for a room, asked for a tub of hot water to be sent up no later than four, and then, unmindful of the young clerk's startled gaze, swung Shaye into his arms and carried her up the narrow stairway to their room.

After locking the door, he undressed her as if she were a child, settled her into bed, then undressed and climbed in beside her. He massaged her back and shoulders, his big hands gentle, and then he drew her into his arms.

His kiss on the back of her neck was the last thing she remembered before sleep claimed her, and the first thing she felt as she came awake some time later.

"What time is it?" she asked, smothering a yawn.

"Almost four. We need to get a move on."

"So soon?" She rolled over, wishing his face would always be the first thing she saw when she woke up.

"I'm sorry, darlin', but we can't stay any longer."

She sighed, knowing he was right. There could be a posse after them even now. The thought of Alejandro being taken back to jail brought her fully awake. It occurred to her that if they were caught, she would probably be arrested, too. Maybe hanged alongside Alejandro. The thought made her mouth go dry. A moment later, there was a knock on the door.

"That must be the water I asked for," Alejandro remarked. Sliding out of bed, he went to the door and opened it. An older man and a young boy stood there, each carrying two buckets of steaming water. He stood back so they could enter the room.

Shaye sat up, the covers pulled under her chin. She hadn't paid any attention to the room's furnishings that morning. Now she saw that there was a round tub in a corner of the room. There was a pretty crockery pitcher and bowl and a couple of towels on top of the rough-hewn dresser across from the bed, a rocking chair near the room's single window.

The man and the boy emptied the buckets into the tub, nodded at Shaye, and left the room.

Feeling suddenly shy, Shaye looked at Alejandro. They had kissed and come close to making love, but she wasn't sure she was up to bathing in front of him.

Alejandro plucked a bar of soap out of the bowl. "Want me to wash your back?"

She glanced at the tub, heat climbing up her neck and into her cheeks as she imagined his big hands spreading lather over her back and shoulders and . . .

He grinned at her as he tossed the soap onto the bed. "I'll wait for you downstairs," he said, and left the room.

She watched him go with mingled relief and regret; then, knowing it was important for them to be on their way, she picked up the soap and threw the covers aside. Feeling as if she were doing a scene from *Little House on the Prairie*, she stepped into the tub and sat down, her knees practically under her chin. She didn't know how Alejandro would fit in the tub, small as it was. The water barely came to her waist. She washed and dressed quickly, ran a brush through her hair, pulled on her shoes, and went in search of Alejandro.

She found him in the lobby, reading a copy of the *Aurora Tribune*.

Alejandro looked up and smiled when he saw Shaye coming down the stairs. Damn, he thought, but she was a pretty woman. Laying the paper aside, he stood up and walked toward her.

"Feeling better?" he asked.

"Much. Better hurry, before the water gets cold."

He nodded. "Why don't you go order us something to eat?"

"All right." She ran a hand over the rough bristles on his jaw.

"Guess I need a shave."

She cocked her head to one side. "Oh, I don't know. I kind of like you this way."

"Good, 'cause I left my razor in Bodie." He dropped a kiss on her forehead.

"What do you want to eat?"

"Steak."

"Of course," she said with a grin. "Rare."

"I won't be long," he said.

Shaye went to the hotel dining room. It was small and crowded. She paused in the doorway while her mind followed Alejandro upstairs. In her mind's eye, she could see him taking off his shirt, exposing his broad shoulders and chest. Her palms tingled with the desire to touch him, to feel the warmth of his skin beneath her fingertips. Her longing for him continued to amaze her. Never before had she felt such a strong desire for a man. She couldn't help wondering if part of the reason her marriage to Josh had failed was her lack of desire for him. She had enjoyed their love-making, but she had never longed for it, or for him, the way she longed for Alejandro. If his kisses made her feel like this, what would it be like to make love to him?

Warmth engulfed her at the mere idea. With a shake of her head, she hurried across the room to an empty table. She gave their order to the waitress, then sat back in her chair, her thoughts again turning to Alejandro, always Alejandro. He had moved into her mind and her heart, and she was content to have him there. She had been obsessed with him ever since she had first seen him in the jail. Had she known, even then, that they would meet? Perhaps it had been her own intense longing that had propelled her into the past.

Her heartbeat increased and she felt a familiar sense of excitement uncurl in her belly when she saw Alejandro walking toward her. Tall and broad-shouldered and sexy as all get out. No wonder every feminine eye in the place tracked his progress across the room. Toward her.

He pulled out a chair and sat down across from her. "What's going on?" he asked.

"Nothing. Why?"

"You look like the cat that swallowed the canary."

"I feel like one, too," she replied tartly.

He frowned at her. "Want to tell me what that means?"

"Not really," she said, laughing.

"Shaye."

She shrugged. "I guess I'm gloating because every woman in the room would like to be where I am right now."

"On the run?" he asked wryly.

"No, silly. With you."

He made a sound of disbelief.

"It's true, and you know it. Lily, Addy Mae, Lottie, all the girls at the saloon—"

"Lottie!" he exclaimed. "Darlin', you're seeing things that aren't there."

"No, I'm not. They're all crazy about you. Even Madame Sophie."

"Sophie! She's old enough to be my mother."

"Uh-huh."

Alejandro laughed. "You look mighty pretty when you're jealous, darlin'."

"Good," she retorted, resisting the urge to stick her tongue out at him, " 'cause that's most of the time."

He leaned across the table, his dark gaze intense as he took her hand in his and kissed it. "You've got nothing to be jealous of, Shaye."

It was a good thing their dinner came then, she thought, because if he'd kept looking at her like that, she would have melted from the heat of his gaze.

After dinner, they stopped at the mercantile, where Alejandro picked out a couple of bedrolls, two canteens, a coffeepot, a sack of coffee, and some other supplies. Shaye paid the bill, and then they went back to the room to collect their things. There was a moment when his gaze met hers, hot and filled with yearning, that she thought they might put off leaving for an hour or two. But then, from somewhere in the distance, a clock chimed the hour as if to remind them they had no time to waste. Alejandro swore under his breath as he grabbed her valise and their supplies and headed for the door.

Shaye grinned as she picked up her backpack and followed him out of the hotel. "I know just how you feel," she muttered.

Their horses were ready and waiting when they reached the livery. Alejandro stowed their supplies in the saddlebags, lashed their bedrolls in place, draped her backpack over one saddle horn and her valise over the other.

"Ready?" he asked, and when she nodded, he helped her mount, then swung effortlessly aboard his own horse.

Shaye settled her skirts around her, then leaned forward and patted her horse's neck. It was a pretty little bay with a small star on its forehead and one white sock. Alejandro's horse was as black as the ace of spades.

A short time later, they were riding out of town.

"Where are we going?" she asked.

"There's an outlaw hideout not far from here. I think we'll hole up there for a day or two, then head for Frisco. We can catch a train in Carson City."

"Outlaw hideout!" Shaye exclaimed. "Are you kidding?"

Alejandro grinned at her. "I know the fella who runs the place. He'll put us up, no questions asked."

"But outlaws?" She was sorely afraid that real outlaws were not as humorous or easygoing as the ones portrayed in movies like *Butch Cassidy and the Sundance Kid.*

"It'll be all right, darlin', don't worry. Calder still owes me one for saving his life a few years back."

Apparently she didn't look convinced, because he reached over and gave her arm a squeeze. "Trust me, darlin'. Everything will be all right."

They rode for several hours, then stopped to rest the horses. Alejandro loosened the saddle cinch on his horse and then Shaye's while she pulled some bread and cheese from the valise and they picnicked in the shade of a scrawny tree while the horses grazed on a patch of sparse yellow grass.

"What else have you got in there?" Alejandro asked when she delved into the valise again.

"Oh, some apples and candy. Some canned stuff. I'm going to have an apple. You want one?"

"Yeah, thanks."

She tossed him one, took one for herself. As soon as she took a bite, her horse wandered over, snuffling softly. "Want some?" Shaye asked, then laughed as the horse plucked the apple from her hand.

"Guess he wanted the whole thing," Alejandro remarked.

"Humph! I guess so." Shaye pulled another apple from the bag. "Oh, no, you don't," she said, jerking her hand away as her horse lowered its head. "Go on, get! You had yours."

Alejandro fed his apple core to his horse, then stood up and tightened the saddle girths on both horses. Offering Shaye his hand, he pulled her to her feet, grinned when she gave her apple core to her horse.

"Ready?" he asked.

She groaned softly. "I guess so. How much farther is this place?"

"We should get there sometime tomorrow night." He lifted her onto the gelding's back and handed her the reins.

Alejandro glanced at Shaye. She was a beautiful woman, and spunky as hell, he thought admiringly. He grinned at the memory of her showing up at the jail in the middle of the night, armed with that useless derringer. Were all twenty-first century women as gutsy as she was? Hard as it was to believe, he no longer doubted she had come to him from the future. How and why didn't matter. She was here now, and she'd saved him from more than hanging. Foolish as it sounded, she had saved him from the loneliness he had felt as far back as he could remember. He had always been an outcast, an outsider, never quite fitting in anywhere, never having a place, or a woman, to call his own. Shaye had teased him about all the women in his life, and there had been a few, but nowhere near as many as she seemed to think. And yet, in spite of all the women he had known, he had never loved any of them enough to settle down. Until now.

Was it possible he had seen her through the mists of time? Had his soul felt her spirit? Had he looked into her eyes and known they were meant to be together? Had his soul's longing for her been so strong that he had pulled her back in time?

He grunted softly, thinking how ridiculous his thoughts would sound if he put them into words.

They rode until midnight, then took shelter in a shallow draw. Shaye spread their bedrolls side by side, hoping as she did so that there weren't any snakes nearby. A short distance away, Alejandro hobbled the horses. He built a small fire to warm them, and they dined on bread, canned meat, peaches and coffee, with peppermint sticks for dessert.

She shivered when a wolf howled in the distance. She remembered reading somewhere that wolves didn't attack people. She just hoped the wolves had read the same book.

"He sounds lonely," she remarked.

"Maybe he's just serenading his lady love," Alejandro said.

"Maybe."

"Don't worry, darlin'. The only thing out here that's likely to take a bite out of you is me."

She grinned at him across the fire. "Is that right?"

He patted the place beside him. "Come and see."

She pretended to consider it a moment before asking, "Is it safe?"

"What do you think?"

Laughing softly, she went to sit beside him. His arm slid around her shoulders, drawing her closer. His kiss, when it came, tasted of coffee and peppermint.

They spent a pleasant few minutes necking, something Shaye hadn't done since high school, and then grinned at each other when they both yawned.

"I reckon we'd better turn in," Alejandro said.

"I reckon."

"Saucy wench," he said with a decidedly wicked grin. "Just because I'm letting you off easy tonight doesn't mean you'll be so lucky tomorrow."

Shaye's hand flew to cover her heart. "Oh, my," she exclaimed in mock horror, "I'm all aquiver!"

His laughter echoed in the night as he drew her head down on his shoulder. "Ah, darlin', what did I ever do without you?" he whispered as he brushed a kiss across her lips.

And what will I do if Fate takes you away?

It was nearing midnight the following night when they reached the hideout.

A lookout hollered a challenge when they reached the narrow passageway that led into the canyon. Alejandro answered with the password Calder had given him, and a few minutes later he led the way into the hideout, which was located in a shallow valley surrounded by high canyon walls. There were a half-dozen shacks, a saloon, a stable, and a large peeled pole corral. All the buildings were dark except the saloon.

"Are you sure this is a good idea?" Shaye asked dubiously.

"Sure, darlin', don't worry."

"I can't help it," she muttered as they rode toward the saloon. "It's what I'm good at."

Alejandro tethered their horses to the hitch rail in

front of the saloon, then lifted Shaye from the saddle. She groaned softly as her feet hit the ground, grateful for his support at her waist. It was, she thought, the only thing that kept her upright.

All activity in the saloon came to a halt when they walked through the door. Shaye took it all in in one long glance: the bar opposite the entrance, the huge man standing behind it, the half-dozen rough-hewn tables, the two painted women, the raw plank floor, the oil lamps hanging from the ceiling.

"Well, I'll be go-to-hell!" exclaimed the mountain behind the bar. "Look who's here!"

Taking a firm hold of Shaye's arm, Alejandro walked to the bar and shook hands with the mountain. "How the hell are ya, Calder?"

Calder's laugh was as big as he was. "Fine as a pig in swill. Damn, Rio, I ain't seen you in a coon's age." He glanced at Shaye, then grinned at Alejandro. "Guess I don't have to ask how you're doing."

"Take it easy, Calder."

"Ah," Calder said, "so that's how it is. Pleased to meet you, ma'am, whoever you might be."

Shaye grinned at him in spite of herself. "Shaye Montgomery," she said.

"Jack Calder."

He was even bigger than Moose, Shaye thought. His shirt seemed in danger of bursting at the seams with every movement. He had a shock of curly brown hair, pale blue eyes, and a nose that looked like it had been broken at least once.

When it was obvious that the newcomers posed no

threat, the other occupants went back to their own pursuits. Soon a low hum of conversation filled the air, punctuated by the slap of cards and an occasional burst of feminine laughter.

"So, Rio, what brings you here?"

"I need a place to hole up for a few days."

"Sorry to hear that," Calder said. "I never figured you to take to the owlhoot trail."

"I didn't," Alejandro said curtly.

Calder nodded, the look in his eye saying he wouldn't pursue the matter now but promising questions later. "Can I get you two a drink? The first one's on the house."

"I could use some whiskey to cut the trail dust," Alejandro said.

"Me, too." Shaye shrugged at Alejandro's look of surprise.

"Whiskey, huh?" he said with a grin. "Well, I guess you deserve it after the last two days."

Calder placed a pair of shot glasses on the bar, pulled a bottle from underneath, and poured two drinks.

Alejandro downed his in a single swallow and asked for a refill. Shaye took a sip of hers, coughed as the raw whiskey burned its way down her throat. She had never been much for hard liquor, but she wasn't sure this stuff really qualified as whiskey. Paint thinner, maybe.

"You look all tuckered out," Calder remarked.

"That we are," Alejandro replied. "You got room for us?"

"Sure. The last cabin's empty. Make yourself t'home."

"Thanks, Jack."

"Don't mention it."

"Okay to leave our horses in the corral?"

"You can put 'em up in the barn, iffen you want. There's a couple of empty stalls."

"Obliged," Alejandro said. "You ready to turn in, Shaye?"

She nodded, wondering if she would ever be able to speak again the way her throat was burning.

Outside, Alejandro took up the reins of their horses and they walked to the barn. Shaye unsaddled her horse, then led it into an empty stall and removed the bridle. Alejandro forked the horses some hay, picked up her valise and backpack, and then they followed a dusty path to the last cabin.

"Don't expect too much," Alejandro warned as he opened the door.

He found a box of matches on the mantel and lit the lamp on the kitchen table, then closed and barred the door.

Shaye grimaced as she looked around. The place had definitely looked better in the dark. There was a small square table, two rickety-looking chairs, a shelf made of empty wooden crates. A narrow bed covered with a dull gray blanket was pushed up against one wall. A faded blue gingham curtain covered the single window; there was a rag rug in front of the hearth.

"We won't be here long," he said. "Think you can stand it for a day or two?"

She nodded, and hoped she wasn't lying.

"Do you want me to wait outside while you undress?" he asked.

"No."

With a nod, he shrugged out of his coat and began to unbutton his shirt.

Suddenly shy in spite of herself, Shaye turned her back to him. Stripping off her dress and undergarments, she pulled her long cotton nightgown over her head, then sat down on the edge of the bed and took off her shoes and stockings.

When she looked up, Alejandro was standing beside her wearing only the bottom half of a pair of long johns. He might as well have been naked, she thought, the way they clung to him. He was beautifully formed, from his broad shoulders and well-muscled arms to his flat stomach and long, long legs.

She pulled down the blanket, more than a little surprised to see that the sheets, though not Tide white, were at least clean. She scooted across the mattress, her heart pounding as Alejandro extinguished the light, then slid into bed beside her. It was a very narrow bed, barely big enough for the two of them.

"I'm sorry, Shaye," he said.

"Sorry? For what?"

"For getting you involved in all this."

Turning on her side, she laid her hand on his shoulder. "I'm not."

"I don't know much about the future," he said, "but I'm sure it's better than this."

"Everything is different, that's for sure," she said.

"But not everything is better. People are always in a hurry. They don't take time to enjoy life anymore. Everything has to be done faster than before. We have microwave ovens that can cook a meal in no time at all, and cars to get us to our destinations faster, and computers and calculators that can add and subtract in the blink of an eye." She shook her head. "You may not believe it, in fact I don't believe it myself, but I kind of like it here, in your time." She paused, her gaze moving over his face. "With you."

He sucked in a deep breath, let it out in a long, slow sigh, and then gathered her into his arms and held her tight. When he spoke, his voice was so low she could hardly hear him.

"Dammit, Shaye, what am I going to do if you go out of my life the same way you came in?"

"Rio . . ."

His arms tightened around her. "Don't leave me, darlin'."

"I don't want to."

"Shaye."

His voice was filled with fear and longing, the same longing she felt, the same fear that she would suddenly be sent back to her own time. She clung to him, knowing, in that moment, that she didn't want to live in a world without him in it, that she would rather stay here and make do without all the comforts she was accustomed to than go back to her old life.

She wrapped her arms around him, overcome by a sudden sense of foreboding. What if she had been sent here to save him from the gallows? What if, now that she had accomplished that, she was sent back to the future?

"Hold me, Rio. Hold me and don't ever let me go!"

"Shaye?"

Her name was a question. Her kiss was the answer.

Driven by the fear of separation, they clung to each other. She moaned with pleasure as his hands and lips moved over her face, her shoulders, her breasts, softly caressing, sweetly arousing. He drew her nightgown over her head and tossed it aside. And she, suddenly bold and unafraid, divested him of his long johns and sent them sailing across the room.

"Beautiful," he murmured. "So beautiful."

"So are you."

He laughed softly and then he was kissing her again, and when the desire that had sparked between them could no longer be denied, Alejandro rose over her, his dark eyes blazing. She lifted her hips to receive him, and now, joined to him heart and soul and body, she felt complete for the first time in her life.

He moved within her, each stroke filling her with pleasure, building, building, until she thought she might explode from the wonder of it, the beauty of it, the unbelievable ecstasy. She was a writer. Words were her forte, yet she knew she would never find the words to express the joy of his touch, the sense of belonging, of having finally found what she had been searching for her whole life. "Alejandro . . ." She cried his name as she tumbled over the edge, her arms holding him tight, her body convulsing as wave after wave of ecstasy pulsed through her. Alejandro threw back his head, his eyes closed, as he reached his own climax; and then, his body still shuddering, he buried his face in the curve of her neck.

Shaye held him close, relishing his weight, pleased that he was in no hurry to shatter the sweet afterglow of their lovemaking. Josh had always rolled away as soon as he was finished, often leaving her feeling bereft. She stroked Rio's hair, awed by the intensity of her feelings. She longed to tell him she loved him, but something kept her from voicing the words aloud.

"I must be getting heavy," he remarked after a while.

They were not the words she wanted to hear.

Rolling onto his side, he cradled her against him, one arm around her waist, one hand cupping her breast. He brushed a kiss over her shoulder, his breath warm on her skin.

"Sweet dreams, darlin'," he murmured.

He did care for her, she thought. It was there in his eyes, in his voice, whether he put the feeling into words or not.

"Same to you," she murmured. A moment later, wrapped in the warmth of his arms, she drifted to sleep.

Chapter Twenty-three

Alejandro listened to the soft, even sound of Shaye's breathing. For the first time since his mother passed away, he was content, and yet even that contentment was edged with despair. What would he do if he lost her? He had been a drifter his whole adult life, never settling long in any one place, never sinking roots, never letting anyone get close to him, never feeling the need for a forever woman in his life. Until now. From the first time he had seen her, he had known Shaye was the one he had been searching for his whole life. The first time, he thought, and felt a chill slide down his spine. He had been a ghost the first time he had seen her. His arm tightened around her waist. Her skin was soft and smooth. Her hair was silky where it fell across his chest. Her breast was warm in his hand. Shaye.

Unforgettable

Her name was like the soft sigh of the wind whispering through the cottonwood trees, reminding him of the carefree days of his childhood with the Lakota. Long summer days when he had wanted nothing more than to be a warrior like his grandfather, Elk-Who-Runs-in-the-Night. He had listened in awe to the old stories and to the tales of battle the men told around the campfire at night. In his mind's eye, he had been one of them, a seasoned warrior riding into battle against the Crow, stealing ponies from the Pawnee, hunting the curly-haired buffalo in the summer, boasting of his exploits around the fire during the long winter nights.

And then his mother had died, and she had taken with her all the security he had once felt. His mother. She had been the one constant in his life. Whether at the ranch or the reservation, she had been there, loving him, encouraging him, helping him to have faith in himself, assuring him that he was as much a Lakota as anyone else in the tribe in spite of his mixed blood. Rightly or wrongly he had measured his worth in her eyes, counted on her to always be there. When she died, he had vowed never to depend on anyone but himself.

He had gone back to his mother's people in the summer of sixty-seven. He had spent the summer there, in the Black Hills, gradually coming to the sad realization that there was no going back. With his mother dead, nothing had been the same as he remembered. Even his grandparents were gone, killed in the massacre at Sand Creek, along with most of the other people he had known.

Shaye stirred against him, bringing him back to the present. Nothing that had happened in the past mattered now. Nothing mattered but Shaye and whatever time they might have together. He would take her to San Francisco, he thought, buy her a house overlooking the bay.

It wouldn't last, he knew that. Sooner or later, he would lose her. Either she would realize he was no good for her, or Fate would send her back where she belonged. But until then . . . until then, she would be his.

Shaye woke slowly, aware of a long, lean body pressed against her back, of a well-muscled arm draped over her waist. Turning her head, she saw that Alejandro was still asleep. Lord, but the man was gorgeous! Just looking at him made her feel all soft and squishy inside. She smiled, remembering how only a few months ago she had sworn she never wanted to have anything to do with another man. Now, she couldn't imagine a life without Alejandro in it. She loved him, she thought, loved him desperately. She only hoped and prayed that he felt the same.

She smiled as his eyes opened. "Morning."

"Mornin', darlin'." He kissed the tip of her nose, the corners of her mouth. "You look beautiful in the morning."

"Right."

"I mean it. There's a glow about you. It's very becoming."

"Well, if I'm glowing, Mr. Valverde, you're the one who deserves all the credit."

"Why, thank you, ma'am," he drawled.

"Thank you." Happiness bubbled up inside her and spilled over in a froth of laughter.

He looked at her, one brow arched in question. "Something funny?"

"No. I'm just happy, that's all."

His arm tightened around her. "Me, too," he said quietly. And for the first time in more years than he cared to recall, it was true.

She heard the faint note of surprise in his voice. She rolled over so they were lying face to face. Lost in the depths of his eyes, she murmured the words she had been holding back for so long. "I love you."

"I can't imagine why."

She brushed a lock of hair from his brow. "Does anyone ever know why?"

"You've got a good heart, Shaye Montgomery, a good soul."

It was by far the nicest compliment she had ever received, and yet she couldn't help wishing that he would say the words she so longed to hear.

His finger traced the outline of her chin, her cheek, her nose, drifting slowly over her lips. "And you're beautiful, darlin'. So beautiful."

"So are you."

He laughed at that.

"You are, and you know it. You turn heads everywhere we go. Stop laughing! It's true. Saloon girls, Addy Mae, Lily, Sophie . . ." Her voice trailed off and she frowned at him. "Have you made love to a lot of women?"

He shrugged. "A few. I'm not a monk, and a man has needs, you know." His gaze moved over her face, seeing the hurt she tried to hide. "Shaye, darlin'," he said fervently. "I've made love to other women, but it's never meant anything, until now."

"Rio . . ."

He knew what she wanted to hear, but he couldn't put his feelings into words. Cupping her face in his hands, he kissed her, hoping somehow that she would know how he felt. They were both breathless when he took his lips from hers.

Lifting his head, he smiled down at her. "Will you marry me, darlin'?"

"Marry you," she exclaimed softly.

"Say yes, darlin'."

"Yes," she murmured. "Oh, yes, yes, yes!"

"Shaye!" He wrapped his arms around her and held her tight. "Name the day, darlin'."

"Is today too soon?" She loved the way his body felt against hers, the way they fit together, two imperfect halves that made a perfect whole. His hands moved over her back, his lips left trails of fire on her lips, down her neck, across her breasts. She felt the evidence of his desire against her thigh, saw his need reflected in the depths of his eyes.

He drew back a little, his gaze searching hers. "You mean it? You'll marry me today?"

"Of course I would. But it's impossible."

"Is it?"

"Isn't it?"

He grinned at her. "I'm calling your bluff, darlin'."

"What do you mean?"

"Calder's a preacher."

"An outlaw preacher?" Shaye asked dubiously.

"Yep."

She grinned up at him, intrigued by the idea of being married in an outlaw camp by a rogue minister. "I'm game if you are."

He winked at her. "I'll see what I can do," he promised, and kissed her again.

"Rio . . ." Her hands clutched his shoulders, her own need building deep within her, fanned by the intensity of his kisses, by the erotic abrasion of his skin against her own.

He rose over her until all she saw was him, all she wanted was him, for now, and forever . . .

Shaye snuggled against Alejandro. He had asked her to marry him. The thought made her smile inside and out. By tonight, she could be Mrs. Alejandro Valverde. She sighed with contentment, thinking how wonderful it would be to spend the rest of her life in the warm haven of his arms. And then she realized that, as pleasant as the idea sounded, she had to get up.

"Hey!" Alejandro caught hold of her forearm when she sat up. "Where do you think you're going?"

"Nature calls."

"Ah," he said, releasing her arm. "It's under the bed."

Grabbing the top blanket, she wrapped it around her shoulders and slid her legs over the edge of the mattress, wishing, as she pulled the battered chamber pot out from under the bed, that the shoddy little cabin came with a nice modern bathroom complete with hot running water and a flush toilet.

"Turn around," she said.

With a grin and a shake of his head, Alejandro rolled over and faced the wall.

She grimaced as she made use of the chamber pot. Wherever they eventually settled down, she was going to insist on indoor plumbing, even if she had to install it herself. And one way or another, she was going to get her hands on some toilet paper, even if she had to invent it. Grinning at the thought, she ripped a page off the catalog under the bed. She could get used to just about everything else, she thought, but she really missed toilet paper.

Her stomach growled as she sat down on the edge of the bed. "I'm hungry."

"I heard," Alejandro replied. He rolled over, sat up, and pressed a kiss to her shoulder. "Let's go see what Calder has to offer."

Twenty minutes later they strolled into the saloon. The place was practically empty. Jack Calder stood behind the bar, playing a game of solitaire. Two other men were sitting at a corner table, playing blackjack.

Calder looked up as the door closed behind them. "Mornin', Rio. Miss Shaye."

"Got anything to eat in here?" Alejandro asked.

"Lucy usually cooks for us, but she's gone off to San Francisco, visitin' her sister." Calder glanced at Shaye. "You're welcome to use the kitchen, if you've a mind to."

"How about it?" Alejandro said. "You think you could rustle us up something to eat?"

"I guess so."

Calder jerked his thumb toward the door behind him. "Kitchen's in there. Help yourself."

"This should be interesting," Shaye muttered. Walking around the bar, she opened the door.

It was a kitchen like no other she had ever seen. The walls had a thin coat of whitewash. There was no curtain at the single window. The stove was a black behemoth. A battered washtub atop a long wooden counter served as the sink. There was a supply of canned goods on a rickety shelf. She found flour and sugar in sacks on the floor. There were a dozen eggs in a cracked blue bowl, no doubt provided by the red hens she could see scratching out in the yard. There were a couple of loaves of bread in a tin bread box. She found a crock of butter, a pot of honey.

"French toast it is," she muttered.

After washing the frying pan and the utensils, and after much trial and error and more than a little cussing, she managed to produce five slices of edible French toast, three for Rio and two for herself. She poured two cups of coffee, added sugar to hers, put everything on a tray, and carried it into the other room.

Alejandro was sitting at a table, playing a game of solitaire. "What's this?" he asked as she set a plate in front of him.

"French toast."

"Looks good," he remarked. He cut off a piece. Took a bite. And grinned at her. "Tastes good."

"Thank you." She sat down across from him, wishing she had some cream for her coffee.

Calder walked over to take a look. "What in blazes is that?" he asked.

"French toast," Alejandro replied. "Want some?"

"Sure," Calder said.

Alejandro cut a slice in half. Shaye was about to offer to get Calder a fork, but before she could say anything, he picked the bread up in his fingers and took a bite.

"Damn!" he declared. "Iffen that don't taste like a piece of heaven. How'd you like to take over the cookin' chores while you're here?"

"Me?" Shaye exclaimed. She hated to cook and ate most of her meals out.

Calder nodded vigorously. "For something like this, I could charge double. Is there any more in the kitchen?"

"No, but it's easy to make," she said. "Only takes a few minutes. I'll show you how, if you like."

"I surely would. What was it you called it again? French toast?"

Shaye nodded.

Calder ate the last bite and smacked his lips. "Yep," he muttered, smacking his lips. "Pure heaven."

Shaye grinned as he went back behind the bar. Who would have thought something as ordinary as French toast would be such a big hit?

"I asked Calder if he'd marry us," Alejandro said, "if you're still game."

"Oh, I am."

"Tonight, after supper?"

"Tonight," she agreed.

Later, while Alejandro was sitting in on a poker game, she took Jack Calder into the kitchen and showed him how to make French toast. She watched in disbelief as he cooked up five slices and wolfed them down one by one.

"Damn!" he declared, dragging his hand over his mouth. "I never tasted nothing like this in all my born days."

"Well, I'm glad you like it. Are you really a preacher?"

"Yes, ma'am, I surely am." He looked at her, a lopsided grin on his face. "Don't you worry none. It'll be all nice and legal. So what're you gonna fix fer dinner?"

"I'm not a cook, Mr. Calder," Shaye protested.

"Well, now, that makes two of us. I know you ain't planning to stay here long, but maybe you could give the boys a treat tonight. I know they're plumb tired of my cookin'."

Shaye shook her head. "Really, Mr. Calder, I wouldn't know where to begin. At home, I usually eat out."

He brushed her excuses aside. "Just do the best you can." He laughed. "Hell, you can serve 'em that there French toast. They won't complain none."

"Do you have any ham or bacon?"

"Sure, got some 'round here somewheres. Got some beef, too."

She looked around, but there was no refrigerator, no icebox. "How do you keep it from spoiling?"

"We pack it in snow in the winter. In the summer, we keep it in a bucket of buttermilk down in the cellar."

Shaye nodded. "All right. French toast for dinner. We'll need more bread, though."

"Got a batch rising now," he said.

"You make your own bread?" Shaye asked.

He nodded. "I worked in a bakery in Pittsburgh back when I was a young'un. Bread's the only thing I recollect how to make, though. Must have made a thousand loaves in my time."

"Well, I'm impressed," Shaye said, meaning it. "I never could get the hang of it." After trying a time or two, she had given up and bought a bread machine. All the fresh-baked goodness with none of the fuss.

She glanced around the kitchen, amazed that anyone would eat anything prepared there.

Calder cleared his throat. "It's a mess, ain't it?"

"Oh, no—"

"Sure it is. I tried to get the girls to do the cookin',

maybe clean up in here a little, but hell," he said, shrugging, "they work all night." He reached into a drawer and plucked out a book. "This is what Lucy uses."

It was a cookbook. There was no cover; the pages were creased and torn. Shaye glanced at the table of contents: Cowboy Muffins, Irish Soda Bread, Johnny Cake, Lumpy Dick . . . she shook her head as she turned the pages. She had to know what Lumpy Dick was. The recipe called for four cups of milk, a half cup of butter, and one cup of flour.

"Cut butter into flour (as for pie)," she read, "leaving butter in pea size lumps. Bring the milk to a boil. Add butter and flour mixture all at once. Reduce heat and cook until thick. Do not stir. Lumpy Dick tastes best when the butter is left in lumps. Serve with cinnamon and sugar, cream or milk."

Somehow it didn't sound very appealing. She turned the page and found some Handy Household Hints, among them how to clean the keys of a piano using alcohol, how to remove fly specks from wood using water and skim milk. She learned that hot sour milk would put a shine on silver, and that lemon juice and salt would remove rust.

She closed the book and handed it back to Calder. "I'll see you at dinner."

With a nod, he dropped the book back in the drawer.

Shaye went out into the main room. Alejandro was still playing cards. He smiled at her as she approached the table.

"Hey," one of the men said, "looks like old Calder finally hired himself a new filly."

"Watch your mouth, Dawson," Alejandro said mildly.

"What'd I say?"

"She doesn't work here." Alejandro caught Shaye's hand in his. "She's my woman. Got it?"

"Sure, sure," Dawson muttered. "I didn't mean nothing."

Alejandro looked up at Shaye. "Wanna sit in, darlin'?"

"No, I don't think so."

"Damn right," Dawson said. "We don't need any women at the table."

Shaye glared at Dawson. He had shaggy dark blond hair and pale brown eyes. Lines bracketed his mouth, making her think that a scowl was his perpetual expression.

"I suppose you're one of those macho jerks who think a woman's only place is in the kitchen or on her back in the bedroom." She spoke without thinking. There was complete silence at the table for a moment; then Alejandro and the other man, who had been quiet until now, burst out laughing.

"That's telling him, honey," the man said. He patted the chair beside him. "Come on, join us."

"Thank you, Mr. . . . ?"

"Jim Hoffman," he said.

"Pleased to meet you, Mr. Hoffman. I think I would like to sit in," Shaye said sweetly. "Thank you for asking."

"Call me Jim."

"Jim." Ignoring Dawson's scowl, she sat down.

Alejandro pushed half his stack of chips toward her, then handed her the deck. "Deal for me, will ya, darlin'?" he asked with a wink. "My arm's getting sore."

She smiled at him, knowing he was giving her a chance to show off. And that was just what she did. She shuffled the cards expertly, then slid the deck in front of Dawson, sitting to her left. "Cut?"

Dawson cut the cards, and Shaye dealt the hand. She stared at her cards in complete astonishment, unable to believe her eyes. Four jacks. What were the odds? "Cards, gentlemen?" she asked.

Alejandro took one, Hoffman took one, Dawson took three.

Alejandro tossed a twenty-dollar chip into the pot.

"Your twenty and five more," Hoffman said.

Dawson scowled at Hoffman and raised it another ten.

Shaye met the last raise and raised it ten more.

Alejandro looked at her a moment, and raised it ten more. Hoffman folded. Dawson raised it another ten.

"Five more," Shaye said calmly, and put chips into the pot.

There was the faintest of smiles on Alejandro's face as he tossed his cards on the table.

"I call," Dawson said. "Let's see what you've got."

Shaye laid her cards on the table, one by one. Four jacks and a trey.

Dawson stared at her cards, muttered a crude oath,

315

and slapped his cards down on the table.

"Looks like you won," Hoffman mused.

"Looks like," Shaye agreed. She raked in the pot, then looked at Alejandro, who grinned at her.

"Guess that makes it my deal," Hoffman said. Scooping up the cards, he shuffled them, offered the cut to Shaye, and dealt the hand.

It was amazing, Shaye thought, how quickly the time passed. One hour became two and then three. Dawson called for a whiskey, Alejandro and Hoffman ordered beer. Shaye didn't really want a beer, but the only other beverages Calder had to offer were water and goat's milk, neither of which sounded tempting, so she opted for a beer. Calder brought them some hard-boiled eggs and bread along with the drinks, and then decided to sit in for a hand or two.

The chair creaked as Calder lowered his bulk onto it. The chair must have been a lot sturdier than it looked, she decided, since it didn't splinter under his considerable weight.

Calder was a talker. He told them about his Army days, when he had been in the Seventh Cavalry. "Rode with old George Armstrong Custer hisself, I did." He picked up his cards, studied them a moment, and tossed a twenty-dollar chip into the pot.

"Custer!" Shaye exclaimed. "Really?"

"Sure 'nuff. I was with Reno's command at the Little Big Horn. That was some fight, I can tell you. I never thought any of us would get out alive."

Alejandro sat forward, his dark eyes alight with interest. "Go on," he said. "Start at the beginning."

Calder dragged a hand across his jaw. "Old Custer, he was in an itching hurry to meet the Sioux. He'd testified in a government investigation about some scandal that involved President Grant's brother, and Grant declared Custer wouldn't be allowed to accompany his troops. Custer begged Grant to reconsider, and the president allowed as how Custer could go in command of his own regiment, instead of commanding the entire column. I reckon Custer figured a major victory would be a right good thing about then. He never believed there were as many Injuns as his own scouts claimed there was, and when we was about fifteen miles from where the village was s'posed to be, Custer sent Benteen and his men off in one direction and Reno in another. That was the last we saw of Custer and his men."

Calder shook his head. "The battle might have turned out differently if Custer hadn't split his command, and if Reno hadn't retreated, but then again . . ." He shrugged. "We was badly outnumbered. If we'd stayed with Custer, I reckon as how we would have all been killed."

Alejandro sat back, his expression thoughtful. Shaye knew what he was thinking as clearly as if he had said it out loud. If he had stayed with his mother's people, he would have been at the Little Big Horn.

Alejandro rose abruptly, reaching for her hand. "Let's go outside. I need to stretch my legs."

"You're not sorry you missed the battle, are you?" Shaye asked as they left the building.

"Not as sorry as I used to be," he said with a wry grin.

"Men! I've never understood their fascination with war and fighting."

"It's a way for a man to prove his courage."

"It's a good way to get killed."

"There are worse things than death."

"Maybe," she said, but at the moment she couldn't think of any, couldn't think of anything but Alejandro, the brush of his thigh against hers, the warmth of his hand. She looked up at him, trying to imagine how he would look in a loincloth and moccasins, with a feather in his long black hair and his face painted for war.

He looked down at her, his gaze meeting hers. He arched one brow. "What's wrong?"

"Nothing."

"Is that right? Looks like something to me."

"I was just trying to picture how you'd look..." She lifted one hand and let it fall. "How you'd look in a loincloth and feathers."

"Well, darlin'," he said with a wink, "someday I'll show you."

As Calder had predicted, the men loved her French toast, loved it so much she feared she might have to spend the rest of the night cooking it. Most of them had four slices, some five, Calder had six, not to mention the bacon and coffee that went with it. By the time she finished, she didn't think she would ever be able to look at another piece of French toast as long as she lived.

She left the dishes for Calder. She had done the cooking, she thought as she carried their plates into the kitchen, he could do the cleaning up. Besides, she couldn't worry about anything as mundane as dirty dishes now. She was getting married!

Chapter Twenty-four

She was getting married. The inside of a dilapidated cabin wasn't exactly the setting most brides dreamed of, but it didn't matter. Shaye saw nothing but the man standing beside her. And if she was dressed in cotton instead of white satin, well, that didn't matter, either. She had worn white to her last wedding, she thought ruefully, and look how it had turned out. Maybe black would bring her luck.

She stood beside Alejandro, her hand tightly clasped in his, while Jack Calder read the words that changed her name from Shaye Elizabeth Montgomery to Mrs. Alejandro Valverde. It took only minutes, but the instant she said, "I do," she knew, deep in her heart, that her whole life had been irrevocably changed.

Calder smiled at them expansively, then winked at

Alejandro. "You can kiss the bride now."

"My pleasure," Alejandro murmured, and drawing Shaye into his arms, he kissed her, long and deep, the kiss more binding than any of the words that had been said.

She was breathless when he took his mouth from hers.

"That'll be ten bucks," Calder said, punching Alejandro on the shoulder.

"Best money I ever spent." Alejandro slapped a couple of greenbacks in Calder's hand. "Now get the hell out of here."

"Not till I've kissed the bride," Calder said. Placing his hands on Shaye's shoulders, he kissed her soundly on both cheeks. Then, whistling softly, he left the cabin.

Shaye grinned up at Alejandro. "Alone at last, Mr. Valverde."

He grinned back at her. "And what would you like to do, now that we're alone, Mrs. Valverde?"

"Gee, I don't know."

"Maybe I could help you think of something."

"Like what?"

"Well, darlin'," he drawled, "if I kissed you here . . ." He kissed her forehead. "Maybe you'd ask me to kiss you here . . ." He kissed the tip of her nose. "And if you liked that, maybe you'd ask me to kiss you here . . ." He kissed her cheeks, first one, then the other. "And if you liked that—"

"I'd ask you to kiss me here." Shaye cupped his face in her hands and pressed her lips to his. Honey and fire flowed through her veins, warming her, engulfing her as he wrapped her in his arms and deepened the kiss until they were both breathless.

"Oh, darlin'," he murmured, "do you know what you do to me?"

She slid her hands under his shirt, wanting to feel the heat of his skin. "Show me."

"My pleasure, Mrs. Valverde."

His clever hands quickly removed her clothing and shoes, his lips brushing across her shoulders, her breasts, her belly. She giggled when he kissed her knees. Grinning, he began to tickle her, until she fell back on the bed. He sank down on top of her, but she pushed him away.

"Oh, no," she said. "You're way overdressed." And so saying, she removed his coat and began to unbutton his shirt.

Alejandro fell back, his gaze hot as he watched her. She tossed his shirt aside, tugged off his boots, yanked off his socks. He lifted his hips so she could pull off his trousers, wriggled out of his long johns.

And then there was nothing between them but heated flesh and an urgent desire that could not be ignored.

Alejandro wrapped her in his arms, and she clung to him with a wild desperation born of a yearning too long denied and the knowledge that what they had found could be lost in a heartbeat.

He caressed her with hands that trembled, kissed her fervently, hotly. They writhed on the bed, time and place melting away, until nothing mattered but the two of them and the love they had one for another.

She ran her hands over his back, his shoulders, his chest, down his thighs until he rose over her, his eyes smoldering with passion. She was ready for him, more than ready. She moaned softly, an utterly feminine sound of pleasure as he sank into her, filling her, filling the hollows of her heart as his body merged with hers, uniting them, completing them.

Her hands moved over his back, her nails lightly raking his skin as he moved within her, deeper, harder, faster, until the explosion came, a white heat that shimmered through her, engulfing her, pleasuring her, until she thought she might die of the joy that filled her heart and soul. And when his release came and he convulsed deep within her, she knew a sense of satisfaction and completion she had dreamed of but never believed truly existed.

With a kiss and a sigh, Alejandro rolled onto his side, carrying Shaye with him, his body still part of hers, his arms holding her tight. He had made love to women before, but it had never been like this. Damn, she satisfied him like no other, filled an aching emptiness in his heart and soul he had never known was there until he felt her warmth seep into him, chasing away the dark. His woman. His bride. His wife.

He still couldn't believe she had accepted his proposal. They had known each other such a short time, yet it seemed as if he had been waiting for her all his life, as if his soul had always been searching for hers. And suddenly, it didn't seem so far-fetched to believe that his spirit had traveled down the long, misty corridors of time and seen her standing outside a lonely jail cell.

Shaye woke slowly, aware of a weight across her stomach, a warmth against her back. It was still dark outside, but she was suddenly wide awake. Smiling, she rolled over, her finger tracing the stubbled outline of her husband's jaw. Husband. What a beautiful word!

She ran her fingertips over his lips, remembering how he had kissed her only hours before, his mouth hot and hungry on hers.

Her hand moved over his chest, slid down his stomach, which was hard and flat and ridged with muscle. He was in remarkably good shape for a man who earned his living playing poker, she mused. If she didn't know better, she would swear he spent his days pumping iron at the gym.

Her hand slid lower, lower, delighting in the warmth of his skin, taking pure feminine pleasure in his nearness, in touching him while he slept.

She shrieked as she suddenly found herself flat on her back, looking up at him, though she couldn't see his face. "Didn't your mother ever warn you about awakening sleeping tigers?" he growled.

She shook her head, her eyes filled with laughter. "Are you going to eat me now, Mr. Tiger?"

"Most definitely," he said. "From the top to bottom and back up again."

And that was exactly what he did.

Twice.

In the morning, she awoke wrapped in his arms, a smile on her face.

"Mornin', darlin'," he drawled. "About time you woke up."

"Why didn't you wake me?"

"You were smiling so pretty I didn't want to disturb you, in case you were dreaming about me."

"Oh, I was."

"Want to tell me about it?"

"No."

"No?"

She smiled seductively. "I'd rather show you."

It was much later when they left the cabin and went to the saloon in search of food.

Calder grinned at them as they approached the bar. "Well, well, looks like I won the bet."

"What bet?" Alejandro asked.

"We had us a bet going about how long it would be afore you two come up for air. I said not before two o'clock, and I was right."

"I'm happy for you," Alejandro said dryly. "You got anything to eat?"

"I reckon I can rustle up something if you ain't too fussy." He grinned at Shaye. "I don't reckon your missus will want to cook, seein' as how it's your honeymoon and all."

"You got any coffee?" Alejandro asked.

"Sure. You want a cup, Mrs. Valverde?"

Shaye smiled. Mrs. Valverde. She loved the sound of it. "Yes, thank you."

Calder grunted softly. "Coming right up."

Shaye and Alejandro took a seat at a corner table. She couldn't stop looking at him. Her husband. Last night had been the most incredible night of her life. Now she knew why so many songs were written about love, why poets extolled it, why Juliet couldn't live without Romeo, why the Prince had been able to awaken Sleeping Beauty with just a kiss. Her gaze moved to Alejandro's mouth, remembering how his kisses had aroused her . . .

Alejandro lifted one brow. "You keep looking at me like that, darlin', and I'm gonna take you right here on the table."

"Promise?"

Alejandro threw back his head and laughed. He was still laughing when Calder arrived with their coffee. "Ham and eggs okay for you two?"

"Sure," Alejandro said. "And plenty of it." He winked at Shaye. "I've got to keep my strength up."

Calder laughed out loud as he lumbered into the kitchen.

"When are we leaving here?" Shaye asked.

"You in a hurry?"

"Well, I was thinking how nice it would be to check into a ritzy hotel in San Francisco. We could get a suite and lock ourselves in."

"Go on."

"And we wouldn't have to go out for days and days."

"Not even to eat?"

Shaye leaned forward, trailing kisses down the line

326

of his cheek to his chin. "Haven't you ever heard of room service?"

Alejandro grinned at her. "Sure, but I've never tried it."

"You'll love it, I promise."

"I'd love a cave if you were in it," he said, "but that fancy hotel sounds expensive. I think I'd better see if I can't win a few dollars before we settle down to a life of decadence."

They spent the rest of the day in their cabin, making love, sleeping, talking, and making love again.

At dusk they went back to the saloon for dinner. There were cheers and catcalls as they sat down at one of the tables. Shaye couldn't help it, she blushed from the soles of her feet to the roots of her hair, disconcerted by the knowledge that every man in the room knew what she'd been doing for the last two days. Alejandro, she noted, was grinning from ear to ear.

After dinner, she went into the kitchen to ask Calder if she could borrow a large pan so she could wash their clothes. Calder told her to help herself to whatever she needed. Thanking him, she left the kitchen. Tonight, before going to bed, she would wash Alejandro's shirt and socks, her blouse and underwear. His trousers and her skirt would have to wait, she decided, since she wasn't sure the heavy material would dry overnight.

Returning to the main room, she found Alejandro playing poker with three other men.

He drew her down onto his lap, one arm slipping around her waist.

"Are you winning?" she asked.

He looked offended. "What do you think, darlin'?"

"You gonna sweet-talk your woman, or deal the cards?"

"Hello, Dawson," Shaye said with a grin.

"You're not gonna sit in again, are you?" he asked irritably.

"Afraid I'll bring you bad luck?"

"Damn right."

"Don't pay any attention to him, darlin'," Alejandro said.

"Why don't you sit this hand out," she asked, "and dance with me, instead?"

"Deal me out, Saunders," Alejandro said. He grinned at Shaye as the piano player hit a sour note. "He plays the way I dance."

"Baloney," she said, standing. "You dance divinely."

"Divinely?" Alejandro said. "Well, well."

Taking her hand, he led her to a small clear area on the far side of the bar. The doves, Shaye noted, were also dancing. Several men were lined up at the end of the bar, waiting their turn. Seeing the two heavily painted girls brought Daisy to mind. She wished she could have done something to prevent Daisy's death. What a horrible life she'd had, and then to have it end so prematurely, and so horribly. It was such a waste.

They had been dancing for several minutes when

one of the men tried to cut in on Alejandro.

"The lady's with me," he said.

"Hell, man, it won't hurt you to share. All I want is just one dance. Just one little dance with this pretty lady."

"Forget it. You're drunk." Alejandro looked at Shaye and smiled. "And this lady is my wife."

"Drunk? Who? Me?" The man waved his hands in the air. "Nah, I ain't drunk. I just feel like dancin'."

"Dance with someone else."

"Lousy 'breed."

The man muttered the words under his breath, but not so low that Alejandro didn't hear them. Shaye felt the sudden tension flow through his arm.

"What did you say?" Alejandro bit off each word, his tone low and deadly.

The atmosphere in the room grew still, like the quiet before a storm.

The man looked at Alejandro and blinked like someone just waking and realizing he was in danger. "I . . . I didn't mean anything by it," he mumbled.

Shaye tugged on Alejandro's arm. "Rio, let's go."

He looked down at her, his eyes dark and dangerous.

"Please, let's go."

Slowly the tension drained out of him. With her hand firmly in his, they left the building.

They kept to themselves for the next few days, only leaving the cabin for their meals. Shaye told Alejandro of her childhood, and how she had always wished she had brothers and sisters, how she had always envied her friend Leslie who came from a large family. She told him how she had always loved to read, and had devoured the Black Stallion books, and *Lad, a Dog*, and Nancy Drew; how she had secretly wished to be an actress but had been too shy to try out for the drama club.

In return, Alejandro told her how he had dreamed of being a warrior, and how disappointed he had been when he went back to his mother's people, only to find that those he knew were gone, and that, as much as he wished it, he no longer had a place there.

She admitted she was afraid of the dark.

He told her he had always been afraid of dying alone.

She confessed that she was a chocoholic and an incurable romantic.

He admitted there were two things he couldn't live without. "A cup of black coffee, first thing in the morning," he said. "And you." He tapped the end of her nose with his forefinger.

"Little ole me?" she asked, immensely pleased.

"You," he repeated. "You made me believe in love, darlin'."

"Ah, Mr. Valverde," she said, deeply touched, "you do say the sweetest things."

"My pleasure, Mrs. Valverde," he replied, and then burst out laughing as her stomach growled. "Sounds like it's time for dinner."

Shaye felt her cheeks grow warm and then she

laughed, too, as his stomach made a loud rumbling sound. "I think you're right."

After dinner, they played a few hands of poker with Calder and a couple of the other men. Luckily, Dawson was engrossed in conversation with another man at a back table. She caught both of them glancing their way more than once. The other man was whipcord lean, with long brown hair and hard brown eyes. She didn't know what they were discussing, but she would have bet every dollar on the table that they were up to no good.

It was late when they left the saloon. Overhead, a bright yellow moon played hide-and-seek with a few wispy clouds.

They walked in silence for a while. Shaye wrapped her arms around her body, shivering a little, not so much from the cold but from a sudden sense of foreboding. As soon as they were out of sight of the saloon, the night wrapped itself around them, engulfing them in a darkness that seemed ominous somehow. She heard the distant hoot of an owl and, further off, the faint wail of a coyote.

"Rio . . ."

"What is it?" he asked. "What's wrong?"

"I don't know." She reached for his hand, overcome by a sense of impending doom. And even as the thought crossed her mind, Alejandro was pushing her to the ground.

There was a bright flash, a popping noise. It took her a moment to realize someone was shooting at them.

There was another gunshot.

She felt the spray of something warm against her cheek, and realized in that instant that Alejandro had been shot.

Chapter Twenty-five

He swam through layers of pain and darkness, calling her name. "Shaye. Shaye."

"I'm here."

He groaned softly as he opened his eyes. Shaye was kneeling beside him, her brow lined with worry, her eyes filled with anxiety. Dawson and another man were staring down at him.

Alejandro tried to sit up, only then realizing that his hands and feet were bound. A sharp twinge lanced through his left side when he tried to move. "What the hell's going on?"

"Norland here rode in from Aurora last night," Dawson said. "He overheard me mention your name. Seems there's a nice reward out for you. Fifteen hundred dollars." He looked at Shaye and grinned. "And another hundred for the woman. We aim to turn the two of you in and split the take."

Alejandro glanced at Shaye. This was all his own fault. He remembered seeing Norland in the saloon, playing cards with Dawson.

"I'm gonna get some sleep," Norland said. "Wake me in a couple hours and I'll relieve you."

Dawson nodded.

Norland tossed Dawson a length of rope. "Best tie up the woman. Keep her from getting any ideas."

"I'll take care of it."

Alejandro glanced around. "Where are we?"

"Couple miles south of the hideout. We'll be leaving for Bodie first thing in the morning. Norland put some supplies together while I dug the bullet out of your hide. Better get some sleep. Gonna be a long day tomorrow."

Anger boiled up inside Alejandro as Dawson grabbed Shaye's hands and lashed them behind her back.

"That oughta hold you till morning," Dawson muttered, and turning away, he walked over to the fire and poured himself a cup of coffee.

Alejandro's gaze moved over Shaye. "Are you all right?"

"I'm fine. How do you feel?"

Guilt ate at his soul. He had kept her with him when he knew he should let her go, and look what it had gotten her. He was a man on the run, and now, because of him, because she loved him, there was a price on her head, as well.

They would hang him, and all his troubles would be over, while hers would be just beginning. They'd lock her up, who knew for how long. The thought of Shaye behind bars cut like a knife, sharp and deep. She would probably curse the day she had met him for the rest of her life. Dammit. He had to get her out of this mess, one way or another.

"Rio, what are we going to do now?"

"Scoot over here."

She did as he asked, felt his fingers tugging at the rope that bound her wrists.

Dawson was on his second cup of coffee when Alejandro managed to free her hands.

Shaye kept her arms behind her back. "Now what?" she whispered.

"I want you to get the hell out of here."

"What?"

"You heard me. If you get a chance to escape, take it."

"I'm not leaving you."

"Listen to me. Do you want to go to jail?"

"Of course not, but—"

"Dammit, Shaye, we can't have any kind of life together. You must know that."

"But . . . but we just got married."

"It was a mistake."

"I love you, Rio. Do you love me?"

He wanted to say yes, wanted to tell her he loved her more than his life, but the words stuck in his throat. She loved him, and what had it gotten her? A price on her head. "No."

"Then why did you marry me?"

He shrugged, his expression blank. "Seemed like a good idea at the time."

She stared at him, her hurt turning to anger. She had been a fool to love him, a fool to think he loved her. She had been nothing but a diversion, just one more woman in a long string.

"Yes, it did," she said. "But I can see now that it was a mistake." She took a deep breath. "I wish I'd never met you," she said, choking back her tears. "Don't worry, if I get a chance to make a break for it, I'm gone . . ."

And she was gone, just like that.

"Alejandro!" She cried his name as darkness enveloped her. "Alejandro! Where are you?"

Where are you . . . where are you . . . The sound of her voice echoed and re-echoed in the thick darkness.

Frightened and uncertain of what had just happened, she turned in a circle, looking for him, but he was nowhere to be seen, and she was alone in the dark.

A familiar noise drew her attention. Looking up, she saw an airplane passing overhead.

No, it couldn't be, she thought. But it was. She was back in her own time. But how? Even as the thought crossed her mind, she knew the answer.

I wish I'd never met you. The words she'd spoken in such haste roared like thunder in her mind.

"Oh, but I didn't mean it." She stared up at the night sky. "I was hurt and angry. I didn't mean it."

She wrapped her arms around her waist and rocked back and forth while grief splintered through her.

"Please," she murmured, "please let him be all right. Please send me back to him. Please, please, please . . ."

She repeated the words in her mind over and over again as she huddled against the weathered boards that had once been part of the saloon. "It can't end like this," she whispered. "Please, don't let it end like this . . ."

The tears came then, sobs that wracked her body until her eyes burned and her chest ached, and still she cried, unable to stem the tide of tears.

And always, in her heart, the urgent plea . . . *Don't let it end like this . . .*

Dawson looked around, frowning. "Where's the woman?"

Alejandro shook his head. "I don't know." But he did know. Despair settled on his shoulders as Shaye's voice echoed in his mind. *I wish I'd never met you.* The pain in his side throbbed with each breath, each movement, but it was the pain in his heart, his soul, that tormented him now, because he knew, in that moment, that what he had feared most had happened. She had gone back to her own time. And it was his fault.

"Well, hell, she can't have just disappeared."

A faint smile crossed Alejandro's lips, because that was just what she'd done. And it was no more than he deserved.

* * *

His arms were warm around her, his breath fanning her cheek as he whispered that he loved her, would always love her. She clung to him, afraid to let him go as she told him of the horrible dream she'd had. He laughed softly, his kisses filled with reassurance as he whispered that they would never be parted. And she believed him. Even when his body shimmered and he began to disappear, she believed him, because she couldn't imagine life without him . . .

"Alejandro!"

She woke with the sun in her face and his name on her lips, hoping it had all been a bad dream, but the sight of another jet passing overhead proved beyond a shadow of a doubt that she was back in her own time.

Please, please, send me back . . . please, I love him so much . . . I'll do anything . . . I'll stay with him forever . . . please, please . . .

Heavy-hearted, she pulled herself to her feet and glanced around. Nothing but desert as far as she could see. This was California, she told herself. There had to be a road or a freeway somewhere close by.

She glanced at the rising sun. Okay, she thought, that's east. Bodie was to the south, as near as she could tell. Turning, she started walking. Nikes might not be good for horseback riding, she mused, but she was glad to be wearing them now. After a mile or so, she fervently wished she had that last bottle of water in her backpack, that her dress had a shorter skirt, that she had a broad-brimmed hat to shield her face from the harsh desert sun. Her stomach growled loudly; her mouth was as dry as the desert around her. How long could a body go without water anyway? One day? Two? Certainly not more than three or four.

She put the thought behind her, her spirits lifting as she came upon a rutted road. She had to get back to Bodie, had to find Clark McDonald, had to find out if Alejandro had been hanged.

She shook her head. She had been so certain she had gone back in time to save him. Could she have been wrong? She frowned, wondering if she had been sent back to save his life, or to save him from a life of loneliness. He loved her, she knew it, even though he had never said the words, might never say the words. He had proved how much he cared at the risk of his own life. If he hadn't pushed her out of the way, she could have been killed. And now he was badly wounded, could be dying. Dead.

She felt a burst of hysterical laughter rise in her throat. Of course he was dead. He had been dead for more than a hundred years.

She quickened her pace in spite of the growing heat of the day. She had to know how he'd died, had to know if he'd succumbed from a bullet he had taken in her place, or if he had been hanged for Daisy's murder, or miraculously died of old age. She had to get back to Bodie. Had to find her way back to the past. And if she couldn't find her way back to his time, then she would just have to stay in Bodie. Maybe she could become a park aide, she thought desperately. Alejandro's ghost would be waiting for her at the jail. If she stayed in Bodie, she would be able to see him. She didn't care if he was a ghost, didn't care if she sounded crazy. She didn't want to live without him. Couldn't live without him.

Gradually, her pace slowed. Sweat trickled down her back. She tripped over a rock, almost falling when her feet got tangled in the hem of her skirt, a skirt that seemed to grow heavier with every step.

She looked skyward, her heart and soul aching. "I need him," she said. "And he needs me."

It seemed as though she had been walking forever instead of only a few hours when she became aware of a rumbling noise that bordered on a low whine. Glancing behind her, she saw several small dark shapes. As they drew closer, they took shape, and she saw three men on dirt bikes riding in her direction.

"Here!" she hollered. "Over here!" It was hopeless, she thought. They would never hear her over the roar of the bikes. She jumped up and down, waving her arms like a madwoman. "Here!" she screamed at the top of her lungs, and felt a surge of relief as the bikes turned in her direction.

She watched them move toward her, then lost sight of them as they descended a small hill. Help was on the way. Maybe they would give her a ride into Bodie, or at least drop her off in the nearest town.

I'm coming, Alejandro. Wait for me . . . wait for me . . .

She frowned as the hum of the motors seemed to take on a new sound, like that of . . . no, it couldn't be . . . hoofbeats.

A dark cloud of dust filled the sky, blotting out the sun. She stared at the motorcycles, now indistinct in the swirling dust. For a moment, she thought she saw men on horseback. She shook her head, wiped her eyes, hoping to clear them. "You've spent too much time in the past," she muttered, then gasped, choking, as the cloud enveloped her, smothering her. The sound of hoofbeats grew clearer, more distinct. As from far away, she heard a voice mutter, "What the hell?"

And then she heard another voice, a voice that proved that prayers were answered. "Shaye?"

The dust cleared and she found herself in the middle of the three riders. But she had eyes only for the one in front of her. "Alejandro. Thank God." Her gaze swept over him. "Are you all right?"

"I am now."

"Well, well, look who's here." Norland glanced at Dawson and grinned. "I told you she'd come back."

Dawson dismounted and walked toward her. "Let's go, girlie. You ain't worth much, but a hunnerd bucks is a hunnerd bucks."

"Get your hands off of me!" Shaye exclaimed as he grabbed hold of her.

Dawson dropped his hands from her waist. "Fine. Walk."

"Shaye, come here."

She hurried toward Alejandro. He took his foot from the stirrup. Grasping his arm, she put her foot in the stirrup and pulled herself up behind him, then wrapped her arms around his waist and held on tight.

Dawson swung into the saddle and urged his horse forward.

Alejandro followed, and Norland brought up the rear.

Shaye pressed her cheek against Alejandro's back, a silent prayer of thanksgiving rising in her heart as she clung to him, determined never to be parted from him again. He felt warm, she thought; too warm.

"What happened?" he asked quietly. "Where'd you go? And why the hell did you come back?"

Before, his question would have upset her, but not now. "It doesn't matter what happened," she said. "All that matters is that we're together again." She closed her eyes for a moment, thanking the Fates that had returned her to him. "Are you all right?"

He nodded. "Nothing to worry about."

Nothing to worry about, she thought. He had been shot. They were on their way back to Bodie to face a trial where he would be found guilty, and then hanged, and he told her not to worry! She wished she had kept her derringer with her. Even though Alejandro had told her that the gun was too small to be of much use at a distance of more than two or three feet, it might have come in handy. Unfortunately, she had left it in her backpack back at the hideout.

They rode for hours. Shaye dozed, her cheek resting on Alejandro's back, her arms wrapped tightly around his waist. Drifting in and out of sleep, she thought about what had happened, trying to find some logical explanation, but none was forthcoming.

The sun was high overhead when Dawson reined

his horse to a halt beside a shallow stream. Shaye slid off the back of Alejandro's horse, resisting the urge to offer him her hand. He dismounted slowly, his jaw rigid. She knew he was in pain and trying not to show it.

Norland dismounted. Taking up the reins of all three horses, he led them to the stream to drink.

Alejandro moved upstream, and Shaye followed him. He lowered himself slowly to the ground and took a drink, then buried his head in the water.

Shaye quenched her thirst, then laid a hand on his arm. His skin was hot. "You've got a fever."

He nodded. "Be careful, Shaye. If you get a chance to make a run for it, take it."

"Don't start that again," she warned.

"Shaye—"

"Forget it! I'm not leaving you, and that's the end of it."

His expression softened. Lifting his bound hands, he stroked her cheek. "It damn near killed me when I thought I'd lost you."

Reaching up, she covered his hand with her own. "I know. I felt the same. I've never prayed so hard in my life."

His smile, though faint, warmed her clear through. "I did a little praying of my own." He shook his head. "You know you would have been better off staying in your own time, darlin'."

"I know. But you're here."

She glanced up as Dawson appeared beside her.

"Let's go," he said.

He reached down to grab her arm, but she jerked away. "I don't need any help."

"Suit yourself," he growled.

She gained her feet, hovered near Alejandro while he stood up.

A short time later, they were riding south, toward Aurora and an uncertain future.

Chapter Twenty-six

She had no idea what time it was when they reached Aurora. Like Bodie, the town was apparently open all night.

Dawson drew rein in front of a hotel. Shaye slid to the ground, her legs weary after hours of riding. Alejandro dismounted. He looked a little unsteady. Going to stand beside him, she slipped her arm around his waist.

Dawson dismounted and handed his reins to Norland. "Take the horses down to the livery. I'll get us a room."

With a curt nod, Norland headed down the street.

Dawson jerked his chin toward the hotel. "Let's go."

Shaye followed Alejandro into the hotel, remaining close to his side while Dawson asked for a room with

345

twin beds. The clerk looked at Alejandro, his gaze lingering on his bound hands.

"He's my prisoner," Dawson said.

The clerk cleared his throat. "Maybe we'd all rest better if he spent the night in the jail."

"Maybe so," Dawson agreed, "but I'm not letting him out of my sight."

The clerk blew out a breath as he pulled a large, leather-bound register from under the counter. "Sign here." He handed Dawson a room key after Dawson signed the book. "Down the hall, third door on the left."

"Obliged," Dawson said. He tossed the key in the air. "My partner'll be along in a few minutes. Name's Norland. Let him know what room we're in."

"Yes, sir, I surely will."

Dawson nudged Alejandro. "Let's go."

The room was fairly large, with whitewashed walls. Dingy white curtains hung at the window, faded brown spreads covered the beds. There was a scarred rocking chair in one corner. Shaye could see the handle of a blue enamel chamber pot under the bed nearest her.

Alejandro crossed the floor, sank down in the rocking chair, and closed his eyes. Going to stand beside the chair, Shaye placed her hand on his brow. "He needs a doctor."

"A doctor!" Dawson snorted. "I ain't shellin' out no money for a doctor. Anyway, the reward says dead or alive."

"Why, you . . ." The words died in her throat when Alejandro took hold of her hand.

"Let it go, Shaye."

He was right. There was no point in arguing with a cretin like Dawson. Kneeling, she lifted Alejandro's shirt. Unwrapping the bandage swathed around his middle, she stared at the ugly hole in his side. The skin around the wound was red and swollen. "It looks infected," she murmured.

Dawson shrugged. He glanced over his shoulder as Norland entered the room and closed the door behind him.

"We can pay for the doctor," she said firmly.

Dawson shook his head. "Forget it."

"What's going on?" Norland asked.

"She wants a doctor for the Injun."

"At least let me go get something to treat the wound so it doesn't get worse."

Norland snorted. "Why bother? He's a dead man either way."

Shaye swallowed her anger and her pride as she glanced up at Dawson. "Please."

Dawson jerked his head toward the door. "Go ahead."

"Are you crazy?" Norland said. "Are you forgetting there's a reward for her, too? What if she doesn't come back this time?"

"She'll be back, won't ya, sweetheart?"

"If she doesn't come back, I'm taking fifty bucks outta your share."

Dawson grinned. "She'll be back."

Norland's gaze locked on Shaye's. "He'd better be right, 'cause if you're not back here in twenty minutes, we'll be collecting that reward on a dead Injun."

"I understand." Shaye reached into Alejandro's pocket and withdrew a handful of greenbacks. "I'll be back soon," she promised.

"Remember what I told you," Alejandro said softly.

"I remember," she replied. Rising, she left the room. "I remember," she muttered as she crossed the lobby toward the door. "But if you think I'm leaving you here like this, you're sadly mistaken, Mr. Valverde."

The doctor's office was located in a small two-story house at the end of Main Street. Shaye knocked on the door, and when no one answered, she hammered her fist on the wood. "Damn!" She glanced up and down the street. Where was the doctor? Well, she didn't have time to wait for him, or to go looking for him, either.

Chewing on her lower lip, she turned the doorknob, and was surprised when the door swung open. She stuck her head through the opening. "Hello? Is anyone home?"

No answer.

Taking a deep breath, she stepped into the foyer. Hard to believe she had once prided herself on being a law-abiding citizen, she mused ruefully. Since coming to the past, she had broken a man out of jail and stolen a horse. Did they still hang people for that? And now she was guilty of breaking and entering.

Well, she amended, maybe just entering, since the door had been unlocked.

She wished fleetingly for a flashlight as she moved through the darkness. She grunted softly as her shin hit the corner of a low table. A moment later, she came to a hallway. The first door opened on a small bedroom, the next room held four beds. Two were occupied. The next door opened on what looked like an examination room. A small lamp, turned low, illuminated the whitewashed room.

Crossing the floor, she went to stand in front of a large glass-fronted cupboard filled with jars and bottles.

She read the labels, looking for something that sounded familiar. She spied a box of powders marked "salicylate of sodium." She frowned, trying to recall where she'd heard the name before. If she wasn't mistaken, salicylate of sodium had been a forerunner to aspirin. Opening the cupboard, she took a couple of the packets and put them in her skirt pocket. She needed something to fight the infection, but what? Nothing else looked or sounded familiar. Where the heck was the doctor? She found a roll of bandages and took that, too; then, thoroughly discouraged, she headed for the front door. Pausing in the foyer, she dropped a couple of dollars on the table beside the door to ease her conscience, then hurried out of the house.

Dawson and Norland were playing cards when she entered the hotel room. Alejandro was still sitting in the chair, his eyes closed.

Dawson glanced down at his pocket watch. "Didn't think you were coming back."

"I said I would."

She poured a glass of water from the pitcher on the dresser, opened the aspirin packet, and poured the powder into the glass. She shook Alejandro's shoulder gently. "Here. Drink this."

He looked at her through eyes glazed with pain and fever. "Dammit, Shaye, why didn't you leave?"

"Just drink this. We can discuss it later. And you know why."

A faint smile touched his lips. "Because you're stubborn?"

"Exactly. Now drink this."

He took a sip, grimaced, and drained the glass. "Don't suppose you brought me any whiskey?"

She shook her head. "Sorry."

There was a knock at the door. Dawson and Norland exchanged glances.

"Who do you suppose that is?" Dawson asked.

Norland shrugged. "Answer it and see. We've got nothing to hide."

The knocking came again, louder this time.

Dawson jerked his chin at Shaye. "See who it is."

Rising, Shaye opened the door to find a tall, frail, gray-haired man standing there. "Yes?"

"Who the devil are you?" the man asked brusquely. "And what were you doing coming out of my house?"

"Are you the doctor?" Shaye asked. She noted the leather bag he carried.

"Yes, and I saw you leaving my house. I want to know what you were doing there."

"Looking for you." She took a deep breath, her nose wrinkling at the smell of whiskey. "Guess I should have checked the saloons."

The doctor glared at her. "Why were you looking for me? Someone sick?"

Shaye could feel Dawson staring holes in her back, but she didn't care. Alejandro needed help, and she intended to see he got it. "Yes," she said, hoping Dawson wouldn't get mad and kill them all. "Come in."

The doctor glanced at Dawson and Norland, nodded, and went to stand beside Alejandro. "This man's been shot."

Dawson nodded. "He's an escaped prisoner. We're taking him back to Bodie for trial."

"I see. You," the doctor said, speaking to Alejandro. "Stretch out on the bed. I need to examine your wound."

Norland started to object. Shaye could see it in his expression, but Dawson silenced his partner with a glance.

Alejandro stood up. Shaye slipped her arm around his waist and helped him to the bed, silently thanking God that the doctor had followed her.

She stood next to the bed while the doctor examined the wound. Muttering to himself about bullets and the stupidity of men, he swabbed the area with carbolic, then probed the wound. A few moments later, he withdrew a tiny piece of fabric from the infected area. When he was certain there was no other foreign matter in the wound, he filled a syringe with carbolic and water and flushed the wound, then covered it with a compress soaked with carbolic.

"Don't move him for a day or two," the doctor ordered as he snapped his bag shut.

"Thank you, Doctor. How much do I owe you?"

"Five dollars." He handed her three packets of salicylate of sodium. "Give him one of those every six hours. If the fever doesn't go down, come get me, and I'll give you a couple more."

Reaching into her pocket, Shaye withdrew the two packets she had taken from his office. "I have some."

He grunted softly. "You steal those from my office?"

"Yes. I left two dollars on a table." She reached into her pocket, counted out three dollars, and handed them to the doctor.

"Well, I guess that makes us square. Call me if you need me."

"Thank you."

With a nod, he patted her shoulder. "He'll be all right. Don't worry."

Shaye saw him out the door, then went to sit on the bed beside Alejandro. "How do you feel? Can I get you anything?"

"I could use something to drink."

She poured him a glass of water, lifted his head while he drank. Setting the glass aside, she brushed a lock of hair from his brow. "Get some sleep."

"Just a damn minute!" Dawson said. "He can sleep on the floor."

She whirled on Dawson like a mother bear defending her young. "He's hurt. And you're the one who hurt him. *You* sleep on the floor."

"The hell I will."

Shaye glared at him, her hands fisted on her hips.

Norland chuckled. "Let him have the bed, Dawson. It's only one night. You take the other bed, and I'll sleep in the chair."

Dawson gave Shaye a push and she stumbled backward, sitting down hard on the edge of the mattress. She looked up at him, suddenly frightened, as he pulled a strip of leather out of his back pocket.

"Lie down," he said curtly.

"Why?"

"Dammit, just do it!" he said.

She lay down alongside Alejandro. Dawson proceeded to tie her hands to the brass headboard.

Moving to the other side of the bed, he jerked Alejandro's arms over his head and secured his hands to the headboard, as well.

"Is that necessary?" Shaye asked.

"Damn right. Now go to sleep, both of you. We're leaving first thing in the morning."

Norland extinguished the lamp, plunging the room into darkness.

Shaye listened to the two men settle down for the night; then she whispered to Alejandro, "Are you all right?"

"Sure. Dammit, I'm sorry about all this."

"It's not your fault."

"Shut the hell up, you two," Dawson said irritably. "Or I'll plug ya both."

Shaye woke slowly, wondering why her shoulders and wrists hurt, and then she realized her hands were tied to the headboard. She turned toward Alejandro and found him watching her.

"How do you feel?" she asked.

"Better." His gaze moved over her, warm and filled with love. "Don't worry, darlin'. I'll get you out of this."

"I'm not worried."

He grinned at her. "No need for you to be. I'm worrying enough for both of us."

She couldn't help it. She smiled back at him.

She heard a distant clock chime the hour . . . five . . . six . . . seven. A short time later, Dawson entered the room carrying a covered tray. He set it on the rickety table beside the bed. He untied Shaye's hands, then drew his gun. "Untie him," he said, "and don't try anything stupid. He's wanted dead or alive. I got no problem killing him here and now."

She didn't doubt him for a minute.

The knot was stubborn, but she finally managed to get it untied. Alejandro sat up slowly and rubbed his wrists. "Where's Norland?"

"Getting the horses."

Shaye uncovered the tray, revealing two plates of ham, scrambled eggs, baking powder biscuits, and two cups of coffee, black.

She carried the tray to the bed and sat down, the tray between herself and Alejandro.

"Hurry it up," Dawson said.

"The doctor said he shouldn't be moved for a day or two."

"Tough."

"He needs to rest."

Dawson snorted derisively. "I ain't wasting my time mollycoddling him. Ain't no point in it anyways. He don't have to be healthy to face the hangman. Just alive."

She stalled as long as she could. She took small bites, chewed each one carefully. When she finished eating, she informed Dawson that she needed to use the privy.

"Go ahead," he said.

She took as long as she dared in the outdoor privy, and when she returned to the hotel room, Norland was there. She could hear Norland and Dawson arguing even before she went in the room.

"What the hell's taking her so long?"

"That damn woman," Dawson replied. "She's more trouble than she's worth."

She opened the door, putting an end to the argument. She insisted on giving Alejandro another dose of salicylate of sodium before they left; then she tucked the remaining packets in her skirt pocket.

"You ready now?" Dawson growled.

She nodded, unable to think of any plausible excuse to delay their departure. Norland tied Alejandro's hands in front of him, and they left the hotel. Their horses were waiting outside.

Alejandro took hold of the saddle horn. She saw him take a deep breath, and then, jaw clenched, he put one foot in the stirrup and pulled himself into the saddle. She shrieked as Dawson grabbed her around the middle and lifted her up behind Alejandro.

She leaned forward, resting her cheek against Alejandro's back, and tried not to think about what might be waiting for them in Bodie.

It was slow going, what with Alejandro and Shaye riding double. With the sun beating down on her, Shaye felt as if she might melt into a puddle and slide over the horse's rump. Sweat ran down her back and pooled between her breasts. She wished she had a hat, wished she was wearing her shorts and a tee shirt instead of a long-sleeved shirtwaist, a heavy skirt, and petticoats.

From time to time, she overheard bits and pieces of conversation between Dawson and Norland, who couldn't agree on how to split the fifteen-hundred-dollar reward. Dawson felt he was entitled to an extra cut, since he was the one who had told Norland that Alejandro was at the hideout. Norland felt he was entitled to a bigger share because he was the one who had told Dawson about the reward in the first place.

She tightened her hold on Alejandro's waist. She could almost feel Fate bearing down on them, had a terrible premonition that there was nothing she could do to keep Alejandro from hanging, just as she had been able to do nothing to prevent Daisy's death. Despair settled on her shoulders. They would be back in Bodie all too soon. Alejandro would be tried and found guilty. Norland had said she was wanted, too. She doubted they would hang her for breaking Alejandro out of jail. There was, however, the very real possibility that they might hang her for horse stealing.

They had been riding about three hours when Dawson drew rein beside Bodie Creek. Dismounting, he tossed his horse's reins to Norland. "I need to piss, and the horses need a rest."

So saying, he walked downstream until he was out of sight behind some scrub brush.

Shaye slid off the back of the horse. Alejandro dismounted slowly, grimacing as the movement tugged on his wound.

"Are you all right?" she asked.

"Sure, darlin', no worries."

"I hate it when you say that, 'cause I know it means just the opposite."

He grinned at her. "Not much of a honeymoon, is it?"

"Don't change the subject."

"Shaye, I'm fine. A little sore, that's all."

She moved close to him. With his hands bound, he couldn't hold her, but she held onto him, finding reassurance in his nearness. Lowering his head, he brushed his lips across hers, a kiss that was no less potent for being butterfly soft and gentle. She looked up and saw everything she had ever dreamed of, wished for, yearned for, in the depth of his eyes.

Lost in the moment, she was only dimly aware of Dawson leading the horses down to the creek, or Norland hovering behind them, one hand resting on his gun butt.

"I love you," she murmured.

Alejandro nodded. "I know, darlin'."

Dawson swaggered up, leading the horses. "If you two lovebirds want a drink, you'd best get it now."

Shaye put her arm around Alejandro's waist and they walked down to the creek. The water was clear and cold. Alejandro braced himself on his forearms and buried his face in the water. Shaye drank from her cupped hands. Rising, she took Alejandro's arm and helped him to his feet.

A short time later, they were riding again.

They were about an hour away from Bodie when Norland's horse pulled up lame. Dawson swore as he reined his horse to a halt. "You two, get down."

With a weary sigh, Alejandro climbed out of the saddle. Shaye slid over the animal's rump, then moved to stand beside Alejandro. He had to get her away from here, but how?

Dawson dismounted and walked over to Norland. "How bad is it?"

"Stone bruise."

Dawson swore again.

"Let's rest him for an hour," Norland suggested. "Maybe it's not as bad as it looks."

"Maybe," Dawson muttered.

Alejandro lowered himself slowly to the ground, his back against a rock. The pain in his side ached

like all the fires of hell, aggravated by every movement he made. And riding was only making it worse.
Shaye sat down beside him, her shoulder brushing his.
He kept his expression carefully blank under her anxious scrutiny.

Dawson and Norland hunkered down on their heels
a short distance away.

Alejandro leaned toward her, pretending to kiss her
cheek. "Shaye," he said quietly, "I don't want you
going back to Bodie."

"What?"

"Shh." He nuzzled her cheek. "You heard Norland.
There's paper on you, too. You need to get away from
here."

"I'm not leaving you!"

"Shaye, darlin', listen to me."

"No! You listen to me. I'm not leaving."

He drew in a deep breath, admiring her loyalty, her
stubbornness. She was a fighter, no doubt about it. He
swore softly. He couldn't abide the thought of her
being locked up because of him. Dammit! What was
he going to do? And then it came to him, the one
argument she might accept.

"Darlin', if we're both locked up, neither one of us
has a chance."

Her eyes widened. "I never thought of that."

He winked at her. "That's why I'm the boss." He
laughed when she stuck her tongue out at him. "All
right, now, listen, darlin'. This is what we'll do . . ."

Shaye didn't like the idea one bit, but Alejandro

was right. If they were both locked up, he was as good as dead.

At his signal, she stood up and walked toward the creek where the horses were grazing on a patch of short grass.

"Hey, where you going, girl?" Dawson called.

Shaye paused and looked over her shoulder. "I need to take a leak," she said, being purposefully vulgar in the hope that it would keep him from suspecting her true motive.

"Well, make it quick."

With a nod, she hurried toward a patch of brush and ducked behind it. A moment later, she heard Dawson's voice.

"Where the hell do you think you're going?"

"I need to stretch my legs," Alejandro replied.

"You just stay where you are."

She peered through the brush. Alejandro had moved a few feet away from where they had been sitting. Dawson and Norland were both standing now, facing him. Dawson's hand rested on the butt of his gun.

"Maybe we can make a deal," Alejandro said.

"What kind of deal?" Dawson asked, and Shaye could hear the sneer in his voice.

"I've got some money in the bank," Alejandro said. "If you let us go, I'll double the reward."

"Go to hell."

"Wait a minute," Norland said. "Let's hear him out."

Alejandro glanced past Norland. Meeting Shaye's gaze, he nodded slightly.

Taking a deep breath, she tiptoed out from behind the bushes. Using the lame horse for cover, she caught up the reins of the other two horses. Pulling herself into the saddle of the nearest one, she reined the horse around, slammed her heels into its sides, and took off running downstream, leading the second horse behind her.

She heard Dawson shout, "What the hell!" followed by the sound of a gunshot. Was it her imagination, or had she felt the heat of the bullet streak past her cheek?

She didn't dare to look back. Bending low over the horse's neck, she rode as if all the demons of hell were barking at her heels.

Her horse was breathing hard and covered with sweat when she finally felt safe enough to stop. Leaning forward, she patted the horse's sweaty neck, then wiped her hand off on her skirt. Well, part one had gone as planned. Now all she had to do was find a hiding place in Bodie, wait for Alejandro to show up, and bust him out of jail.

Again.

Chapter Twenty-seven

Alejandro glanced out the coach window, though there was little to see but desert and sage and a brassy blue sky. Dawson and Norland had both been as mad as hell when Shaye took off with the horses. He grinned inwardly. The three of them had spent the night camped by the stream, and set out walking this morning with Dawson and Norland cussing a blue streak the whole way. It had been sheer luck that they'd been able to flag down a stage this morning, otherwise they would still be walking.

Alejandro glanced from Dawson to Norland. He had offered them two thousand dollars each to let him go. Norland had jumped on the offer like a frog after a fly. Alejandro had little faith that they'd actually let him go, but there was always a chance, and it was the only chance he had.

When the stage reached Bodie, they were the last three to climb down from the coach. Dawson jammed his hat on Alejandro's head. "Keep your head down," he said brusquely. "We'll go straight to the bank and get the money. Then you're on your own."

Alejandro nodded. No one paid them any mind as they made their way down Main Street, which seemed even more crowded than he remembered. He wondered if Shaye had made it back to town, and, if so, where she was now.

They stopped outside the Bodie Bank. "We're gonna have to untie his hands," Norland said.

Dawson nodded. Drawing his gun, he moved behind Alejandro. "Don't try anything stupid. Just get the money. One wrong word, and I'll shoot you where you stand. Got it?"

"Yeah."

"Let's go."

Alejandro opened the door and stepped into the bank. It was still early in the day. There were only three men in the place. He went to the end of the line, acutely aware of Dawson and Norland standing directly behind him. He knew the chances that they would keep their end of the deal were probably a thousand to one, but at the moment, they were his best hope.

The men in front of him moved up one. Alejandro glanced over his shoulder.

"Don't even think about it," Dawson warned.

Alejandro muttered a vile oath. "No," he said, his

gaze resting on the man just entering the bank. "I won't."

Dawson looked over his shoulder, and drew his gun. "Morning, Sheriff," he said. "Look what I caught."

She had ridden through the night fervently praying that she was going in the right direction. Nothing looked familiar, and yet everything looked familiar, since one clump of gray-green sagebrush looked pretty much like any other.

Fear snaked through her as she wandered in the dark. She had no food, no water, no blankets, no weapon. All things considered, jail was looking better all the time.

"Rio," she murmured, "this was not a good idea."

Not knowing what else to do, she gave the horse its head, hoping the animal had a better sense of direction than she did. How had the pioneers managed to cross the whole United States, when she couldn't go a few miles without getting completely turned around? If she had been in charge, no telling where the pioneers would have ended up!

Finally, she had stopped to rest a few hours, then mounted up with the dawn. Now she sat staring at a squat square building with a heavy heart. Impossible as it seemed, she was back at the hideout.

She dismounted at the stable. Leading the horses inside, she found two empty stalls. Removing the saddle, blanket, and bridle from first one and then the other, she forked the horses some hay, made sure both stall doors were latched, then left the stable.

She stood outside a minute, wondering what to do next. She never got lost in the city. Of course, there were signs on every street back home, and a handy Thomas Guide when entering unfamiliar territory. Out here, there was nothing. Even if there were signs, what would they say? Turn left at the big rock? Go south for three miles and turn right at the cottonwood tree?

With a sigh, she headed for the saloon. Maybe she could find someone who would take her to Bodie. Then again, maybe not. How could she trust any of the men who frequented this place? They were all outlaws and ruffians, no better than Dawson and Norland.

The first person Shaye saw when she opened the door was Jack Calder. He smiled as he came around the bar to greet her.

"Damnation, girl, I was wondering where you went." He glanced past her. "Where's Rio?"

The question, and the concern in Calder's face, were her undoing. Feeling like a fool, she burst into tears.

Calder muttered an oath as he placed a beefy arm around her shoulders and led her out of the saloon and around the back to his cabin. He sat her down in the room's only chair. "All right, what's going on?"

Sniffling, she told him what had happened. "And now they're taking him back to Bodie, and I've got to get there to save him before it's too late."

Calder shook his head. "Rio wouldn't kill no

woman." He looked at Shaye and grinned. "He might love 'em to death, but he wouldn't put no gun to their head."

"I have to get to Bodie right away."

"Sure, sure. Settle down now." He pulled a dingy kerchief from his back pocket and dabbed at her eyes. "Cryin' never solved nothing. Just let me think a minute."

Hours of riding and worrying had taken their toll, and she sat back in the chair, suddenly exhausted.

"You look all done in," Calder said sympathetically. "You lie down and get a little rest, and I'll go see what I can do about getting you back to Bodie."

"Thank you, Jack."

He dismissed her thanks with a wave of his hand. "Use my bed. And don't worry. I'll think of something."

She woke to the sound of someone knocking on the door. For a moment, she didn't remember where she was, and then it came back to her. She was in Calder's cabin.

"Shaye, you awake?"

"Yes, Jack," she said, sitting up. "Come in."

"Brought you some food," Calder said, grinning. "French toast."

"You didn't have to do that."

Calder handed her a tray, then sat down in the chair. "Least I can do for Rio's wife. Man saved my life. I talked to Hoffman. He's willin' to take you to Bodie." He held up a hand at her look of apprehension. "He's a good man, Hoffman is. You can trust him. I'd take you myself, but I can't leave the saloon. I know what you're thinkin'," he said with a broad smile. "Why can't Hoffman look after the place? Well, here's the truth of the matter. He ain't the kind of man who would hurt a woman, but he'll rob ya blind iffen he sees the chance."

Shaye nodded. "Thank you."

"How's that Frenchy toast? I been getting lots of practice makin' it."

"It's perfect."

Calder slapped his hands on his thighs. "Well, then. You finish eatin' and I'll go tell Hoffman to get hisself ready. I reckon you'll want to leave right away?"

"Yes."

So it was that, an hour later, Shaye found herself riding away from the outlaw hideout with Jim Hoffman. She had collected her gear from the cabin she had shared with Alejandro. Her backpack and valise were tied behind her saddle. Calder had generously supplied them with food and drink.

She looked over at Jim Hoffman. He was best described as average, she thought. Average height, average looks, with an infectious Billy Crystal grin.

They rode in silence for a time, and then Hoffman started talking, first about the weather, which was, he said, "damn hot, even for July." He went on to reminisce about the last winter he had spent in Bodie. "A rough one," he said, "so cold they threw the horses out of the barn and rented out the stalls. Yep," he said, "I'm hightailing it outta here before the snows come."

Shaye nodded. She was trying to think of something to say, but no reply was needed. Hoffman was a talker, and he rambled on for hours, telling her about his childhood in Tennessee, his growing-up years in Texas.

"Met my wife there," he said. "She was purty as a black-eyed Susan and sweeter than molasses. I sure do miss that gal."

"What happened?"

Hoffman shook his head. "She was a good woman. Too good for me. She wanted me to settle down, take up clerkin' in her father's store. I tried. I really did. But stealing was so much easier than workin'. Second time I got caught, she left me. I ain't blamin' her, mind you. She was a churchgoing, God-fearing woman. I just couldn't be what she wanted."

"I'm sorry."

"Hey, don't fret yourself on my account. Nobody's fault but my own that I lost her."

He fell silent after that, leaving Shaye to her own thoughts, all of which were centered around Alejandro, and a sudden, overpowering fear that she would arrive too late.

Alejandro paced the floor, his long, angry strides carrying him quickly from one end of the cell to the other. Damn. Damn, damn, damn! Of all the rotten luck. Conner had been only too happy to pay Dawson and Norland the reward money. The lawman had grinned like a man who had just hit pay dirt when he locked the cell door, and he was still grinning that afternoon when he escorted his prisoner to court.

The trial had been over practically before it started. Alejandro's lawyer was no match for Pat Reddy. There were only a few witnesses, but in the hands of Mr. Reddy, their evidence was damning. The clerk at the hotel had testified that he remembered seeing Alejandro and Daisy leave together on the night in question. When asked, he stated he had been called away from the desk for about an hour and hadn't been there when Alejandro returned to the hotel. Several miners testified that they had seen Alejandro going into Daisy's house.

But the most damning piece of evidence, aside from the fact that his derringer had been found near Daisy's body, had been Dade McCrory's testimony. McCrory had sworn that he had been passing Daisy's house that night, that he had overheard Daisy arguing with Rio, that he had heard a gunshot, and then seen Rio hurry out of the house.

The jury had deliberated for less than twenty minutes, and he had been found guilty of murder and sentenced to hang. And because he had escaped jail the last time he had been arrested, the judge had decreed that his sentence was to be carried out the following morning at ten by the clock.

He had no hope now, except Shaye, and little hope there unless she could bust him out of jail tonight.

Going to the window, he gazed out at the setting sun. Where was she? Had she made it back to Bodie?

And what were the odds that she'd be able to bust him out a second time? He had no doubt at all that she would try, but he had a feeling, deep down in his gut, that his string of luck had played out.

His thoughts turned to Daisy. Shaye had told him Daisy would be killed on the ninth of August, but Daisy had died more than a month earlier. It looked like Shaye had been wrong about the date of his hanging, too.

He swore softly, his hands gripping the bars. Somehow, her presence in the past had altered certain events. She had told him he had been hanged on the twelfth of August, but that, too, was about to change.

Damn. He lifted a hand to his neck, imagining the weight of a rope there, the rough feel of it, the thick knot behind his ear, the terror as he waited for the hangman to spring the trap, his body dropping through the hole. What would his last thought be as he plummeted toward eternity?

Shaye.

He shared her name with the emptiness of his cell. "Shaye." An urgent whisper. A heartfelt prayer. A wealth of regret that he would never see her again. "Shaye . . ."

Chapter Twenty-eight

The sun was setting in a riotous blaze of crimson and pink when they reached Aurora. Shaye felt a growing sense of urgency as they threaded their way through the noisy crowd on Main Street, dodging wagons and carts and hundreds of people who were all in an itching hurry.

Hoffman pulled up in front of the nearest hotel. Shaye stared at the building. She was weary right down to the bone yet certain she would not sleep a wink.

She slid gratefully out of the saddle to stand on legs that felt like overcooked spaghetti.

Hoffman reached down and took the reins from her hand. "Why don't you go get a room? I'll look after the horses."

"Thanks." She lifted her backpack off the saddle horn.

With a nod, Hoffman rode on down the street toward the livery barn.

She stepped onto the boardwalk. She brushed off her skirts, ran a hand through her hair, then opened the ornate front door and entered the hotel. Crossing the carpeted lobby, she approached the front desk.

A short man with a balding pate and a handlebar moustache greeted her with a smile and a friendly, "Hello. Can I help you?"

"I'd like two rooms," she replied. "And a bath."

"Yes, ma'am. That'll be five dollars. In advance."

Slinging her backpack over her shoulder, she pulled a handful of crumpled greenbacks from her skirt pocket and placed five of them on the counter top. Slipping the rest back into her pocket, she signed the register for herself and Hoffman, picked up one of the keys.

Room 122 was small and square, with pale blue walls, gingham curtains, a single ladder-back chair, and a brass bed topped by a wedding-ring quilt. She dropped her pack on the floor, took off her shoes, then fell back on the bed, legs hanging over the edge of the mattress, arms stretched out at her sides, and immediately fell asleep.

She woke with a start, not knowing what had awakened her. Sitting up, she glanced around the darkened room, her heart pounding wildly. And then she heard it again. Alejandro's voice, whispering her name.

"Rio?" She glanced around the room. "Rio?"

"*Shaye.*"

His voice again, filled with a yearning that reached into her very soul.

"I'm coming!" Rising, she hurried toward the door, stumbling in her haste.

A single lamp lit the hallway. Hoffman had the room across from hers. She knocked on the door and when there was no answer, she knocked again, harder.

A moment later the door swung open to reveal Jim Hoffman clad in a pair of faded red long johns. Seeing her standing there chased the sleepy look from his face.

"What's wrong?" he asked.

"We have to leave."

"Now?" He blinked owlishly. "Hell, girl, it's not even daylight yet."

"We have to go. Get dressed. Hurry!"

He frowned at her. "What's wrong? The hotel on fire?"

"Please, just get dressed. We have to go. Right now."

"All right, all right." He scratched his jaw and then his chest. "Give me ten minutes."

"Make it five," she said, and hurrying back to her own room, she splashed some water on her face, put on her shoes, grabbed her backpack.

When she stepped into the hallway again, Hoffman was waiting for her. "Do you want to tell me what the hell is going on?" He shoved his shirttail into his pants.

"I don't know. I can't explain it. You wouldn't

believe me anyway. All I know is we have to get to Bodie right away."

He looked at her as if he thought she'd lost her mind, and maybe she had, but he didn't argue.

Ten minutes later, they were riding out of town.

Alejandro took a deep breath as a clock chimed the half hour. It was nine-thirty. He hadn't slept the night before; had done nothing but pace the floor, or stare out into the darkness. How quickly the last hours of his life had gone by! He had few regrets. He had lived his life as he pleased, and if it had been less than perfect, he had no one to blame but himself. He had ridden some lonely trails, seen some beautiful country, always found work when he needed it, always had money in his pockets. But it was Shaye who had made the deepest impression in his life. Shaye, with her beautiful deep green eyes and earth brown hair. Shaye, with her sweet spirit. She had shown him that there was more to life than whiskey and cards. She had shown him what love was, made him realize that, until he met her, he hadn't really been living at all.

"Shaye." He whispered her name, hugging it close, remembering how easily she had fit into his life, how quickly she had become important to him. He wished he could have held her one last time, told her how much he loved her. His biggest regret was that they had had such a short time together. Did she know how much he loved her?

He closed his eyes, his mind conjuring her image. She was all woman, from the top of her head to the tips of her funny shoes. Would she go back to her own time when he was dead? He wished he had asked her more about the future. He was intrigued by the things she had told him about: vehicles that moved without horses and, even more astonishing, vehicles that flew through the air; pictures that moved and talked; indoor privies; hot and cold running water; machines that washed and dried clothes.

But Shaye was the most amazing thing of all. It wasn't only iron bars that kept them apart, he mused; it was a hundred and twenty years.

Damn. Surely she hadn't been sent to him only to have it end like this.

The sound of Conner's footsteps proved how wrong he was. The sheriff regarded him a moment. "Do you want to see a priest?"

"No."

"Cigarette?"

"No."

"All right then, let's go. The hangman's waiting."

"Empty? What do you mean, the jail's empty?" Shaye grabbed Hoffman's arm. "Where is he?"

"I don't know."

Shaye stared at Hoffman. Was she too late? Where could he be? He wasn't dead, couldn't be dead. She would know it, feel it, if he were.

On the edge of panic, she stepped out of her hiding place. He was here somewhere, and she would find him. She frowned as she watched a bunch of men hurrying down the street, felt her heart drop when she overheard a man telling his friend that if they didn't hurry, they would miss the hanging.

With a cry of despair, Shaye followed them. Turning a corner, she came to an abrupt halt. The top of the gallows rose above the hundreds of men crowded around it. She pushed and shoved her way through the throng, hardly daring to breathe. And then she saw him, standing on the platform, his arms tied behind his back, his expression blank as he stared into the distance. The sheriff stood on one side of him; the hangman waited on the other.

Frozen by the horror of the moment, she watched the hangman drop the noose over Alejandro's head, saw him arrange the knot behind his ear, take up the slack in the noose.

She had to do something, but what? Tears welled in her eyes, blurring her vision. Her heart pounded frantically. It couldn't end like this. It couldn't! She glanced at the people around her. It didn't make sense. Why had she been sent here if not to save him?

She looked up at the platform again, felt her heart skip a beat when she met his gaze. He shook his head, and she knew he didn't want her to be there, didn't want her to watch him die, but she couldn't leave, not when she would never see him again.

"I love you." She mouthed the words, hoping he could read her lips, hoping he knew the feelings of her heart and soul.

He smiled faintly, his eyes dark, smoldering, filled with a thousand things unsaid between them. And then he mouthed the words she had waited so long to hear. "I love you."

She filled her eyes with the look of him, imprinting his image in her mind as he stood there, tall and straight, with the early morning sun casting gold highlights in his black hair. He must be terrified, she thought, yet he looked calm, at peace.

The courthouse clock chimed the hour. It was time.

A man standing next to her shouted, "Get on with it, Conner. Some of us have got work to do!"

Shaye turned to look at him and found herself staring into Dade McCrory's cold blue eyes. "You!" she hissed. "It should be you up there."

"Me? What the hell for? I didn't kill her."

Shaye stared at McCrory. He was telling the truth. She knew it. But if not McCrory, and not Alejandro . . . "Then who did it?" she murmured.

"She killed herself."

Shaye's eyes widened. She had suspected that Daisy had committed suicide, but there had been no proof, no note. "How do you know?"

Dade pulled a crumpled piece of paper from his pants pocket. "She left a note."

She looked up at the platform again, hope rising within her. If Daisy had left a note, they would have to free Alejandro. "You lied!" she exclaimed.

McCrory laughed coldly, bitterly.

"If you've got any last words," Conner said, "now's the time to say 'em."

Alejandro shook his head, his dark eyes fixed on Shaye's face. "Just get on with it."

The sheriff took a step backward, one hand resting on the butt of his gun, as the hangman slipped a hood over Alejandro's head.

"Wait!" Shaye screamed, but no one paid her any attention. She was Alejandro's woman, after all.

The hangman reached for the wooden lever that would spring the trapdoor and put an end to Alejandro's life.

"No! Wait! He didn't do it! I can prove it!" She grabbed the note from McCrory's hand and raced toward the platform, but it was already too late.

As if in slow motion, she saw the hangman's hand close around the lever. She screamed as the trapdoor beneath Alejandro's feet fell away. There was a collective gasp from the crowd as his body plunged through the opening.

"No! No!" Her hand fisted around the note. Too late, too late.

It should have been over, but it wasn't. He was still alive, his legs twitching convulsively as the rope tightened around his neck.

A hush fell over the crowd as they watched the life being slowly strangled from his body.

"No! No! No!" Hardly aware of what she was doing, Shaye ran toward him, the note falling from her hand as she wrapped her arms around Alejandro's legs. She lifted upward to ease the awful tension on the rope. He was heavy, so heavy.

Why didn't someone help her? She couldn't support him much longer. The world began to spin out of focus, the faces of the crowd blurring, fading. She staggered beneath his weight, tears of frustration running down her cheeks. Why didn't someone help her?

Bright lights exploded behind her eyes and she felt herself spinning down, down, into a deep black void.

Chapter Twenty-nine

Feeling as though she were waking from a long sleep, Shaye opened her eyes. The sun was high in the sky. And it was quiet, so quiet. A glance to the left showed the Methodist Church. Had it all been a dream, then, she wondered. But it had all seemed so real, the people, the town. Alejandro . . .

She closed her eyes, and his image sprang to mind: Alejandro striding toward her in the saloon, smiling at her across the table, teaching her to play poker, dancing with her on the Fourth of July, making love to her . . . swinging from the gallows.

Choking back a sob, she opened her eyes, banishing the last gruesome image.

She looked away from the church that proved beyond a shadow of a doubt that she was back in the present, and saw Alejandro lying on the ground a short distance away, the ugly black hood still in place, his hands tied behind his back, and she knew it had been all too real. She didn't stop to wonder what he was doing in her time, or how he had got there.

Scrambling to her hands and knees, she ripped the hood away, then placed her hand over his chest, reassured by the steady beat of his heart. He was here, alive, in the flesh. She fumbled with the rope binding his wrists and tossed it aside, then sank back on her heels, weak with relief. The how and the why of it didn't matter, she thought. He was here.

She wondered what day it was, and how long she had been in the past, and knew, if it weren't for Alejandro lying there beside her, she would have been certain she'd dreamed the whole thing.

She thought briefly of Clark McDonald, wondered what he would say, what he would think, if she and Alejandro were to walk into the museum. Perhaps she would write Clark later. Of all the people she knew, he was the only one who was likely to believe what had happened. It would make a great story, but of course, it was one she could never write, except as fiction. Who would believe it? She could hardly believe it herself.

She glanced past Alejandro, surprised to see her backpack and overnight bag, both of which had been left in the past, sitting a few feet away. How had they gotten there?

Alejandro groaned softly, then jackknifed into a sitting position, his hand going to his throat. "What happened?" he asked, his voice low and raspy.

"I'm not sure, but somehow we seem to have been zapped back to my time."

"Your time?" Alejandro's gaze rested on Shaye's face for a moment, and then he glanced around, taking in his surroundings. Across the way stood the Bodie Chop Shop. It had been a new building when last he saw it. Now the paint was gone, the roof was sagging, there were boards nailed across the windows.

He stood up, his hand absently massaging his throat. Then, leaning down, he took Shaye's hands and pulled her to her feet. Feeling a little dazed, he began to walk down Green Street, past the morgue and the Boone Store, past the Swazey Hotel, past the schoolhouse. So many buildings were missing, he mused, with nothing left to show where most of them had stood. He recalled Shaye telling him that fires had decimated much of the town.

It took some getting used to, this idea of being in the future. He supposed it wasn't any more impossible for him to be in Shaye's time than it had been for her to be in his, but, damn . . . he shook his head. It was downright disconcerting to see the town the way it was now, to realize that the life he had known no longer existed, that everyone he had ever known was dead. Lottie, Sophie, Philo Richardson, Rojas, the men he had played cards with, Addy Mae and Lily, the doves at the Queen, all gone. Dead and gone.

It was quiet, he thought, so quiet without the ever-present thumping of the stamp mill, without the boisterous shouts of the teamsters, the rumble of heavy-laden wagons and carts, the rowdy banter of the miners as they swarmed over the hills. The stillness was oppressive. Nothing stirred save a faint warm breeze. The town looked old, he thought, old and tired, as if a good strong wind could blow it all down.

"Are you all right?"

He turned to see that Shaye had followed him down the street. She was his reality now. Standing on the gallows, with a rope around his neck and his future measured in heartbeats, he had realized that he loved her with a forever kind of love. He'd just been too damn stupid to realize it until it was too late. It had been his last thought when the hangman dropped the hood over his head, his last thought as the trap was sprung. Why had he waited so long to admit it? Why hadn't he told her sooner?

"Shaye." He drew her into his arms.

She looked up at him, her heart shining in her eyes.

"I love you, darlin'."

"And I love you," she replied tremulously. "More than anything in this world or any other."

And perhaps that was the magic that had brought him here, he thought, the magic of their love, a love that was strong enough to defy death, strong enough to bring him across time and space to the only woman he had ever loved. Would ever love.

Her smile faded. "I thought I'd lost you forever."

"I know." He gazed down at her, needing her in a way he couldn't quite explain. "I want to make love to you here, one more time." Everything and everyone else he had known was gone, but Shaye remained, a link between his past and his future.

"I wish we could." She glanced around. The town seemed deserted, but even so, there was no place where they could be alone.

The words were barely out of her mouth before Alejandro swung her into his arms, striding purposefully toward one of the houses that was located up a side street well away from the others. The doors were locked, but that only slowed him down. Going around to the back of the house, he broke a window and they went inside. The interior was dark and quiet. There was a mattress on the floor in the bedroom. Alejandro spread an old quilt over the mattress, then took Shaye in his arms again, the need between them humming like a live wire.

He kissed her gently, softly, tenderly, his hands moving ever so slowly, ever so lightly, up and down her back before he pulled her up close against him, letting her feel his desire. He deepened the kiss, and she opened for him like a flower reaching for the sun, felt his heat flow into her and through her. His desire fueled her own, and she clung to him, everything else forgotten but the wonder of his kiss, the magic of his hands moving over her body. She didn't remember undressing him, or being undressed, but somehow they were lying on the quilt, arms and legs entwined, moving toward that moment when two become one. His skin was fever hot beneath her fingertips.

He rose over her, his long black hair brushing against her breasts, his dark eyes blazing with a need she knew was reflected in her own.

"Now," she whispered urgently. "Now, now, now!"

She closed her eyes, a wordless cry of pleasure on her lips as his body merged with hers, filling her with delicious heat, completing her. She grabbed the moment, that one moment when there was no telling where she ended and he began, that one moment when two hearts beat to the same wild pulsing rhythm.

She heard his voice whisper that he loved her and she knew, in that single perfect moment in time, that the love they shared had forever bridged the gap between her world and his.

It was near dark when they left the house. Alejandro glanced from side to side as they made their way back down Green Street. It seemed impossible, yet here he was, in the twenty-first century, walking through what was now a ghost town, he mused with a wry grin. And soon even the ghost would be gone.

He paused when they reached the Methodist Church, which hadn't been built during his lifetime. His old lifetime.

When they reached the top of the hill, he glanced over his shoulder one last time, bidding a final goodbye to everything he had ever known.

And then he swung Shaye into his arms and twirled her around and around, eager to begin their new life together, to see for himself all the wonders she had told him about, knowing in his heart and soul that nothing the future held could be more wonderful than the woman in his arms.

Epilogue

Shaye placed her hand on her father's arm. Clad in an old-fashioned gown made of ivory antique lace and a shoulder-length veil, and carrying a bouquet of white roses and baby's breath, she smiled up at her dad, her heart beating in anticipation. Today was her wedding day.

She hadn't felt the need to be married again, but her mother had wished it, and Alejandro had agreed, stating he wanted proof in writing that she belonged to him and no other. How could a girl argue with that?

It was a small wedding, with just her parents, her boss, a few coworkers, and Clark McDonald in attendance. She had called Clark when they got to L.A. He had been surprised to hear from her, relieved that she was all right, amazed by her story. But, just as she had known he would, he had believed every word.

It had been more difficult to convince her parents that her future husband was from the past. They had been certain it was some kind of joke, but after talking to Alejandro and seeing the photographs Shaye had had developed, her parents had come to believe the truth. It had been, Shaye thought, the pictures that had convinced them. The photos had come out bright and clear: the picture of Alejandro taken in his room; a view of Main Street crowded with people and freight wagons taken from Alejandro's hotel room window; another picture of Main Street; one of the Queen of Bodie; three of the mine; the photo Alejandro had taken of her; a picture of the two of them taken outside the mine; eight pictures of the Fourth of July parade; three of riders trying to pull the rooster out of the ground. The other roll of film was pictures of the ghost town as it was today. The differences between the town, old and new, were too obvious to deny.

Shaye peeked around the corner. She could see Alejandro standing at the altar, looking more handsome than ever in an old-fashioned frock coat made of fine black broadcloth, black trousers, and black cowboy boots.

Fake ID for Alejandro had been a lot easier to get hold of than she had thought it would be, thanks to her father, who still had some connections with some rather shady characters he had arrested a time or two when he worked for the police department.

Yesterday they had gone to the library and there, in a chapter on Bodie in an old history book, they had found a reference to Alejandro.

"One of Bodie's more colorful characters was Alejandro Valverde, a professional gambler by trade. Valverde was convicted of killing Daisy Sullivan, known prostitute and former business partner. Though he professed his innocence to the last, Valverde was hanged on July 15, 1880. Several hundred people witnessed the hanging, which took place as a violent windstorm swept through the town. When the dust settled, the body was gone. Ironically, a suicide note written by Sullivan was found immediately after the hanging. For a time, Valverde's ghost was said to haunt the town . . ."

Shaye smiled as the organ began to play.

"Ready?" her father asked.

"Oh, yes," she replied tremulously.

Alejandro stood in front of the altar, unmindful of the guests in the church, only dimly aware of his surroundings as he gazed at the vision walking down the aisle toward him. Never had she looked more lovely. Her gaze met his, and a swarm of emotions flowed through him: admiration, desire, anticipation, gratitude to whatever Fate had sent her to him, but most of all a deep surge of love. She was every dream he had ever had, every hope, every desire.

He stepped forward, taking her hand in his, hardly aware of the phrases the minister spoke until it was time for him to say the words that made Shaye his wife.

"I, Alejandro, take thee, Shaye . . ."

He looked into the depths of her beautiful green eyes as he spoke the solemn, heartfelt words that

would bind them together for now and all eternity,
and knew that he had come home at last.

Ever After

The explosion of my soul
now freed into her keeping
carried us into reality
where we had dreamed
where I had
wished

to hold her close
to fly through time
as one
skin so easily tasted with kisses
from lips so eagerly awaiting
my touch

my hands raised with freedom
life coursing through my veins . . .
come with me, my love
our travels now begin
we fly into the clouds
never looking back
never looking down

for time has healed its mistake
and folded you into my embrace
now my arms

Madeline Baker

stronger than bars of iron
will hold you close
keep you near
for now and
evermore

Dear Reader:

I hope you enjoyed Shaye and Alejandro's story. When I visited Bodie in the summer of 1999, I fell in love with the town and hated to leave. It had a "feel" impossible to describe. In some otherworldly way, I felt at home there. I was especially intrigued by the jail and lingered there for some time.

Like most of my books, this one is a blend of fact and fiction, of actual places, and those I made up, of people both real and fictional. I took some liberties with the Bodie Jail, changing part of the interior to fit the needs of my story.

I wish to express my thanks to SpiritWalker for his help. He proofread my manuscript, caught all the mistakes I missed, outlined the jailbreak scene, and gave me several ideas for other twists and turns in the plot.

I would like to urge everyone who reads this book to send a contribution to The Friends of Bodie, which is a volunteer, non-profit organization. Severe winters and time itself are gradually eroding Bodie's remaining buildings. Financial aid is needed to help maintain and preserve the town. If you would like to offer financial support or become a volunteer worker, you can contact The Friends of Bodie at P.O. Box 515, Bridgeport, CA 93517.

The newspaper ads used in my book were taken from reprints of the *Bodie Morning News* and the *Daily Free Press* and were used with the permission of the Department of Parks and Recreation. I also used text from *Bodie's Historical Guidebook,* also with permission from the Department of Parks and Recreation.

I would like to thank the Aides in Bodie for answering numerous questions. I would also like to thank the *Pipe Spring Cook Book* for allowing me to use their recipe for Lumpy Dick.

You can see some photos of Bodie on my website at: http://www.geocites.com/SoHo/Workshop/7309/page4.html

May all your best dreams and wishes come true.

—Madeline

MADELINE BAKER

Beneath A Midnight Moon

Winner Of The *Romantic Times* Reviewers Choice Award!

He comes to her in visions—the hard-muscled stranger who promises to save her from certain death. She never dares hope that her fantasy love will hold her in his arms until the virile and magnificent dream appears in the flesh.

A warrior valiant and true, he can overcome any obstacle, yet his yearning for the virginal beauty he's rescued overwhelms him. But no matter how his fevered body aches for her, he is betrothed to another.

Bound together by destiny, yet kept apart by circumstances, they brave untold perils and ruthless enemies—and find a passion that can never be rent asunder.

_3649-5 $4.99 US/$5.99 CAN

Dorchester Publishing Co., Inc.
P.O. Box 6640
Wayne, PA 19087-8640

Please add $1.75 for shipping and handling for the first book and $.50 for each book thereafter. NY, NYC, and PA residents, please add appropriate sales tax. No cash, stamps, or C.O.D.s. All orders shipped within 6 weeks via postal service book rate. Canadian orders require $2.00 extra postage and must be paid in U.S. dollars through a U.S. banking facility.

Name_____
Address_____
City_____State_____Zip_____
I have enclosed $_____ in payment for the checked book(s).
Payment <u>must</u> accompany all orders. ❏ Please send a free catalog.

RECKLESS HEART
MADELINE BAKER

They play together as children—the Indian lad and little Hannah Kincaid. Then Shadow and his people go away, and when he returns, it is as a handsome young Cheyenne brave. Hannah, now a beautiful young woman, has never forgotten her childhood friend—but the man who sweeps her into his powerful arms is no longer a child. He awakens in her a wild, erotic passion she has never known. But war is about to erupt in the Dakota Territory, a war that will pit the settlers against the Indians. Both Hannah and Shadow know that the time is coming when they will have to choose between happiness and hatred, between passion and duty, in a conflict that will test to the limit the steadfastness of their love. . . .

___4527-3 $5.99 US/$6.99 CAN

Dorchester Publishing Co., Inc.
P.O. Box 6640
Wayne, PA 19087-8640

Please add $1.75 for shipping and handling for the first book and $.50 for each book thereafter. NY, NYC, and PA residents, please add appropriate sales tax. No cash, stamps, or C.O.D.s. All orders shipped within 6 weeks via postal service book rate. Canadian orders require $2.00 extra postage and must be paid in U.S. dollars through a U.S. banking facility.

Name_____
Address_____
City_____State_____Zip_____
I have enclosed $_____ in payment for the checked book(s).
Payment <u>must</u> accompany all orders. ☐ Please send a free catalog.
CHECK OUT OUR WEBSITE! www.dorchesterpub.com

APACHE RUNAWAY

MADELINE BAKER

Ruthless and cunning, Ryder Fallon is a half-breed who can deal cards and death in the same breath. Yet when the Indians take him prisoner, he is in danger of being sent to the devil—until a green-eyed beauty named Jenny saves his life and opens his heart.

___4464-1 $5.99 US/$6.99 CAN

Dorchester Publishing Co., Inc.
P.O. Box 6640
Wayne, PA 19087-8640

Please add $1.75 for shipping and handling for the first book and $.50 for each book thereafter. NY, NYC, and PA residents, please add appropriate sales tax. No cash, stamps, or C.O.D.s. All orders shipped within 6 weeks via postal service book rate. Canadian orders require $2.00 extra postage and must be paid in U.S. dollars through a U.S. banking facility.

Name_____

Address_____

City_____State_____Zip_____

I have enclosed $_____ in payment for the checked book(s).

Payment <u>must</u> accompany all orders. ☐ Please send a free catalog.

THE ANGEL & THE OUTLAW

MADELINE BAKER

Bestselling Author Of *Lakota Renegade*

An outlaw, a horse thief, a man killer, J.T. Cutter isn't surprised when he is strung up for his crimes. What amazes him is the heavenly being who grants him one year to change his wicked ways. Yet when he returns to his old life, he hopes to cram a whole lot of hell-raising into those twelve months no matter what the future holds.

But even as J.T. heads back down the trail to damnation, a sharp-tongued beauty is making other plans for him. With the body of a temptress and the heart of a saint, Brandy is the only woman who can save J.T. And no matter what it takes, she'll prove to him that the road to redemption can lead to rapturous bliss.

_3931-1 $5.99 US/$7.99 CAN

Dorchester Publishing Co., Inc.
P.O. Box 6640
Wayne, PA 19087-8640

By the Author of More Than 10 Million Books in Print!

Madeline Baker

Headstrong Elizabeth Johnson is a woman who knows her own mind. Not for her an arranged marriage with a fancy lawyer from the East. Defying her parents, she set her sights on the handsome young sheriff of Twin Rivers. But when Dusty's virile half-brother rides into town, Beth takes one look into the stormy black eyes of the Apache warrior and understands that this time she must follow her heart. But with her father forbidding him to call, Dusty engaged to another, and her erstwhile fiance due to arrive from the East, she wonders just how many weddings it will take before they can all live happily ever after....

_4069-7 $5.99 US/$6.99 CAN

A WANTED MAN.
AN INNOCENT WOMAN.
A WANTON LOVE!

Renegade Heart
Madeline Baker

When beautiful Rachel Halloran took Logan Tyree into her home, he was unconscious. A renegade Indian with a bullet wound in his side and a price on his head, he needed her help. But to Rachel he was nothing but trouble, a man whose dark sensuality made her long for forbidden pleasures; to her father he was the answer to a prayer, a gunslinger whose legendary skill could rid the ranch of a powerful enemy.

But Logan Tyree would answer to no man—and to no woman. If John Halloran wanted his services, he would have to pay dearly for them. And if Rachel wanted his loving, she would have to give up her innocence, her reputation, her very heart and soul.

_4085-9 $5.99 US/$6.99 CAN

Spirit's Song

MADELINE BAKER

She is a runaway wife, with a hefty reward posted for her return. And he is the best darn tracker in the territory. For the half-breed bounty hunter, it is an easy choice. His was a hard life, with little to show for it except his horse, his Colt, and his scars. The pampered, brown-eyed beauty will go back to her rich husband in San Francisco, and he will be ten thousand dollars richer. But somewhere along the trail out of the Black Hills everything changes. Now, he will give his life to protect her, to hold her forever in his embrace. Now the moonlight poetry of their loving reflects the fiery vision of the Sun Dance: She must be his spirit's song.

___4476-5 $5.99 US/$6.99 CAN

MADELINE BAKER

The West—it has been Loralee's dream for as long as she could remember, and Indians are the most fascinating part of the wildly beautiful frontier she imagines. But when Loralee arrives at Fort Apache as the new schoolmarm, she has some hard realities to learn...and a harsh taskmaster to teach her. Shad Zuniga is fiercely proud, aloof, a renegade Apache who wants no part of the white man's world, not even its women. Yet Loralee is driven to seek him out, compelled to join him in a forbidden union, forced to become an outcast for one slim chance at love forevermore.

___4267-3 $5.99 US/$6.99 CAN